May you always be surrounded by REAL friends

F.A.K.E.!

A Novel

By

Vivian Luke

F.A.K.E.! A Novel by Vivian Luke

This is a work of fiction.

ISBN-10: 1722362146
ISBN-13: 978-1722362140

DEDICATION

To God.
Thank you.

CONTENTS

ACKNOWLEDGMENTS

My heartbeats - Raiven and Elle

Mom & Dad
Aunt Cav
Uncle Doc
Uncle Connie
Junie R.
Luke Family
Edwards Family
Calvin
Kyle and John
April Ryan
STC Moms
GSM J&J Moms
Ladies of AWWG
People of Antigua & Barbuda

These FABULOUS women who have been on this journey with me and
ALWAYS had my back:
Lisa P.; Paula D.; Wanda G.; Tamara M.; Donna S.;
Michelle H.; Kishia B-H; Angie B.; Dr. Tanek J.; Dr. Marilyn C.; Tia W.;
Nicole C.; Danielle H.; Kimberly M.; Edda A.; Dr. Sandra H.;
Monique A-W.; Georgette L.; Sheronda P-W.; Wanetta H.;
Debra M.; Carla P.; Julie B. (aka "Jukie")

In loving memory of Kim H.

PART 1

Section 1 - Hopes and Dreams

Busted! My mother always said, "*What you do in the dark ALWAYS comes to the light!*"

CHAPTER 1

EVEY – "SUPPORT IS EVERYTHING!"

"It's back, Evelyn. The cancer is back. But this time we found spots on your pelvis, as well as your left kidney, right femur, two ribs and your lower spine. That's why you've been experiencing the pain in your leg. I'm so sorry."

With these words and tears in her eyes, Dr. Maxine Monroe, my oncologist, told me once again, my diagnosis was *cancer*. She and I had been down this road twice before but both times before she'd told me *The Bitch* (the term I use for my cancer) was confined only to my breasts – first the right, then the left three years later. Now I'd been cancer free for four and a half years and with the exception of the pain in my right leg I'd started experiencing recently, I felt fine and I was looking forward to training and running in my first triathlon.

Besides my husband and children, running is my life. I'm convinced that in addition to my faith, it is what kept me sane and alive after my second bout with cancer.

I had attributed the pain in my leg to simple fatigue from my daily training regimen but thought it was best to get it checked out. Given my history of cancer, Dr. Monroe decided to run both a CAT scan and MRI to be thorough. I've always been an optimist and I'd become familiar with the drill so I wasn't at all nervous about going through these tests but as usual I felt anxious until I received the results. Frankly, I wanted the process to be over quickly so I could get back to my life and not be further interrupted or distracted by the looming threat of *The Bitch*.

For some odd reason, hearing the results this time felt nothing like the others. The first time, I was so shocked I literally collapsed into a heap onto the floor of Dr. Monroe's office after hearing this unbearable news.

The second time, I was angry and blamed myself for not allowing my doctors to take both of my breasts during my first surgery because my vanity couldn't come to terms with having *both* of them surgically removed. Implants or not, I couldn't fathom it. I'd identified myself with having breasts as part of being a woman, mother, and nurturer. The ones *God* gave me, not some fake man-made versions. I wanted *my* breasts. Not just for me, but for my husband, for *us*. They were *my* breasts but I shared them with him and I felt as if *The Bitch* - via my breasts - was chiseling away at our relationship and us. I held on to that anger until I couldn't any longer and when they finally removed my other diseased breast, it seemed like my anger was cut out with it.

When I awoke from that surgery, I no longer felt anger and pain. Instead, I was awash with an indescribable peace and calm that has remained within me to this day. Since that moment, I've known for sure God is truly living inside of me because this thing called *cancer* no longer frightens me, worries me, or is permitted to take over my life. God is in control and I trust HIM!

After getting through the treatments that followed my *second* diagnosis, I committed myself to LIVING – with or without my natural breasts – and started walking at least thirty minutes every day. My walks progressed to light jogs and before I knew it, I had entered my first 5K race. I've since completed three marathons and was beginning to train for my first triathlon. I'd lost forty pounds (a healthy forty, not just from the chemo), had reconstructive surgery, was thrilled with my perky new ta-tas and feeling better and hopeful I'd finally beaten *The Bitch*.

Our sons were doing well in their respective schools and their graduations rolled in one after the other. My relationship with Len, my husband, was solid and we were enjoying each other again sans the dread of *cancer* lurking in the shadows. I'd completed a dual Masters Degree in Public Health and Business Administration and was looking forward to forging ahead in a new career as a hospital administrator. Our family was healthy again because we didn't have to engage and be beholden to that unwanted visitor, *The Bitch*, any more. I'd been cancer free for four and a half years! Life was good!

When Dr. Monroe told Len and me my cancer was back, my reaction to this news surprised both of them. You never know how you'll react to hearing something like this. As Dr. Monroe spoke, I began to laugh. I leaned forward in my chair, elbows on my thighs shook my head repeatedly and just laughed hysterically. I laughed so hard, I began to cry. At one point in between my laughter and the tears I blurted out,

"Are you fucking kidding me? I'm doing a triathlon in eight months. I don't have time for this *Bitch* now!"

The combination of my reaction to the news and uncharacteristic use of the "f bomb" shocked Len and Dr. Monroe. There was a stunned silence in the room as they tried to gauge my reaction; probably assuming I was in shock. Perhaps I was. Perhaps not, but laughing at the news felt good and it made me feel in control. I *needed* to feel in control of this *Bitch* who, without invitation or permission, had blasted her way back into my life *again*.

I continued, addressing them directly.

"I just found out I have cancer *again*, for the *THIRD TIME!* I think I'm entitled to curse if I want to!"

"It's... it's just you *never* curse, that's all," Len stuttered out in a hushed tone.

"The Lord understands my reaction. I'm already forgiven!" I retorted, dismissing his observation and waving him off.

I got up from my seat and started pacing the floor. Len stood up too. I think he did it in order to catch me should I collapse again. I convinced him I wouldn't require his help and got him to take his seat. I calmly asked Dr. Monroe to repeat the areas where the new cancer was found.

"We found hot spots on your pelvis, left kidney, right femur, two ribs and your lower spine," she repeated.

"What the hell did *The Bitch* do, Maxi? I asked. "Dip a paint brush into a can filled with cancer and just splatter me with it?

"Unbelievable! You're really trying to kill me this time, huh?" I audibly addressed the cancer that had invaded my body again. "But you won't win! I'm telling you *right now*. **YOU** WON'T WIN!"

This was when I first started talking to the disease as if it had taken on a human form. It had invaded me once more, but this time it wasn't contained to my breasts because I didn't have those any longer. Now I felt this had become a personal war with a demon that was hell bent on ruining, if not killing, me. When this realization landed in my spirit, I immediately made the decision to fight and *win*! I started by seeking the blessing in the devastating news my doctor just gave me.

"OK, so what's the good news, Maxi? What's the blessing?"

"Well, the good news is that we know what type of cancer it is. It's what you've been battling from the beginning, breast cancer, so we know how to treat it. Although your breasts were removed and we tried to get all of the cancerous cells, there were some we couldn't reach. We had hoped the chemo and radiation would have eradicated those but..."

I knew how her sentence would end so I interrupted her. I was ready to move onto the next phase.

"Game plan, game plan. We need a game plan," I rapidly paced the floor and like a coach preparing her players for a big game, I began clapping my hands in excitement. I was getting "the team" and myself ready for battle. I was getting in the zone.

"So, see, there *is* a blessing in this news. God is GOOD! He is *GOOD*! I'm not going to die, at least not yet. I told you a long time ago that *cancer will not kill me.* I believe it. Do *you* still BELIEVE, Maxi? We're a TEAM, right? Do you STILL BELIEVE? God has my back! I BELIEVE IT! If you don't or if you have any reservations at all, I need to know RIGHT NOW so I can assemble the *right* team!

"So, Dr. Monroe, are you in? You're my girl, but I gotta hear it straight from you. Do you still BELIEVE?" I calmly, yet pointedly, asked.

Without hesitation she responded, "Yes, Evelyn, I *still* believe. You're an amazing woman. God bless you."

I turned to Len and with the same level of energy, vigor and a bright smile, asked him the same question.

"Ok, babe, I know I don't have to ask you this question, but I will. Are *you* in? Do *you* still *BELIEVE?*"

I asked the question assuming and expecting my husband of twenty years would respond quickly and affirmatively. We'd been down this road twice before and he had been there every step of the way. I had no reason to think this time would be any different. Instead, he paused, covered his mouth with his right hand and slowly shook his head. He took two deep breaths, looked up at the ceiling and shook his head again; this time a tear fell down his right cheek. He looked at me and just continued shaking his head; the words trapped inside his mouth.

"Len? I need to hear you tell me you're in and *you* still believe I can beat this thing – *WE* can beat this thing, Len!"

Sensing the tension, Dr. Monroe excused herself and told us to take all the time we needed to talk. Once the door closed, I walked over to the chair I had been sitting on and pulled it closer to him. Leaning in, I found myself pleading with him, or better yet, doing my best to convince him of what I knew was true, I was going to be fine. The journey wouldn't be easy but I'd survive it.

"Len? We'll get through this, babe. Cancer is NOT going to kill me!"

As I reached for his hand, he jumped out of his chair and pointedly said to me, "I, I can't do this any more, E. I just can't go through this again. *Your cancer is killing **me**...* and I want a divorce."

The forced smile on my face disappeared immediately. While I wanted to believe the enormity of the situation had just momentarily overwhelmed him, in that moment, I believed every word he'd said. There was no doubt in my mind he meant it and for the first time since I had been diagnosed with this disease all those years ago, I felt abandoned and unsupported.

He left my cancer and me alone in the room and did not return.

I've always viewed Len as my rock and best friend so his reaction to my diagnosis was shocking and worse than hearing the news that the cancer was back. Leonard Montague, MD, my husband, an anesthesiologist and co-owner of a popular medical spa, had always been available to me -- emotionally, physically, mentally, and spiritually and that's what made our marriage so incredible. From the very beginning of our relationship, Len was always very attentive and doting and loved only me.

We met the month before I graduated from nursing school.

Unbeknownst to me, my college roommate Faith had set me up on a blind date with him. For weeks, she had gone on and on about Len who was a friend of her boyfriend and how she thought we'd make a great couple. I refused to meet him because I hated being fixed up on blind dates. I found them awkward because inevitably the other person didn't measure up to how they were described so ultimately I'd walk away disappointed and possibly dodging some weirdo for several weeks.

I wasn't interested in that happening again and repeatedly made that clear. But Faith is like a dog with a bone. Once she gets something in her mind, she won't let go. In this case, it was matching Len Montague up with me and in an effort to get her way, she'd managed to get us both to attend a Memorial Day cookout at a friend's house.

As fate would have it, Len and I found each other at the cookout without

Faith's introduction. He noticed me mingling among some friends and made an obvious "Bee line", landing him next to me. He introduced himself and we spoke for some time.

I learned a lot about Leonard Montague that afternoon. I was intrigued by his sense of purpose. He was confident but not a braggart. He listened attentively when I spoke and seemed genuinely interested in my opinions and me. He encouraged my dreams of becoming a surgical nurse and then later moving into hospital administration. He was adamant about his plans of becoming a doctor – specifically, an anesthesiologist– and expressed his desire to do a brief stint in the "Peace Corps" or maybe "Doctors Without Borders" at some point in his career.

"You never know," he said. "One day we may find ourselves working on the same case."

We smiled at the thought and toasted our plastic cups.

He was excited about an upcoming humanitarian trip to Haiti he was planning to take with other pre-med students after graduation. Len beamed when he talked about starting medical school in the fall and how demanding the curriculum was certain to be. He seemed focused, driven and very much a giver. Those qualities put him in a different light compared to the other self-centered and self-serving guys I'd met since moving to the United States from Antigua, West Indies and I was intrigued.

Len was altruistic and God-fearing. Originally from New Orleans, his paternal grandfather was Trinidadian, so we had similar family values and backgrounds. He, like me, is an only child and both of us came from large, well-to-do extended families. His parents are both doctors, while my mother, Marguerite, is an ophthalmologist and my father, David, a civil engineer.

We exchanged numbers but things stalled after graduation. He left for Haiti and I went home to Antigua for the summer until my nursing practicum started in September. In the spring of the following year, I saw him at a luncheon for the volunteers of a children's mentoring group and we reconnected. He was excited to see me and asked me out that day. We dated for two years before he proposed to me over Memorial Day weekend on Broadway in New York City. He told me I was the brightest star in his universe and what better place to propose to a star than on Broadway where stars are made and dreams come true every day.

There, in the middle of Times Square, Len Montague asked me to make his dreams come true by becoming his wife for a lifetime. I said, "Yes!" and the crowd that had gathered and witnessed the proposal cheered and applauded. A wonderful stranger even took a picture of him proposing and our long kiss immediately after I accepted. We gave him our address and he sent the photos to us a few days later including one in a beautifully matted frame that said, "She said *YES!*" inscribed at the bottom. While his proposal was amazing, that photo of this memorable event has always remained most special to me. It remains prominently displayed in our home and I believe it symbolizes we'll be together for a lifetime.

For the first time since Len and I married, I felt completely alone. He'd abandoned me to deal with this diagnosis and all that was to follow. But before the door could completely close behind him, Adrienne walked in. In a barely audible whisper, I told her the cancer was back, Len couldn't handle it and he wanted a divorce. I could hear Faith's voice in the hallway saying "OK, Krish, we'll see you when you get here," while immediately asking, "Len, where are you going?"

I couldn't hear his reply.

Faith continued, "What do you mean you're *leaving*? What the *Hell* is wrong with you? You can't leave *now*, she needs you!"

"E, are you OK? What did the doctor say?" Faith shot out those questions as she entered the room.

In a near whisper, Adrienne, cradling me in her arms, told her my diagnosis.

"It's back, Faye. The cancer is back."

8

Poor Faith. I couldn't speak or acknowledge her, my oldest and dearest friend. I was numb. With every step Len had taken as he exited the room, the energy to fight this disease seemed to drain out of me. The realization that my "best friend" had just walked out on me when I needed him most left me in shock. Len's abandonment was without a doubt more devastating and difficult to accept than hearing the actual diagnosis.

Faith dropped onto the floor next to my legs and feet as if the news had deflated her. Her black patent leather "red bottoms" folded like pretzels under her St Johns suit and she shook nervously as she clung to my legs, her head on my knees while Adrienne continued to envelope me in her arms.

The love I received from my girlfriends that afternoon felt like heavenly angels were holding and lifting me up. Even though no words were spoken, I no longer felt alone or frightened. Instead, I began to feel at peace and embraced by an overwhelming and indescribable feeling of *love*. It was spiritual and it penetrated every fiber of my body. It felt pure and cleansing and healing all at the same time; calming me and making me feel safe. Words cannot describe this and I've *never* felt anything like it before or since. Faith eventually got up from the floor and anchored herself to the other side of me. My girlfriends did what my husband would not do, could not do. They just held me as the three of us sat there and cried.

The tears I shed were for my sons Zeke, Timothy and Isaiah and the fact they would have to live with this demon again. I allowed myself to feel sadness because it was real, but I clung to the peace and calm that engulfed my spirit because at that very moment, I realized that God was present within me and the peace I felt was His way of telling me I was going to be OK. I knew my healing – through God's grace – had already begun. His love filled the void Len had left behind.

As we sat there in a pool of all of our tears, I somehow managed to lighten the mood by saying to Faith, "Girl, I'm glad you got up off of that dirty floor in your suit!"

"Shut up," she laughed and wiped the tears from her eyes.

"I love you, E.," Faith said. "This suit doesn't mean anything to me. You're all I care about. But you better believe I'm taking it straight to the cleaners in the morning, 'cause you *know* I'm a germ-phobe!"

The three of us laughed wiped each other's tears away and clung to each other as dear friends. They were ready to support my fight and knew I would be fine.

I first met my *sister-girlfriends*, Faith, Adrienne, and Krishna in college when we were all wide-eyed co-eds eager to take on the world and leave our mark in it. Faith St. John was the very first person I met on campus during freshman move in day at our Ivy League university. She was one of my three suitemates but the only one I connected with immediately. During a mandatory freshman workshop, we met our other two sister-girlfriends, Adrienne Moran and Krishna Williams. The four of us were grouped together for an icebreaker exercise and have been stuck together ever since. Faith was a pragmatic, polished, and well-spoken New Yorker who loved Hip Hop. Adrienne, a true "old money" Southern Belle, was hilariously funny and not afraid to get her hands dirty while Krishna was a petit beauty that didn't take herself too seriously and had a great sense of humor. We worked well together, and laughed and giggled during the entire orientation.

Four different women from different walks of life; we're all very independent, have pursued various professions and we're close enough to allow each other to grow as individuals – encouraging and supporting one another along the way. I realize now how truly rare this type of connection is between women. We are honest but never deliberately hurtful; we push and encourage each other without secretly competing against one another and we are the cornerstones of each other's lives.

Admittedly, the four of us have been slaves to fashion and all things designer since college – even when some of us couldn't afford it! It's one of the many interests we share and have no shame in admitting. We've lived by our labels for decades and everyone who knows us knows it.

Faith, Adrienne, Krishna and I graduated from college together; attended every graduate school graduation for each other since; we were bridesmaids in each others weddings; and we are all godmothers to the collective brood of nine children between the four of us.

As the years passed by and our lives with husbands, children and careers began to solidify, our sister-girlfriend bond has grown stronger. Together, we are all living the dreams we'd set for ourselves and have supported each other through every milestone and challenge.

CHAPTER 2

FAITH – "TRUST IS EVERYTHING!"

With experience under my belt and Len making himself virtually invisible, I decided to manage my third set of treatments differently. I allowed myself to rely on my girlfriends more than him on treatment days or when I needed help managing my household. Typically on chemo days, Faith and I would go to the hospital while Adrienne came over to my house to prepare her amazing all natural green smoothies because they energized me and were the only thing I could keep down at one point. Krishna always made sure my portion of the bills were paid, saw to the housekeeper and scheduled visits from the masseuse and acupuncturist she'd hired for my benefit. I knew this battle wasn't going to be easy but I was hopeful, positive and did my best to remain upbeat in spite of everything. My girlfriends made sure I was emotionally, mentally, physically and spiritually "healthy" and ensured my household stayed afloat the way it would if I were cancer-free.

We had dinner and drinks together every Thursday night from 6:00p to 9:00p so we could catch up on what was happening in every one else's lives. I counseled them when asked and this definitely helped me take my mind off of my battle.

We also got together with our families for church on Sundays. Church has always been special to us because it's an opportunity to forget about our problems and focus on our faith.

While my parents wanted to be with me, I respectfully asked them not to visit during this chemo and radiation regimen but instead to take our sons home with them to Antigua for the summer. It was the best graduation/summer vacation gift I could give the boys and their doting grandparents because I felt none of them should have to endure cancer and its effects on me any longer. I also thought that with the children away, Len and I could work on our marriage and move forward from this setback together.

Initially, my parents didn't want to agree to this request because they wanted to be with me, but I didn't want the additional stress of them worrying over me and blaming themselves in some way for my health problems. In the end we compromised. I agreed to allow Mrs. Olive Samuels, a friend of the family and a widowed, retired nurse stay with me during my treatments in order to keep a "medical eye" on me and to report to my parents.

Mrs. Samuels was definitely an angel. A soft-spoken, gentle, kind and very young seventy-two year old West Indian woman who formally trained as a nurse in the United States Air Force over thirty-five years ago; she was the perfect person to take care of me. Widowed after forty-five years of marriage, she returned to working part-time three years ago to stay active. Before I received my diagnosis, she had been considering moving to the West Coast to be closer to her children and grandchildren but when my parents asked her if they could hire her to be my full time caretaker she immediately said yes. I must admit Mrs. Samuels was a Godsend.

I was not feeling my best as I approached the tail end of my treatments. I was tired of being sick, lethargic and wanted it all to end. While my plan worked great as far as my children and parents were concerned, unfortunately, Len proved to be less than supportive and virtually nonexistent. He repeatedly made himself unavailable on treatment days and often came home too late to make any meaningful contributions to my care when I needed him and his help the most.

We seldom spoke and no longer shared a bed. We were nothing more than roommates who shared a domicile and children. It was sad, but this situation quickly became my reality and I had no choice but to face it. After all, it was staring me in the face each and every day. He was *living* another life while I was *fighting* cancer! While I had no concrete proof, I felt strongly he was having an affair but I couldn't bring myself to confront him and fight that battle on top of the one with my health too. I had to concentrate on getting well again for my kid's sake.

With Mrs. Samuel's spiritual guidance, I clung to my faith in God and prayed daily for the emotional, mental, and physical strength necessary to get through my fight against this vicious demon in my body. I also prayed for the wisdom to understand what Len was going through as he too, dealt with my cancer, albeit in his own way. I needed to understand his decision to abandon me the way he did in my time of need.

At this point in my treatment, my parents hated him, our children had lost all respect for him, my friends merely tolerated him when they encountered him at the house and Mrs. Samuels prayed for all of us daily. No one understood Len's callousness but I made the decision not to allow it to consume me because I believed we'd get our marriage back on track once my treatments ended. I knew cancer doesn't affect just the patient, it affects *everyone* and I felt he just needed to deal with it on his own terms even if it meant abandoning me for a short time. So, whatever he was doing and perhaps whomever he was with, I knew was temporary because Len loves *me*. He needed to get through this latest challenge his own way and I'd decided I would give him the freedom and the space to do that. I decided to leave him in God's hands while I focused on beating this disease and getting well in order to be able to be a healthy mother and wife.

As this series of treatments wound down and Len's indifference continued, I was in the awkward position of having to rely on Faith, Adrienne and Krishna for many routine physical tasks but as I got mentally stronger, it was critically important for me to support them as much as possible emotionally as they were doing for me physically.

One afternoon Faith and I were driving back from the gym and I could tell she was distracted and distant. She didn't look like herself and was definitely not the Faith I knew. Once we got back to my house I asked her what was wrong. Strangely, she couldn't even look at me and then through her tears she said, "D is cheating on me, Evey. I didn't want to burden you with my problem; you don't need the extra stress. He's *cheating on me!*

"Van just blurted it out on the phone a couple of days ago," she sobbed and continued,

"She said, 'I hate to tell you this, Faith, but your husband's been cheating on you!' "

Her words took my breath away and I felt all of the pain she was carrying. I grabbed her hand and simply held it tightly as it seemed like her very life was draining right out of her with each tear.

Faith and Van both met and married a Rathers brother: Clyde and DiMarco. Van was the first one to marry into the family through her union with Clyde, while five years later Faith followed in her footsteps and married DiMarco. It wasn't until Faith was officially a part of the family she learned Van's marriage had been compromised by Clyde's womanizing, a situation Van felt she had no choice but to tolerate.

I had known for years Faith believed Van deeply resented her life in comparison to her own. Faith had had a wonderful childhood, a successful career and most importantly, a happy marriage and family while Van's life was pretty much the polar opposite. Although I never told Faith, I always believed the differences in their lives kept them from building a real friendship.

Faith and her brother Luke were raised in an upper middle class neighborhood in Westchester, NY. Their family was close-knit despite their dad, Keith's, constant travels for his job as an airline executive and their mother, Bridgette's, full-time work as a CPA at a mid-size accounting firm.

Unlike similar neighborhoods in the area, which were predominately white, theirs was a melting pot of races, religions, and nationalities. As a result, Luke and Faith always joked how they attended school at the United Nations and she said they never felt intimidated or insecure around people of different colors or backgrounds.

In fact, the opposite was true. Because of their dad's job as an executive with a major airline, they were able to travel to many of the places their classmate's families had immigrated from; places many of them had never been to themselves! They spent summer vacations in Europe, Africa, and Asia and Spring Break was often in the Caribbean. As a result, their classmates often called them "spoiled brats" but it was usually in jest and when it wasn't, they just took it in stride.

Over the years I learned that as Faith was growing up, there was always a perceived pressure in her community to "Keep up with the Jones" but her father would hear nothing of it and he'd always tell her, " We're not *rich*, we are *comfortable*. It can all vanish in a flash if you lose your humility." The message behind this? Life's delicate nature and good fortune should never be taken for granted.

Good fortune smiled on Faith when half way through sophomore year, she realized she had to settle down and declare a major. Her thoughts kept returning to politics.

She had run for class President senior year in high school and lost by only six votes and although the loss itself didn't bother her, she couldn't let go of the "why" and she sometimes wondered what she could have done differently to win.

She decided she wanted to become active in politics, but not as a candidate. Faith decided to become a political strategist and create winning teams while learning how to avoid the mistakes of less successful ones. By the end of her sophomore year, Faith declared political science as her major.

As part of this major, one of the practicums was volunteering for a race at the state or local level. Faith chose to volunteer on the Pierce Johannson campaign; an up and coming candidate for state representative whose headquarters was close to campus. She was happy to work for him because they shared the same ideas about how our communities could be best served.

Faith got two "bugs" working on that campaign. She confirmed politics was definitely where she wanted to make her mark career wise and another bug by the name of DiMarco Rathers.

She first met DiMarco at Johannson's campaign headquarters and they took "baby steps" on the campaign together, albeit on different trajectories. Faith started with door to door canvassing and by the end of the general election, she had worked her way up to doing some debate prep and message development. For his part, DiMarco worked the phone banks and helped tally poll data of likely voters. The nature of their jobs required them to frequently work together.

D didn't impress her the first time they met (it was just the opposite, in fact – she said she found him "annoyingly arrogant" at times), but the more she got to know him, the more she began to like him. As they worked together, she found him to be smart, witty, engaging and driven and that was *definitely* attractive to her. He had set goals for himself she found impressive and realistic. While he was too full of himself sometimes, he was always true to his word and appeared to be thoughtful toward people and causes he cared about. As a result, after working together on the campaign then continuing to date after the election, they got close and while he wasn't her "type", he grew on her and over time they seemed to mesh well.

Once that race was over and their candidate took his place in the state house, Faith immediately wanted to work on another campaign. She continued her classwork but she also sent her resume to her party's state committee and applied to join their pool of paid political workers. They promised to try to place her as soon as the next election cycle began and urged her to finish her BA and then get her Masters degree. She enrolled in graduate school and patiently hoped for her next campaign assignment.

And then fate stepped in. Representative Wilbur Whitestone, the

Congressman from her district unexpectedly died while still in office. A special election had to be held to fill his seat and her political committee contacted Faith and asked her if she would be interested in working for Maureen Van Hudson, a state senator who had announced her candidacy. Faith jumped at this opportunity and became a strategy/media consultant for that campaign which won easily, but as a result of that, *Van Hudson's* state senate seat became vacant, so *another* special election had to be held.

This time, Harry Mitchelson, a state representative, contacted Faith personally and asked her to work on his campaign for state senator and things began to snowball from there. Once the special election cycle was done, the usual primary season was beginning and suddenly, Faith was in high demand not only in our state but also in other races across the country. She had more work than she ever thought possible. It was a dream come true and she thrived on the excitement, long hours and adrenaline.

The next few years were a whirlwind. She went from race to race, state to state, usually working on several campaigns at a time.

Faith also didn't forget her commitment to graduate school and completed her studies despite her hectic work schedule. She knew a lifetime of being on the campaign trail wasn't for her. She wanted more stability: a husband, a family, a house and the myriad of other things the rest of her friends were already way on their way to achieving.

I can't say her relationship with D was typical. Between her hectic travel schedule and school as well as his own pursuit of a graduate degree and advancing in his career as a CPA, they were busier than a lot of other couples their age. I sometimes worried that DiMarco and Faith were too busy for each other and she worried that her frequent trips and fluctuating weight would put him off, but he always assured her he was head over heels in love with her and that his love grew with each election she completed. When things weren't going well on the campaign trail, he'd sometimes pay her a surprise visit and make her shut work down for a few hours while he lavished attention on her.

" Faye, I'm so proud of you. If I'm out somewhere and I see you on TV, I tell everyone around who will listen, 'That's my girl!" he'd tell her.

"You have my heart and you're the only woman in the world for me. I don't expect you to settle down now, but you're going to eventually, and when you do, I'm going to be waiting and I'm going to make you my wife."

Hearing things like that made her feel much better and went a long way to allay any doubts or fears she had that he might be seeing other women during her absences. In hindsight, while I had no knowledge of it, it wouldn't surprise me if he were cheating on her during this period too!

They dated for about three years before he seriously started to talk marriage and settling down.

It didn't take long before Faith found herself being swept up into the marriage mindset. All of us were either already married or making that transition and I think she felt the pressure to marry mounting.

And then, DiMarco proposed. It was memorable because it was also the night of a big "all white" 30th birthday party she had planned for him at the yacht club. Unbeknownst to her, however, he'd planned his proposal that night as well, so it was a spectacular evening neither of them, or their guests, would ever forget.

After their wedding, Faith slowly withdrew from campaign work, obtained her Ph.D., became a tenured political science professor at a highly respected liberal arts university and a political analyst for a local, but nationally syndicated talk show.

As for DiMarco, after their work on Johannson's campaign, he decided politics wasn't for him but he continued to work with numbers. He passed the CPA exam, got his MBA and rose through the ranks of several high profile auditing firms before establishing his own business for a handful of top notch clients. These client's personal finances often garnered media attention for them and (by default for him) for one reason or another.

Eventually, they bought a lovely Tudor style home in Bethesda, MD just outside of Washington, DC and God also blessed them with two wonderful daughters, Kennedi and Harper.

Kennedi was born just a year after their wedding. I think Faith would have liked to have had more "alone time" with D to get used to their lifestyle but Kennedi had other plans and couldn't wait to join them! At first, motherhood was a little overwhelming, but then Faith realized that handling the unpredictability of a child wasn't all that different from handling the unpredictability of a campaign, so she got the knack of it pretty quickly and was an old pro at juggling a child, a husband and her career by the time they had Harper, three years later.

Faith did her best to pattern her loving marriage after that of her parents. Their relationship has always been the envy of most and remarkable to me because after all of these years, they still make time to just talk to one another. It's obvious they enjoy each other's company and being together is no chore for either of them. Their love has been deepened and enriched by the enormous respect they have for each other and Faith wanted that for her marriage as well. She witnessed it growing up, so she knew it was possible and why Van's words, "Your husband has been cheating on you," must have penetrated Faith's heart like acid. I knew how miserable Van was in her own life and so it didn't entirely surprise me she would be cavalier about trying to destroy Faith's.

Faith sighed deeply and continued.

"I asked her to repeat herself and while I was waiting, I flew like an eagle downstairs to the entertainment room where DiMarco, my *husband of fourteen years*, was watching Sunday afternoon football.

"I didn't give him any indication as to what was coming. I simply gestured for him to pay attention as I muted the TV while I sat directly across from him and put the phone on speaker. I was nervous, but calmly repeated the question,

" 'Van, what did you just say?'

" 'I don't want to be the one to tell you this, Faith, but Clyde is my witness and he's right here,'" she said in her strong, Vietnamese accented English. " 'I just want this stuff out of my house. D is cheating on you.'

"Evey, I swear, if I had blinked, I would have missed DiMarco's *only* reaction –his eyes widened a bit– other than that, he just sat there motionless on the sofa and seemed a little annoyed I was interrupting the game."

"Faith! I'm so sorry! I just can't believe it! What did you do?" I asked.

She responded matter-of-factly. I said, " 'Really? OK,' and hung up the phone.

"D kept staring at the television behind me, so I asked him three direct questions.

" 'Are you cheating on me, D?'

" 'No,'" he replied, finally looking at me.

" 'Have you *ever* cheated on me?'

" 'No.'

" 'So *why* would Van say such thing?'" I asked him.

He actually had the nerve to say, " 'I don't know. Go ask her!' Can you believe it?"

I said, "'OK, I will,' and I drove straight over to Van and Clyde's house."

This didn't surprise me. Faith has never shied away from confrontation.

"D's cavalier response made me so livid I forgot about the Sunday dinner I had in the oven, as well as Kennedi and Harper, who had been running in and out of the house, playing with the neighbor's kids."

She paused for a minute and then continued.

"On the short drive over there, I tried to figure out what would motivate Van to make such an absurd accusation. Trying to make sense of this fueled my fury as I pulled into their driveway and knocked on the front door.

"Clyde greeted me with a simple, yet serious, 'Hey, Faith.' I just said 'Hi' and immediately asked to speak with Van.

"You know Van never keeps a tidy home and that day was no exception. Clyde walked me down the hallway and into the kitchen where I could barely see the tabletop under the clutter of mail and other stuff.

"As soon as Van joined us, Clyde actually started to get ready to leave the house and the two of us alone. I was so mad, I said,

"'Clyde, this is *your* house, you don't have to leave.'"

"'Nah, man,' he said to me as he shook his head. 'I've got some stuff to do.'

"'Stick around, Clyde. Don't leave. It's out now', I said to him.

"'You knew what was going on because you were involved too, right? D's your boy, right? You guys look out, or should I say, *lie* for each other. Don't leave your own house, Clyde.'

"Evey, he kept heading for the door and I practically screamed out, 'So, you're just going to *leave*? You don't have anything to say about what's happening here?'

"He paused as he opened the door, turned around, shook his head and only said, 'Nothing good is gonna come out of this,' and walked out.

"As he closed the door, I turned to Van.

"'What's going on?' I asked her.

"Instead of answering my question, she busied herself straightening up the kitchen table like it was suddenly a priority.

" 'Van, what the hell is going on?' I asked her again while I worked to keep my composure.

"She attempted to clear the mess, shook her head and finally, in that strong Vietnamese accent of hers said, 'I don't want to be in middle of this Faith. I'm going to be hated by whole family and I just want it out of my house.'

" 'You're *already* in the middle of it!' I reminded her. '*You're* the one who started it by opening your mouth. You're already up to it chin high. Now just tell me what the hell is going on!' I practically screamed.

"This bitch dropped a bomb on my family and *now* she was telling me she doesn't want to get in the middle of it? Am I right? As usual, she was only thinking about herself. Did she really think I give a *damn* what the family is going to think about her dumb ass when they discover *she's* the one who let the secret out? Evey, I wanted to tear her fucking head off of her shoulders because she seemed to be having second thoughts about telling me what she knew about D's infidelity but I decided to try to appeal to her woman to woman in order to get to the truth. I regained my composure, quieted my tone and calmly began my appeal.

" 'Van, please tell me what you know,' I said. " 'If what you are telling me is true, this situation is going to affect *everyone* but mainly my children. I know you know exactly how I feel at this very moment because you know I know Clyde has repeatedly cheated on you and abused you throughout your marriage. But I only learned what Clyde was doing to you *after* I married into the family and sadly, you and I were never close enough to talk about these types of things openly. Please, from one woman to another, *tell me everything*. Don't worry about what the family will say or think because with the truth on my side, the ball will be in *my* court - no one else's. But I can't make any decisions without *all* the information. Please, just tell me what you know.' "

"I think this appeal struck a cord with her because she finally sat down at the table and slowly began to tell me all she knew (or was willing to share). I grabbed some paper and a pen from atop the mess on the table and took notes.

"I listened to her tell me about the 'Hostess' (a soubriquet Faith created for her husband's mistress). I don't owe this whore the respect of referring to her by name. In fact, in my opinion, by giving her that particular nickname and not something more appropriate like 'bitch ass skank', I'm giving her more respect than she deserves! I learned she had worked part-time as a hostess at a café next door to the novelty shop where Van works and that's how she and D first met.

"Then I learned about her *ten year* affair with *my* husband!

"Van talked about the 'Hostess' and DiMarco; their trips and attendance at sporting events, lunches, dinners and the gifts he bought her. I was shocked to learn about the multiple lies he had told me over the years and the fact he was so brazen about his relationship with her he had no problem taking her around to socialize with mutual friends of ours – except, of course, you girls. She told me how comfortable the 'Hostess' was in publically referring to *my* husband as *her* 'boyfriend' in their social circles and how she made no bones about her plans to marry him.

"Imagine that! And I had no fucking clue any of this shit was going on because I was home doing what I'm supposed to be doing – holding down a *real* job, raising two kids, taking care of a household and being a good wife to him! Trust me, if I was running the streets he would have no choice but to be at home doing what I've been doing – being faithful. I guess it *is* true when they say, 'The wife is *always* the last to know!'

"It was horrible," she cried. "Periods of my life as a married woman flashed before my eyes, and suddenly learning it was all a lie was almost too much to bear. I felt sick to my stomach by the time Van finished. I got up from the table, folded the two double-sided pages of notes I'd taken and stuffed them in my pocket. I was in shock. I think I whispered 'Thank you' and left.

"Oddly enough, I *am* thankful.

"Thankful that after her initial hesitance, Van finally got up the nerve to tell me what she knew. Thankful that I didn't beat the shit out of her, even though that bitch, yellow-bellied Clyde left me alone with her when he knew what was coming!

"Evey, my head and my heart were at war. I felt jarred, like an electric current had shot through my body. Thoughts of betrayal, embarrassment, humiliation, anger and vengeance raced through my mind. I couldn't even tell *you* when it happened. I am so embarrassed.

" 'That mother fucker! He's been *cheating* on me!' I kept saying to myself as I got into my SUV and headed home.

"What's happened to my life?" Faith wailed to me. It was like she suddenly noticed I was still sitting there, listening to her.

"What about our children?" Faith continued, almost hysterical. "How could he do this to us?" "Everything we've worked so hard for is ruined!" "That selfish bastard!" "How will I tell my parents? *Should* I tell my parents?" "My brother, Luke? Oh my God, he's going to kill D when he finds out!"

Faith's reservation about telling her parents and brother, Luke, of DiMarco's cheating was justified. The St. John's are a very close-knit family and this situation was going to cause a problem in the family. Luke is extremely protective of his little sister and the news of D cheating on her was certain to cause a significant rift in the relationship he has with D so Faith's hesitancy was justified.

While Faith pursued a career in politics – albeit as a strategist behind the scenes –Luke had become a successful plastic surgeon and subsequently married and started a family of his own. His relationship with D had always been cautious because like Faith was at first, he felt D was unnecessarily arrogant and therefore occasionally annoying. As the years past, however, Luke began to accept DiMarco because Faith loved him. Learning of D's infidelity was certain to destroy Luke's perceptions of him.

The news of DiMarco's cheating shattered me. Hearing Faith tell the story was literally unbelievable. I thought they were a solid couple. Yes, DiMarco is arrogant but I *never* thought he was capable of cheating on his wife and ruining their lives and family. The only thing I could do was console my friend and remind her I would be here for her as always.

25

I got up from the table, poured her a glass of wine, got myself another green smoothie and asked her if she wanted to continue, which she did.

"As I drove home, I was so incensed I couldn't cry. I felt as if my heart had been ripped out of my chest and then run over by an eighteen-wheeler but I was focused on getting the truth out of D. Based on some of the things Van told me, as well as the timelines I started weaving together, events that had taken place in the past suddenly made sense. I wasn't in denial DiMarco had cheated on me, betrayed me, and destroyed my trust, Evey. I just wanted to know *why* and I wanted *answers*! I deserved the truth and I wouldn't stop until I got it." Faith sobbed uncontrollably and my heart broke for her. As she continued, I couldn't hold back my own tears.

"I pulled into the driveway and ran into the house. Fortunately, Harper and Kennedi were still playing outside on their scooters with the neighbor's kids. I was an emotional wreck and had no idea what would happen if I saw DiMarco or, even worse, approached him again – now that I had all of this new information – so seeing my children playing outside was a relief. I swear I was on the brink of losing it so, having even one of them say 'Mommy' and needing attention would have pushed me over the edge. I was a wreck!" she admitted.

"I ran into the house through the garage and mudroom and nearly tripped over all of the sporting gear and clothing. Honestly, it looked like a combination Under Armour, Nike and LL Bean outlets. As I sprinted through the kitchen and approached the stairs, I saw DiMarco come through the door from the basement and heard him telling someone on the phone, 'Yeah, man, she just walked in.' That comment caught my attention so I stopped in my tracks.

" 'Who the *fuck* is that?' I screamed.

" 'Brian,' he said.

" 'Really? Huh! Just the person I want to speak to because based on what I just found out, he knows you've been cheating on me for years too!' I yelled."

Brian Patterson is DiMarco's cousin and is as close to him as his brother. The three of them talk all the time and when D isn't on business travel, they hang out together. Faith loves Brian like a little brother as he's five years her junior. Over the years, she would give him sisterly advice about his career goals and relationships and this included his marriage and subsequent divorce from his college sweetheart, Sheryl. So when Van told Faith how much Brian knew about D's infidelity, his role in helping him cover it up and his own unfaithfulness to Sheryl, she nearly flipped a gasket over the level of betrayal she was uncovering. She explained how she tried to grab the phone from D, but he snatched it back and quickly said to Brian, "Call her back on *her* phone, man," and ended the call.

"Girl, there was something about his reaction to the phone that immediately struck me as 'off', but I couldn't quite put a finger on it and I had too many other things on my mind, so I let it go at that moment," Faith said. "But I came back to it later and realized what it was. D was already trying to cover his tracks and feared giving me his cell phone for even a few seconds meant all his personal information – text messages, email, phone contacts – would be at my fingertips and that wasn't a chance he was willing to take.

"As I ran up the stairs to our bedroom, my phone rang. It was Brian. I slammed the door behind me, which caused the framed picture of us that hung on the wall over our bed to be jarred out of place. Huh, how visually metaphoric is that?" she openly pondered.

"I answered the call and blurted out, 'Brian, did you know D was cheating on me?' I began pacing the floor; nearly tripping over the pair of Manolos I bought at Saks with you after we left the gym, remember? There was a prolonged silence I let linger until my patience ran out, and then I just freakin' lost it because he wouldn't open his mouth!

" 'Answer me, dammit! Did you *know* D was cheating on me? And don't fuckin' lie about it either,' I yelled at him as if he were a child - not a grown thirty something year old divorcee.

"He had the nerve to say, 'Faith, you know I can't say anything that's not going to make this situation worse than it already is. D's my cousin. Please don't make me do this. I just can't.'

"Evey, I swear, at that point and with those words, I realized Brian Patterson made his decision to protect my cheating husband.

"I said to him, 'Forget it! You just answered my question. You'd rather protect his cheatin' ass because by protecting him you're protecting *yourself* too… you sorry ass mother fucker!'"

"Oh my goodness, Faye, but unfortunately, I'm not surprised. You know that family is going to stick together – rightly or wrongly," I said. As my best friend sat there pouring her guts out to me I sat in shock and amazement that *this* was her life at all! I couldn't believe it because she didn't deserve any of this.

She continued, "I said to Brian, 'Now I know why your marriage didn't last! And why after your divorce you and D tried to keep Sheryl and me apart!'"

" 'Faith I'm…' he tried to interrupt, but I cut him off and snapped,

" 'I loved you like a brother and this is how you treat me, Brian? I've supported every fuckin' thing you've ever done!' I yelled through my tears.

" 'I love you too, Faith, but…' I refused to allow him to continue making excuses and cut him off again.

" '*Fuck you, Brian.* Don't you ever say those words to me again! You're dead to me!' I screamed and hung up the phone. I'd heard enough from him.

"While pacing my bedroom floor, I scanned through my phone contacts for Sheryl's number. During my 'conversation' with Van she told me about an event involving Brian and Sheryl, which had occurred during their marriage. Between that story and the call I had with Brian, I wanted to speak to Sheryl immediately. I was convinced if she could confirm Van's account about her and Brian, everything else Van had told me about D and his years of infidelity would also be true.

"I found Sheryl's number and called her, pacing the floor as the phone rang. My hands were shaking, Evey, and my stomach was in knots. I was so nervous my heart felt like it would pound out of my chest and then she answered the phone.

" 'Hey Faith!' she sounded so excited. 'Girl, it's been forever! How are you?'

"She was her usual bright, cheery, upbeat self. You know, she always sounds like she has a smile on her face."

Sheryl and Faith met through her relationship with Brian. She's a lot of fun and was clearly head over heels in love with Brian so Faith liked her immediately. They got married and for a few years were happily setting up their household and planning to start a family. But for some reason none of us could figure out, it seemed like one day a dark curtain closed on their relationship and they divorced two years later. Of course when Faith asked Brian and D about it, they were very tight lipped and the bits and pieces they *did* tell her never seemed to add up. They even went so far as to subtly discourage her from staying in touch with Sheryl, but because Faith is her own woman, she felt the dissolution of their marriage shouldn't mean the dissolution of their friendship so the women stayed in touch.

Faith went on. "I said to Sheryl, 'I have to ask you something and all I ask is for you to be honest with me.'

" 'Sure, Faith, anything for you, girl. What's up?'

"I paused and it took all I had to ask her, 'As far as you know, did D ever cheat on me?' I sat down on the loveseat in my sitting room, my head in my hand, dreading her response. It was one of the hardest things I've ever had to face.

"Sheryl responded immediately but gently and said, 'Oh, Faith, I'm so sorry.

"My heart sank and a tear ran down my face. Her response confirmed what Van had blurted out on the phone as well as what she revealed in person in our conversation later that day. For over *ten years*, my husband of *fourteen years* had been completely unfaithful! I couldn't believe it and I felt like a complete fool.

"Sheryl explained she became aware of DiMarco's infidelity four years ago while I was pregnant with the twins I eventually lost in utero. She had stumbled across some travel plans on Brian's computer that didn't include her and when she confronted him about it, he confessed he'd allowed D to borrow his computer during a visit to their home so he could plan a trip with his mistress.

"Sheryl told me as soon as Brian told her about DiMarco's cheating she threatened to tell me. Brian begged her not to and promised he'd encourage D to end the affair.

"Sworn to secrecy and not wanting to bring this to my attention during this difficult time, she chose to remain silent.

"She told me, 'Faith, I felt so badly about knowing about D's infidelity and I couldn't let it go. I even said something to my mother-in-law and she told me to mind my business and keep my mouth shut! I was so offended by that and what felt like everyone's part in protecting D, and what he was doing, I couldn't take it. I got the sense that if Brian and I ever got into a similar situation, they'd treat me the same way. It was like this wall went up between their family and me and because I challenged their decision and wasn't on board with their plan to protect D I became the bad guy. It was crazy!'

"Her voice quivered. Her pain was still apparent as she told me how this impacted her marriage, their subsequent divorce and how very ugly it became for her.

" 'It became a real problem and then I got suspicious of Brian's behavior because based on the stories he was telling me about DiMarco, some of *his* timelines weren't adding up either, so I started checking into things. I called you one weekend to talk about my problems and suspicions about Brian but you had just been rushed to the hospital and that afternoon you lost the twins. I just couldn't bring myself to further complicate things for you. The whole thing was a big mess and I felt horrible for you on so many levels. I couldn't imagine what you were going through and I didn't want to add to it. I'm so, so sorry.'

"I believed every word she said. I was sad because I suddenly felt like *her* marriage ended because of DiMarco's infidelity in *my* marriage and her willingness to speak up for me. My respect for her grew exponentially because as she explained things, she never implied any regrets for her stance although I could tell she was still very hurt by it.

"Brian was probably worried some of his own shit would be discovered if the subject of D was raised. As Sheryl and I continued to talk, I could tell this was difficult for her because it brought back so many bad memories she'd buried since her divorce. She tried to comfort me, knowing how new all of this was and how shattered and raw I felt. She reminded me I had always been a prayerful woman of strong faith and that now, more than ever, I would need to rely on my faith to get me through this. Sheryl was comforting and I could tell that after all she'd been through she was healing and regaining her confidence in life. I was happy for her.

"She's a wonderful person and a real blessing. I love her and I'm so happy we've remained friends."

"Oh my goodness, Faye! I need a drink… I swear if I could have a shot of Tequila *right now* I promise you that bottle of Patron would be gone in no time! But, I can't… I'm numb just hearing all of this," I confessed to her.

"Evey, girl, this is just the tip of the freakin' iceberg! I've been numb for a week! And, let me tell you, when Adrienne and Krish found out, they went off! I'll take another glass of wine please.

"I didn't want to bother you, so I called Adrienne who was leaving town on a business trip, but she conferenced Krishna on with us and K agreed to meet me at the house.

"My mind raced as I paced the bedroom floor. I wondered how I'd missed the signs. I wanted to know whom she was and what happened in our marriage *years ago* that caused him to step outside of it and cheat on me. I saw my entire life with D – past, present, and my dreams and hopes for our future flash before my eyes and then a rage began to build inside me.

"I opened the door and made my way down the stairs. I'd planned to grab my purse and car keys, but as I made my way down the stairs I saw DiMarco. Without warning, I caught him completely off guard; lunged at him, slapped him across the face and called him a liar. He grabbed me and attempted to restrain me, which only made matters worse. I tried to pull away but he yanked me back in order to keep me from hitting him again. All of this commotion, yelling and screaming captured the girl's attention and they came running up the stairs. As they tried to pull us apart, D let me go and I screamed, 'You're a *fucking liar*!! How could you do this to us? You selfish bastard! I hope it was worth it to you!'

"As I stood there screaming and demanding answers, Krishna pulled up in the driveway, ran up the walkway, opened the door and yanked me outside. Kennedi and Harper were screaming because they've never seen anything like that between their father and me and they were terrified.

"For my children's sake, I left the house and them with Krishna before things got further out of control. As I walked down the driveway, they were screaming at the door with 'Auntie K' trying to reassure them that 'Mommy will be OK.' Truthfully, her arrival was timely and heaven sent because in hindsight, she likely prevented me from killing D.

"What's happened to my life?" Faith wailed to me. It was like the magnitude of everything that happened hit her all over again.

"What about our children?" Faith continued, almost hysterical. "How could he do this to us?" "Everything we've worked so hard for is ruined!" "That selfish bastard!"

CHAPTER 3

ADRIENNE – "SEX IS EVERYTHING!"

I was so glad I was nearing the end of my treatments when Faith told me about her problems with DiMarco. I could only thank God for getting me through it all so I could be there for my friend. Fortunately, my "not so good days" were becoming fewer and farther between and my ability to continue my modified training regimen was no longer significantly impacted by my cancer treatments. I felt more in control of my life and this was important to me.

Len and I were barely communicating and I saw very little of him. He spent all of his time at the hospital or at our medical spa and little to none at home caring for me. Thankfully, Mrs. Samuels was great support and comfort. As a nurse, not only did she keep a professional eye on me, but she also was a very calming spirit in my chaotic world dictated by disease. Between Mrs. Samuels, my girlfriends and the love and support of my boys who were in constant contact, I really was in the best of hands and was beginning to feel a shift in the energy around me and in my body. I needed it. I deserved it. And I welcomed it all.

Despite all this good news, I couldn't help but think about Adrienne when Faith mentioned her. While I pray for all my sister-girlfriends equally, Adrienne is the one who thinks she needs it the least and is most likely to stifle a laugh when I mention it.

Faith didn't know what I knew. There were now *three* of us with marriages falling apart.

A couple of years ago, Adrienne and I got together before she was leaving for a month long business trip. As Senior Vice President of International Marketing for Ryco Pharma, Inc., a major pharmaceutical company, she was about to leave for Europe, Asia and Africa and navigate more languages and time zones than I cared to think about.

"This job is killing me," she confided.

"You know how much I love to travel and close a deal, but I've had enough. There aren't any places I want to go to I haven't seen already and you know," she blushed a little, "money isn't an issue."

"Have you told Chris? What does he say?" I asked.

"Oh, you know Chris. He just says, 'Stay focused on our future' or 'Tough it out,'" she replied.

Chris, Adrienne's husband, is a workaholic. Working and building their financial portfolio is his primary focus but this comes at the expense of listening to Adrienne's complaints about her job or dreams of switching careers. What's worse, he neglects the physical intimacy she requires in their marriage. This is a huge problem for her and it has been that way for quite some time.

After being on the road for weeks at a time, Adrienne is the kind of woman who *needs* to be intimate with her husband. Sex shouldn't be viewed as some sort of chore, but unfortunately for her, she feels that's how he views it. Everything in their lives is predictable and for someone like Adrienne – a spontaneous, fun loving person who likes to try new things every now and again – it's an annoyance.

With her frustrations growing about their relationship, Adrienne had become a lot more vocal about what's NOT happening in their bedroom! As her girlfriend, I'd rather not know that much about their intimate life, but given how frustrated she is, I let her vent and get it off her chest.

Honestly, though, this is too much information!

Adrienne has told me Chris steers away from trying new things on his own and that includes in between the sheets. Their physical relationship is more routine than exciting. "If I get home after he's asleep, I have to wait until the morning – he doesn't like to be awakened to have sex; it actually annoys him!" she confided. "If I arrive before he's sleeping, I usually have to initiate it, and that's once we're in bed. Then he kisses me, (never passionately the way he used to), climbs on top and within five to ten minutes, it's all over. If I don't rush my climax, I won't reach it because he's reached his and that's the end of the line. I'm starting to wonder if I should stay with him."

What? Isn't it written somewhere if you have to constantly beg your husband for sex and rush your climax with him it's grounds for divorce?! Something is NOT right about that! Over her third martini that night Adrienne went on to admit, "When we were newly married, we had sex several times a week but even then it always lacked the passion I crave but have learned to live without over the years."

"And you married him any way? Basic sex was no surprise," I thought to myself as she poured her soul out to me.

As her girlfriend, all I could say was, "Dre, I'm so sorry. I really hope things get better."

I simply couldn't bring myself to say what I was really thinking which was, "I don't know how you've been holding up all of these years. You settled and now you're paying the price. You knew how important sex was to you from the beginning but you chose to compromise yourself for someone whose sex drive is far beneath yours hoping it wouldn't matter to you over time and now it's driving you crazy. Lord, chile'!"

She continued, "When our sex life becomes an issue, it's because I make it one. If it were up to him, he wouldn't change a thing because he's satisfied with the way things are. I give him hints...I even tell him what I like, but if he's not comfortable with something sexual (and that's most things), he doesn't even try. For a while he did, but I could tell he wasn't comfortable so I stopped pressing the issue.

"Our love life is just fair. We have sex, but there's really nothing to it. You know I'm a very sexual being but Chris' sex drive is nowhere near mine. Over the years, I've tried to convince myself it's not that important. Hmm…I'm beginning to think I was wrong about that!"

"Ya, think?!!!" I thought to myself.

I love my girl to death but I think the lack of activity in her bedroom is adversely affecting her ability to process the obvious.

Adrienne always said she married Chris for more than just the physical part of their relationship. He was a good guy with tremendous potential as a provider (something her father did very well notwithstanding his emotional distance for a time) and, Chris wanted to marry *her*. Now, twenty years later, having plenty of money and realizing the kids will be leaving the nest soon, it's no surprise she wants more from him. Personally, I don't see that happening. That leopard isn't changing his spots any time soon. Don't get me wrong. He's a nice guy but his personality is milk toast boring! She knows that and we've told her that many times over the years.

In general, while Adrienne and Chris are great as a team and share common life goals, the physical intimacy she craves and, frankly, *needs*, just isn't there. She was finally admitting it that night and trying to come to grips with it.

"I wish I was excited about the prospect of having sex with him, especially when I come home after a long trip, but I'm not. When I begin to feel this way, I want to relive the early days of our relationship. It was fun and exciting and I miss it."

When telling the story of how she and Chris met, Adrienne always romanticizes it and recalls the experience of their courtship this way:

It was around 7:00p and I was just getting home from work, standing in the lobby, waiting for the elevator. The doors opened from the basement parking level and there he was. Even if the elevator had been jam packed with people, which it wasn't, I would have immediately noticed his 6'3" frame and chocolate brown skin that looked almost edible.

I got on the elevator and pressed the button for my apartment on the fourteenth floor; his was already selected for the eleventh. As the door shut behind us and we began our ascent, Mr. Tall Dark and Handsome said,

"Excuse me. I hate to bother you, but I just moved into this building and I don't know the neighborhood very well. Could you recommend a place to eat? I'm starving and frankly, I'm not much of a cook."

"Oh, Lord," I thought immediately. "Is that the best pick up line you can come up with Mr. Cutie?" but I decided to play along any way.

"Sure, there are a ton of places just a couple of blocks away. Just take a right from the lobby and then another right when you reach Calvert Street. Pretty much anything you want to eat is right on those few blocks. If you live around here, you don't ever have to cook if you don't want to."

"Thanks so much," he said, flashing a grateful smile. "I'm a fast learner. I'm sure I won't have to rely on the kindness of strangers around here for much longer, even if they are beautiful."

I had to laugh a bit at that corny line but as it was coming from such a handsome stranger, I took the bait.

"Thanks. I'll tell you what," I said, extending my hand. "My name is Adrienne, so there you go, now we're no longer strangers and you know at least one person around here."

Before he had the chance to properly reciprocate, the bell for his floor rang and the doors opened.

He propped it open for a minute with his foot, extended his hand and said, "Nice to meet you Adrienne, I'm Chris" as he firmly held and shook my hand.

"Pleasure. Tell you what, Chris. I'm hungry, too. If you meet me in the lobby in thirty minutes, I'll let you buy me dinner. But thirty minutes sharp. If you're late, I will assume you've gone on without me or have decided you can live on air."

He seemed a bit surprised by how assertive I was but quickly regrouped and flashed another smile.

"Sounds good. And just for the record, I don't have a reputation for being full of air," he said as he released my hand and got off the elevator. I smiled and then blurted out, "We'll see about that," as the doors shut behind him.

"Well, that was easy," I said to myself as the elevator took me up to my floor. The unexpected meeting and exchange of wits made me smile. "And it's not like I feel like cooking or had other plans any way," justifying my sudden plans with this very handsome stranger.

That simple exchange was the beginning of their twenty-year relationship and marriage.

(They say you'll learn everything you need to know about someone in the first couple of hours you spend with them, and looking back on her "first date" with Chris, Adrienne can now fully admit its a truism, in more ways than she'd realized at the time.)

"The neighborhood I took him to that first night had every kind of restaurant imaginable and I had been living around the corner for three months already, so I considered myself a veteran as I'd already been to most of them.

I prepped for this spontaneous date: changing out of my Jill St. John "uniform" and took a quick shower. Since it was a typical humid summer night in Washington, I wore a brightly colored linen dress I bought in Hawaii the year before and paired it with a strappy pair of snakeskin Jimmy Choo sandals with nose bleed high heels. I wasn't surprised he was waiting in the lobby and practically starting to drool when he saw me exiting the elevator, but I *was* a little surprised at what he chose for his casual style, though -- he left on his work pants and had only changed into a polo shirt and loafers. He definitely lacked the sense of style from the types of dates I was used to.

"I thought thirty minutes was enough time for him to shower and give his outfit a bit more thought but I guess I was wrong," she laments when telling the story. "I was used to guys who were much more stylish, even in casual wear, when they took me out so this 'look' was definitely a change of pace for me. But I was hungry so I didn't allow his lack of fashion sense to bother me. Plus, the polo shirt showed off his cut torso and chiseled arms to his advantage and I was certainly OK with that."

"I couldn't keep my eyes off of him and wondered what it would be like to have his chocolate skin pressed into mine."

Prior to dating Chris, we used to tease Adrienne constantly because she used to think about men the way a lot of men think about women – as conquests. If she found a man really attractive, her first thoughts were usually, "How good is he in bed?" and then, "How do I get him there to find out?" Chris Morris had definitely peeked her curiosity in that regard.

"There was a new place I was dying to try because it had gotten rave reviews, but one glance at the line and menu and Chris suggested we try a more relaxed and quieter place. We walked around and checked out a few places, ending up in a corner booth at a typical neighborhood pub having dinner and learning about each other over burgers and beer. I learned Christopher Morris was originally from Atlanta, had just graduated summa cum laude from George Washington University, had fallen in love with Washington, DC during his time here and decided to stay. As a result, he took a position as an entry-level stockbroker for a well-known brokerage firm.

After a few beers, he confided in me, "You mark my words, Dre, one day I'm going to have a portfolio as big as some of the biggest clients there. And I'm going to do it by investing *their* money, making *my* money off of it and investing my own money wisely in order to build my own wealth."

"I admired his drive and the clear-cut goals he had set for himself. Chris certainly was different from many of the other men I was used to dating, most of whom came from old money like me but didn't have goals that went far beyond taking a seat on the board of a family company at best or indulging in a variety of long shot entrepreneurial ventures at worst.

"I didn't say much during the date or the others that followed it before the first time we had sex. I was far more curious about finding out how well Chris performed in bed than hearing about the ins and outs of the stock market but I pretended to listen when he'd talk about it. I even casually mentioned I might know some people who would be willing to take a chance with small investments with him, while I planned to close the deal with him and find out about *his* ins and outs on a much more personal level.

I knew Chris had no idea this was what she was plotting as she sat there wearing her designer linen dress and $750 Jimmy Choo's! She loves working in sales, especially the thrill of the chase part of it and she was gearing herself up for a chase on him!

"When I told him about my job, I admitted to Chris I was low on the corporate rung, too, although not quite as low as him."

Being low on the corporate ladder was absolutely Adrienne's choice. After graduating from business school, she decided she wanted to go out into the world and make it on her own merits and not as a result of her parent's connections. It wasn't always easy for her, but she managed to do it. She had paid her dues at entry-level work through some college internships (the first, she readily admits, landed with the help of her father's connections, but the rest earned entirely on her own), and as a result, when she met Christ she was a small territory regional sales and marketing executive for Ryco with a handful of salespeople answering to her.

"It didn't take me long to find out all I needed to know about Chris in *that* way," Adrienne always says so matter-of-factly. "He wasn't the best lover I've had but I liked how he kissed me passionately and the attention he paid to me. What he lacked in imagination he made up for in frequency and that was fine with me at the time. It also didn't hurt that given we lived only a few floors away from each other, 'connecting' was never a problem.

"I found myself falling for him because he was fatherly and protective. He had a quiet confidence that was very powerful and I found very sexy. Sometimes he could come across as stuffy and aloof but I quickly learned he just wasn't comfortable relaxing and letting loose. That's never been one of my problems and I think that's why I fell for him too. I'm a spontaneous, incurable romantic and I think that balances out his conservative and methodical tendencies.

"To the surprise of my friends and family, within three months of meeting on that elevator, Chris and I were engaged and then married. Our marriage was probably the most impetuous thing Chris has ever done short of betting against his favorite team, the Steelers, in a Super Bowl game when he was in college!

"Given the short amount of time I had known him, and my reputation for making hasty decisions, the girls tried to slow me down and talk me out of it; they feared I was making the biggest mistake of my life.

" 'Dre, I know he's cute and all, but we're talking about a *husband*, not another pair of shoes for goodness sake,' Faith even said over drinks one night a few weeks before my wedding, and while my parents thought I had lost my mind, but they were surprisingly supportive and threw us a beautiful wedding on virtually no notice."

I had met Adrienne's parents, Drs. James and Cecile Moran, a handful of times by the time of their wedding and their kindheartedness and generosity came as no surprise. Adrienne had never been anything less than honest about her upbringing and resultant free spirited nature. When we were in college, she told us that from her perspective, up until the age of ten, her life was perfect. Her days were filled with long hours of horseback riding on the 75 plus acres of their sprawling property in Middleburg, Virginia that had been passed through generations of her father's family after the Civil War. As is customary for those with the means in that area, Adrienne attended a nearby private boarding school and when she wasn't in class, the rest of her time revolved around playing lacrosse, piano and ballet lessons and of course, her horses and her friends who also had horses.

Adrienne's parents were each second-generation physicians; her father is a cardiologist and her mom an internist. They, unlike many of their peers, chose to start a family in their thirties and always knew they wanted only one child. They spent the first ten years of their marriage completing their medical education and training, traveling and giving back to their communities in the form of medical missionary work on tribal lands in the U.S. and Africa. Once Adrienne came along, all of their efforts and energies went into providing her with the very best life any child could wish for. Generally speaking, her parents were the doting type and fortunately, didn't spoil her to the point where she became crippled by their help or the lifestyle they afforded her. They raised Adrienne to be fiercely independent but also conscientious and socially attuned as well as altruistic and she is thankful for this type of upbringing.

Unfortunately, Adrienne's world as she knew it changed dramatically after her father discovered her mother had an affair. Understandably, her parents kept the details of this from their young daughter but the house was always thick with the tension it created. It was evident to young Adrienne however, that all the love in her parent's marriage (and to a large extent in the home) seemed to disappear over night and her father all but completely withdrew emotionally from the household and this included Adrienne. This abrupt change in his behavior made her want to do anything she could to get his attention. When excelling scholastically as well as athletically didn't do this, she began misbehaving, especially when it came to boys. None of this seemed to make much of a difference to her father other than a lovely gift or lavish trip when she did well, or a stern reprimand when he got wind of some of her antics.

By the time Adrienne left for college, her father had more or less recovered from her mother's betrayal and they began to repair their relationship, albeit slowly. But as Adrienne has told me many times, by the time she had begun mending her relationship with her father, she'd established a pattern of behavior that had taken root. Perhaps fueled by the love of the chase from years of riding and fox hunting coupled with the emotional abandonment and need for attention from her father during her youth, Adrienne was constantly chasing wild, passionate relationships with men until she met Chris.

Chris proved himself to be very adaptable to the circumstances marrying Adrienne landed him in. The stuffy, "old money" culture of her parents and many of her childhood friends suited his personality perfectly. Unlike some other men we know, he's never overtly flashy, but as he became more experienced and educated about the finer things in life, he definitely took to custom-made suits from London's best tailors and became an avid collector of watches, expensive cars, cigars and fine wine. Under his supervision their wine cellar rivals those of many in the finer restaurants in Washington, DC.

Chris took professional advantage of the many introductions being a member Adrienne's family afforded him. While her dad initially had reservations about him, I believe over the years he quietly accepted him and even grew to respect Chris' stick-to-it-ness.

Through some of those connections and his talent as a financial broker, Chris quickly rose up in the ranks of several different companies -- each new position bringing in larger signing bonuses and more lucrative clients. In no time, their portfolio grew by leaps and bounds without them having to skimp on anything and trust me, they didn't.

Adrienne is no slouch professionally either. While she stayed with Ryco, her steady trail of promotions led her to international sales and marketing --- a job she truly loved. She was thrilled she was getting *paid* to do things she loves: travel, meeting new people, learning new languages and experiencing different cultures and of course, the thrill of making a deal and beating the competition.

She's also a savvy investor in her own right. During her senior year in college, she used some of her family money to dabble in real estate and as a result, acquired two apartment buildings totaling thirty units. She's kept these properties and pays a property management company to oversee their upkeep. She's proud of this investment because, after paying back her family loan it was the first investment she accomplished on her own and she's made a lot of money from it.

While Chris won't give her credit, the truth is Adrienne has always been very wise about money. She consistently invested in her 401(k) and has never liquidated it for any reason. As a result, over the years, she's been able to squirrel away nearly $1,500,000 in just **one** of her retirement accounts because she's consistently maxed out the amount allowable for contributions and she always invested aggressively. Her personal stock portfolio (the one she started on her own when she was in college) is worth over a million dollars and as a general rule, she tries to keep at least $20,000.00 liquid cash in her personal savings account at all times just in case of emergencies. It's the advice she received from her dad decades ago because it's sound and viable and he's never steered her wrong. While some may view her as a trust fund baby, she never really leaned on her parents for financial assistance once she graduated from college. Adrienne is one of those rare privileged kids who simply wanted to make it on her own merits and without "daddy's help".

She's quite proud of what she's been able to amass on her own because she *does* like to shop. There isn't a designer who makes a handbag or a pair of shoes that doesn't have her name on them, as well as theirs. Her collection of exclusive label handbags plus the shoes is noteworthy and the envy of many, but they're just fun things for her unlike the art she's grown to love collecting as she's gotten older.

Adrienne is a serious and avid collector of original and limited edition art pieces and these days she prefers shopping for art instead of designer clothing. Their home is exquisitely outfitted with Erté lithographs and sculptures, original Romare Bearden oil paintings, original Paul Wegner sculptures, Fernando Botero paintings and sculptures, two signed Andy Warhol lithographs created before he became world famous and other limited edition pieces and collectibles from around the world.

She also has a space in a small warehouse for other artwork she has acquired from her travels over the years. Adrienne's long-term dream upon retirement is to open a large art gallery with artist studios. With all of the items she's acquired over the years and the contacts she's made in the art world, Adrienne is certain to hit the ground running with her magnificent, one-of-a-kind pieces. She's told me her dream gallery will include a workspace for artists and from there, she'll curate art and artifacts from the many places she's traveled as well. Adrienne is very intent on leaving her job and making this venture her primary focus as soon as possible. Her biggest obstacle is the challenge of obtaining Chris' support.

My girlfriend is passionate about her art and the role she sees herself playing in the art world. When speaking of her dream, she has often said her career in sales and marketing gave her the life she wanted but art gives her a purpose. As part of her life in the art world, Adrienne sits on numerous boards and is working diligently to get indigenous art from around the world exhibited in D.C. as part of the first leg of an international traveling art exhibit. While designer fashions are art unto themselves, they just don't excite her like her oils on canvas or the relief paintings and sculptures she owns. Her personal art collection has depth, tells a story and brightens her days.

This is why I can't understand why Chris always gets annoyed whenever she brings up the idea of switching careers. Perhaps he views her work as their safety net should the market begin to tank again; thereby adversely affecting their investments. Adrienne leaves it to him to worry about those things while she concentrates her efforts on her next career move because that's what brings her the most joy at the moment.

It didn't take long, and somewhat surprised Adrienne to learn that the normally reserved, somewhat boring and methodical Christopher Morris *loves* to gamble. She knew he bet on football games like pretty much everyone else does and sometimes he and his buddies would go to Atlantic City for a weekend, but as he started making more and more money, his gambling sprees and habits increased proportionately as well.

Prior to getting the Senior VP position at his current employer, Braithwaite Fielder, LLC, a hedge fund firm, he would travel to Las Vegas upwards of five to seven times per year. Sometimes his trips would be with his gambling buddies, sometimes she would join him and other times, he'd go alone. Because he was such a big gambler, getting rooms comped at the Bellagio or the Venetian wasn't a big deal for him. In any given weekend, it wasn't unheard of for Chris to lose $10,000-$15,000 at the craps table but he would also win anywhere from $15,000 to $50,000 at the blackjack table.

For the first ten or so years of their marriage, Adrienne repeatedly expressed her concerns about this habit, but it wasn't until he started working at B&F she noticed a dramatic change. The thrill of gambling no longer seemed to satisfy him, or perhaps he became concerned about jeopardizing his job, because he significantly cut back on his trips. Thank God, because trying to get him to stop or even cutting back was impossible for Adrienne and I believe it was beginning to take its toll on her and placing a strain on their marriage.

But this was far from the only stress she felt about her marriage. Around their third anniversary, Adrienne began to wonder if marrying Chris only three months after meeting him was such a good idea after all. They were very comfortable in their lives, rarely argued and they enjoyed going out and taking wonderful vacations together but their sexual incompatibility was increasingly an issue for her.

It was a difficult period in their marriage for Adrienne so when she told me about her frustrations back then, all I could do was be supportive, tell her to pray on it, be faithful and not give up.

"God brought the two of you together for a reason, Dre," I told her. "And God doesn't make mistakes. You're only three years into a journey of a lifetime. 'For better or for worse' are in marriage vows for a reason. You can't abandon the ship over a rough patch and let's face it girl, all things considered, compared to how other people have it, your rough patch 'ain't' all that rough."

She took my advice and decided to buckle down and work on being more appreciative of her marriage, not allow Chris' insecurities to become hers and when possible, help him overcome his. Adrienne appreciated my advice and she claims because of it she soon became pregnant – with twins!

The prospect of starting a family and the challenge of twins (girls, no less!) was more than enough to put any mild dissatisfaction Adrienne had with Chris on the back burner.

They immediately bought a large parcel of land in Potomac, MD and started building their dream house - a 10,000 square foot contemporary home with a swimming pool, playground and putting green on ten acres of land. Both Adrienne and Chris have an amazing eye for all things high end – a chef's kitchen with top of the line granite counters, a living room furnished with imported Italian leather and marble, Waterford chandeliers in the foyer and formal dining room and every bedroom has its own sitting room and extreme walk in closets. Decorating their home became a labor of love for Chris so Adrienne agreed he should take the lead on much of it. Shortly after their home was completed, it was featured in an issue of *Architecture Digest* and both of them shared the interior design and decorating credits.

Almost immediately after moving into their new home and getting the hang of juggling the demands of a career and family -- Madison and Madeline were almost three and getting into everything -- Adrienne became pregnant again. Sadly, however, during her second trimester she learned their son, Marc-Anthony, had Downs Syndrome. This news, while shocking, was something Adrienne accepted and she took the challenges that followed with grace and in stride.

Six months after Marc-Anthony was born, they hired Juliza -- a live-in Guatemalan nanny, to keep the children on track. With her travels, Adrienne simply couldn't juggle five people with different schedules. Juliza was 28 years old when she went to work for the Morris family and she's become invaluable. Personable although quiet, Juliza loves children and established an immediate bond with Marc-Anthony who took to her right away. The bond between them helped put Adrienne's mind at ease.

Adrienne and Chris bought Juliza a new Volvo SUV a couple of years ago and that makes it easier for her to drop and pick up the kids from school each day and taxi them around to their various activities. She helps out in general, especially with Marc-Anthony, who requires special attention and the whole family loves her.

Chris has always been a great provider and a good and faithful husband. He loves his children and dotes on his daughters especially, even though their taste in music drives him crazy since he's metamorphosed into someone who listens only to classical music or traditional jazz now. "Fusion jazz is not real jazz," according to him. He no longer enjoys listening to Rap and Hip Hop the way he used to and gets annoyed when he hears Adrienne and the girls playing it in the house or in her car. Adrienne has always loved that kind of music because it started in our generation and it keeps her rooted, so she plays her Hip Hop, Jazz, and frankly, all types of music in order to just have fun, dance around the house with the kids and partially because she knows it drives Chris crazy! His only reaction to this is the same every time.

"Adrienne, these kids have a hard enough time staying focused as it is. Do we really need you to encourage them to run around and dance like little heathens as well?"

The devil in her laughs every time he says "little heathens," and the kids have taken to stomping their feet loudly and whooping every time he says that until he breaks down and laughs a little.

While Adrienne loves the fact he showers the girls with so much affection and attention, she admits to feeling a little jealous of their relationship at times because she didn't have anything comparable to that with her father for a long period in her own childhood.

It's not that Chris doesn't love Marc-Anthony, he just has difficulty showing it. Adrienne believes he's never fully accepted their son's disability and the fact he isn't "perfect". As a result, Chris is often awkward and guarded and doesn't interact with him the way a father should with his son, in my opinion. Generally speaking, I believe Marc-Anthony reminds Chris of imperfections and other things we have no control over in our lives. You can *appear* to have everything, but God has a way of humbling all of us and proving to us that we, His children, really aren't in control of anything. Adrienne immediately accepted Marc-Anthony as one of their three blessings God entrusted to them. She loves him with every fiber of her body and her daily prayer is that one day Chris will love him the same way and this is also my prayer for them.

Chris' work ethic has kept them on the right path financially and has positioned them well for retirement; they have a multi million dollar portfolio, but at what price? Now that Adrienne has accomplished most of her professional goals and is looking forward to leaving Ryco and launching a new venture, she's concluded she's miserable in her marriage because she and Chris have vastly different ideas about sex and money.

She's becoming weary of the constant pursuit of the almighty dollar and strategizing how to save it or make more of it. And unfortunately, that is the only thing that appears to drive Chris. They've always had differing opinions about money: saving it and investing it and he has no problems reminding her of this. Their individual views on saving are vastly different because he sees it as a necessity to the point of it becoming an obsession. Adrienne, in contrast, views it as an option and a means to an end - perhaps because her family is wealthy and she always knew she had a safety net and so the pressures Chris feels to succeed aren't hers. Personally, I think Chris is a huge hypocrite and I'm convinced that as a result of his financial successes and the access to the "exclusives" its afforded him, he has forgotten where he's come from and has assimilated so much into the world of the "c's" as I call it, "cash, cars and clubs", he's completely lost his own sense of identity.

But here they are, a jumble of different personalities, wants, and dreams but after nearly twenty years of marriage and three beautiful children, their marriage was relatively strong and happy.

Adrienne called me after she'd been home for a few days after that crazy intercontinental business trip and said Chris was acting strangely. Somehow he had gone from being relatively even tempered to overly uptight, visibly irritable and on edge while she was away. His interactions with Madeline and Madison were curt and he spent virtually no time with Marc-Anthony. This bothered her because Juliza told her Marc-Anthony had been upset for several days prior to her return home because of an apparent bullying situation at his school.

During this period, Chris and Adrienne barely had time to speak. She immediately dealt with Marc-Anthony's problem while Chris' work schedule seemed to double and he was virtually never at home. He spent countless weekends in the office preparing for an unprecedented audit by the Securities and Exchange Commission (SEC) of Braithwaite Fielder's financials, as they are a publicly traded company. While he'd been through SEC audits in the past at his previous employer, Adrienne said she felt he seemed strangely nervous about this one, but when she questioned him about it, he never wanted to discuss it. The rare times when he *was* at home, the entire household walked on eggshells around him and the tension was unbearable.

After the audit was over and all of the pressures associated with it subsided, Chris' moodiness and sour disposition left as fast as it came, things returned to normal, his schedule settled down, he was in better spirits and everyone was happy about that. He'd even started planning a short impromptu vacation to Costa Rica for the entire family. Typically, Adrienne is the one who plans their family vacations but this time Chris had done all of the legwork and planning. They all needed a fun trip and Juliza certainly seemed like she could use a break from them as well!

The seven-day family vacation in Costa Rica was fantastic! They stayed in a fabulous five star two story beachfront villa with panoramic views of the beautiful sapphire blue ocean complete with a private chef, butler, and maid service. The villa had an Asian Zen feel and it was wonderfully secluded from all things "tourist". Adrienne, Chris and the kids were able to simply unplug and relax; something they *all* desperately needed. They enjoyed all of the water sports, went zip lining and horseback riding. Now that their children are older, these types of get aways enable Chris and Adrienne to enjoy each other's company more than usual. If nothing else, it's a break in the monotony Adrienne has come to expect in their relationship.

She told me that while Chris always seemed preoccupied in his thoughts, there were many times during this trip where he was more outgoing than usual and noticeably engaged with the entire family. He and Adrienne were able to take quiet walks on the beach and sleep in if they chose. For Adrienne, it was really refreshing to watch Chris take the time to simply relax and she did that too. With a private chef in residence, meals were prepared for them whenever the urge or curiosity to eat something tugged at their stomachs and each meal was better than the last. All of the seafood was caught that day so it couldn't be fresher. The fruits and vegetables were locally grown and represented every color of the rainbow with a variety of textures. As a family of true foodies, their palettes did the happy dance for seven days straight! It was truly one of the best family vacations the Morris' had ever taken and it gave Adrienne and Chris an opportunity to reconnect and rekindle some of the dying embers of their relationship. She was hopeful and upbeat about their relationship when they returned and I couldn't have been happier for her.

The day after their return from Costa Rica, Chris left the house early that Saturday morning and headed for the office. On their flight back from vacation he promised the girls he would return in time to attend their late afternoon soccer game. After breakfast, Juliza helped Marc-Anthony prepare for an outing while Adrienne began sorting through the week of mail that had collected in their absence. She caught up with me on the phone and spent over an hour talking to me about her trip and how refreshing it was to get away after the stressful previous weeks.

Always a multi-tasker, she was sorting the mail and making her way into Chris' office to leave his mail on his desk like she always does.

"Evey, you wouldn't believe how messy his office is!" she said to me. "You know how meticulous Chris is about everything. They're boxes and papers everywhere! I can barely see the surface of his desk to put his mail on it. He obviously didn't take the time to get things sorted out or straightened up after the audit and prior to our trip.

"I guess I'll just put it on his chair so he sees it when he gets home. Good grief, I almost banged my shin because he even left some of the desk drawers open!

"Hmm? You should see this beautiful postcard on top of one of the open drawers in his desk. It's has a beautiful picture of the Matterhorn on it. I wonder who it's from."

There was a pause much longer than it takes to read a postcard and then she flatly said, "Oh, shit."

" 'Oh, shit'?" I repeated. "What does the postcard say?"

"Oh my God, I can't believe it. I can't fucking believe it. It says,

> My love,
>
> Switzerland is beautiful! You're all
>
> that's missing on this trip.
>
> I can't wait to see you again in May.
>
> Yours,
>
> Deb

"Who the hell is 'Deb'? 'My love'? … 'see you again'…? 'Yours'? What the hell is going on?" she sputtered.

"Evey, oh my God, the postcard was sent recently, so it was *not* sent from an old girlfriend and it's addressed to him, *Mr. Chris Morris*, at a post office box I don't know anything about.

"Oh my God. That son of a bitch is cheating on me! He has his own post office box? I have to call my dad. I'll give you a call or stop by later. Love you. Don't worry."

With that, she hung up, leaving me almost as stunned as she was but all I could do was pray for her because I had no time to react. While I felt physically helpless, sad and even petrified for her, I knew that praying for Adrienne would greatly benefit her. I asked God to grant her the guidance, wisdom, and protection she would need to deal with the *truth* however painful it may be.

Within one hour, my phone began ringing off the hook. Faith and

Krishna were calling to find out what exactly happened and if I'd heard from Dre since she unexpectedly stumbled on that now infamous postcard. Each of them had spoken to her briefly after calling to find out about her vacation and, instead, learned about what Dre found in Chris' office. Unfortunately, none of us had updates to share. I told them I felt it best we give her the appropriate amount of space to deal with the issue any way she needed to. I sent her a text message from the three of us expressing our concerns, offering our collective support and suggested if she needed us we'd all be at my house later in the evening for her. When Dre responded, she thanked us and said she would meet us after meeting with her father.

When Adrienne walked through the door, she looked as if she had seen a ghost. It was evident that she had spent most of the day crying because the whites of her eyes were pink. She was visibly and understandably distraught and the bright light that always emanated from her was no more. As she crossed the threshold, we all met her there with open arms and did our best to hug her back to life. With tears streaming down all of our faces, we escorted her toward a comfortable chair in my living room and just allowed her to tell us exactly what happened after she had found that postcard and called her father. Through her tears and sobs she recalled what happened next this way:

"I collapsed into Chris' big leather desk chair in shock and covered my face. As random thoughts of his audacity raced through my head, I panicked and suddenly became aware of the time. Realizing I had the house to myself for several hours - with the exception of the twins sleeping upstairs, I got busy searching for any evidence of his cheating and immediately started rifling through the files in that open drawer.

"Chris is so neat and organized that finding evidence of his cheating was like feeding milk to a baby. I didn't have to look far because he had it all neatly filed right there in that drawer! As I scanned the labels on the files, I found a folder with the name *Deb Horton* on it. It immediately caught my attention because it was the only file in the endless rows of files that was identified by a specific individual's name and not by the name of a corporation or some type of business entity. It was also the very last file in the draw – and not alphabetized like the rest of the files.

Chris is so meticulous and predictable that having a file out of
alphabetical order is very odd for him and it stuck out like a sore thumb.
I pulled the file out and found many postcards with the same signature
from a variety of countries with similar provocative inscriptions on them
addressed to him at that P.O. Box. Some of them even commented on
how much fun she'd had with him on previous rendezvous; trips I was
aware of in most cases because he presented them to me as business trips
and we often talked about the deals he was working on. In a few
instances, I even helped that S.O.B. pack his bags, ya'll!

"He'd kept all of her postcards and they were all addressed to that same
unfamiliar P.O. box. The folder also had her account information in it. I
found that odd because I knew that for years he represented and managed
her ex-husband's account. Fortunately, time was on my side. I had no
meetings or appointments to prepare for on Monday because I'd taken
that day off in order to get myself and the family organized after
returning from our trip; Chris was at work, Juliza had several errands to
run after dropping off Marc-Anthony and returning to pick him up later
in the afternoon and the girls were still asleep upstairs and I didn't expect
them to wake up before the middle of the afternoon – just in time to
leave for their 5:00p soccer game. I had several hours alone and that is
exactly what I needed to absorb this shocking news and continue
searching for more evidence. I decided to use the time to collect and
make photocopies of everything in that file."

" 'Deb Horton' *was* a familiar name to me because over the years Chris
had mentioned her in conversations pertaining to her husband, C. Patrick
Horton – a wealthy multi-millionaire 27 years her senior who made his
money in waste management and commercial real estate. Their divorce
was messy and public and you know that behind the scenes Chris was
entrenched in the drama. He was managing Horton's hedge fund
portfolio and other investments in some of his other accounts at the time
and helping him to hide his money from her legal team. I was aware of
the pressure Horton was placing on Chris to ensure his money was
protected and repeatedly warned him that *C. Patrick Horton* couldn't be
trusted. I also repeatedly reminded him he had a moral responsibility to
stay clear of anything illegal while he assisted that asshole during his

divorce.

" 'It'll come back to haunt you, if not land you in jail. You're smarter than that, Chris. Money isn't everything!' I told him," Adrienne continued. " 'You can't be a husband and a father if your ass is sitting in jail for fraud or worse, dead somewhere because Horton got one of his goons to knock you off!' I told Chris this on several occasions but I almost never believed he really *heard* or heeded any of my warnings.

"Instead, he just constantly reassured me everything he was doing was legal and because he'd made himself virtually indispensible in Horton's eyes, the perks he received from him benefited all of us. As Horton's divorce started to heat up and the proverbial mud slinging began, Chris nearly found himself on the outs with Horton.

"During one of the meetings regarding Horton's account, Chris told me Horton accused him of flirting with his wife and said to him, 'I see how my wife looks at you. Are you fucking my wife, Chris? Well, shit, if you are, you wouldn't be the first. That's why we're divorcing, you know! She's a whore! I know she's been screwing around on me, especially after my last heart attack. The only reason why I won't fire you right now is because I don't want you changing sides and telling her where I have all of my money stashed! I have friends everywhere, Chris, remember that… don't ever find yourself on the other side!'

"Chris claimed Horton was drunk when he made those 'baseless accusations' and 'shallow threats' and the following day he was able to smooth things over with him and remain on the account. But I never forgot that story. There was something about the accusations and veiled threats that seemed very real to me. My grandmother used to say, 'Alcohol brings out the truth in people so make sure you listen when people drink and speak' so perhaps deep inside I suspected 'Old Man Horton' knew what he was talking about regarding an attraction between Chris and his wife. Chris defiantly denied all of it and outright dismissed it, going so far as to call Horton 'an old drunk who is jealous of any man who even says hello to his wife,' and claimed he was paranoid because of the age similarity between him and her.

"While I'd never heard that Deb Horton cheated on her husband, the few times I was in her company I was unimpressed by her presentation, found her to be strangely standoffish towards me and a laughable snob. Deb Horton was classified as a social climbing pseudo socialite who became known in some of my social circles because of her marriage to C. Patrick Horton. She was his third wife, decades younger than he, and unfortunately for her, didn't have an acceptable pedigree. As a result, but not for lack of trying, she was never fully accepted in the social circles I've grown up in. She was an outsider, and no matter how hard she tried or how many lavish events she sponsored, she would *never* fit in or be accepted."

Adrienne continued, "My hands trembled as I looked through the *Deb Horton* file and emotions flooded my body. I felt betrayed, hurt, angry and sick all at the same time. Strangely, however, I also felt relieved and oddly vindicated. For the first time in our marriage, I felt as if my 'perfect' husband wasn't so perfect any more. He had flaws and imperfections just like the rest of us! The image of perfection he worked so hard to portray is tarnished. This is the opportunity I need to do whatever it is *I* want to do relative to how I lived my life and pursue the dreams I've put on hold during our marriage and Christopher Morris can't stop me!

"I pored over the various files in the drawer for hours. But his cheating became inconsequential when I discovered several bank statements documenting accounts worth millions of dollars in three separate Swiss banks and one in Belize. All of the accounts were in *his name only* and addressed to him at that P.O. Box. I was in shock. The more I examined the documents, the more consumed I became with learning more. Countless questions regarding the accounts flooded my mind. *Why are these accounts in Chris' name only? Are these his **personal** accounts? Why the account in Belize? Where and how did he get all of this money? Why didn't I know about this money? Why are these documents in the Deb Horton file?* The more I read the documents and bank statements in the *Deb Horton* file, the more I came to realize my husband of twenty years had several private international accounts and *none* of them had any references to *me*.

"I was seething with anger and resentment and I followed up on calling my dad. Sorry, E. At the time I felt like he was the only person I felt could guide me and tell me what I needed to do next.

"When I reached him, he said he was just about to go into a meeting and asked if he could call back in an hour or two but I couldn't wait. 'Daddy, Chris is cheating on me,' I wailed to him. I was hurting and the anger I felt as I initially went through the files had been replaced with sorrow, fear and a gut wrenching pain I'd never experienced before. I told him how I stumbled on the information, the *Deb Horton* file I found and all of the information in it regarding the secret P.O. Box, Swiss accounts and the account in Belize.

" 'Where is Chris now?' he asked calmly.

" 'At the office,' I sobbed.

" 'When is he expected back home?' he queried.

"I told him Chris had promised the girls he'll attend their soccer game so I think around 4:00p but more than likely he'll just meet us at the game.

" 'That gives you just a little over three hours,' my dad replied. Make copies of everything you can put your hands on in those files but be certain to put them back exactly as you found them. Be very careful and mindful of the order of the pages, and what not, OK? Chris is very meticulous so if something is out of place, he'll notice. No matter what, stop everything you're doing at 3:00p. That'll give you time to ensure the office is just as he left it and in case he does come home by 4:00p or earlier, you won't be in there. If he does come home, do your very best to say absolutely nothing to him. Have him drive the girls home after the game and bring all of the files to my house. We'll talk when you get there.'

"I listened to my dad's advice intensely. I could tell he was already formulating a plan and his involvement is exactly what I need.

" 'OK, daddy. I just can't believe this is happening,' I moaned to him.

" 'Pumpkin, listen to me. I know you're in a lot of pain right now and I'm sorry this is happening. But besides his cheating, there could be other issues that are at hand here and we need to find out what's really going on and how deep he's in. I know a really good PI. His name is Don Snyder. He's thorough, discreet and very well connected. He gets information and he can get things done. Trust me, he's very, very thorough. He'll dig up everything you want to know and more. I'll give him a call and have him meet us at the house tonight.'

" 'A PI?' I repeated. 'Oh my God, what has he done?' My question was rhetorical for the moment but this is a question that needs to be answered.

" 'I don't know but we'll get to the bottom of it,' my dad said. 'Don't worry about that right now, we'll talk about all of that when I see you later, OK? Right now, I need you to do your best to act as if everything is normal. You're really good at compartmentalizing. I need you to focus on copying those files and then staying away from him. Say absolutely nothing to him beyond the basics. If that's too difficult, just tell him you're not feeling well and that you think you may be coming down with a cold or something. I know all of this hurts right now but believe me you're going to be fine. You're not alone and you won't go through this by yourself. I'm here for you. I love you, Pumpkin. I have to go now because I need to get back to this meeting but I'll see you later, OK?'

"I told him I would follow his instructions and see him later.

"My thoughts were racing as I copied pages and pages of everything in the Deb Horton file and other files pertaining to the overseas accounts. I don't know how the other documents will be used exactly or what dad has in mind, but I knew I had to be thorough because the opportunity to have unfettered access to everything again might not come again any time soon."

She stopped crying, wiped her tears and I could see the resentment built up inside of her. She could care less about the cheating. Adrienne was incensed about the overseas accounts and the sacrifices she had been making in putting her dreams on hold all of those years in order to appease him and their marriage.

"After everything I've done and everything my family has done to pull his ass out of the gutter, this is how he repays me? Hiding money from me? That son of a bitch! I swear under no circumstances will Christopher Morris see one cent of any of the money in any of those accounts – ever. I'll make sure of it!"

CHAPTER 4

KRISHNA – "MY MAN IS EVERYTHING!"

I left the doctor's office feeling upbeat and hopeful because everything was looking good, my doctor was pleased with my scans and blood tests and the tumors, which had spread throughout my body, were shrinking significantly. Mrs. Samuels and I celebrated by making a quick stop at my favorite smoothie shop before heading home so I could get in a good workout. "God is answering my prayers, Evey," Mrs. Samuels shared with me as we sipped on our Green Tea smoothies. "He's answering mine too, Mrs. Samuels. This journey I'm on, *again*, hasn't been easy – you know that. But, because of you and my girlfriends I've been able to get through it. You're a member of my family now and I sincerely thank you for your love, support and the patience you've shown me through all of it. I love you." I thanked her and got up and gave her the biggest hug I could give because I wanted her to know how much she meant to me. "I love you too, darling," she told me as she hugged me back. "You're going to be just fine. *Everything* is going to be just fine, darling, God told me so. Just have faith." As those unexpected words left her lips and landed in my ears, I paused and looked at her. Our eyes met and she simply nodded.

After my workout, I came home and took a much needed nap. I briefly considered going to Lauren's track meet since it was local but it was Thursday and the day for our weekly "What's the tea?" night, so I opted not to go. Lauren is Krishna and Frank's only child and truly a track star.

Last year she broke the high school record in the 100 meter dash and she's ranked 5th in the nation in the 200 meter race! I'm so proud of her! She's being scouted by all of the top track programs in the nation and she is an amazing young lady.

Sadly, however, neither Krishna nor Frank has made the time to attend her track meets. Now that Lauren is in high school and seemingly more self-sufficient, her parents pour most of their time in to DMTG, the multi million dollar IT company Krishna founded. Adrienne (when she's not traveling) and I try to fill in that gap by supporting her at local meets. While Lauren always appreciates seeing us there, I know she'd rather look into those stands and see her parents.

It's not that they're not proud of her, just the opposite in fact, but it's a problem. Adrienne and I have voiced our concerns about this to Krish, but we also know we have to be sensitive to the other issues she's dealing with, namely Frank's womanizing, but her preoccupation with it comes at Lauren's expense. Krishna has taken on too much – running the business *and* trying to keep track of her husband; a man whose cheating has become a bit of a sport, in my opinion, with poor Krishna in a constant state of denial! As a result, she's an emotional mess as it pertains to him and is ignoring the needs of her only child.

It was Thursday, so the girls would be coming over for our weekly "What's the tea?" happy hour and dinner girls night. Prior to my getting sick, we always made an effort to meet each other for happy hour and/or dinner every Thursday. Since I got sick again Faith, Adrienne, and Krishna decided the tradition would continue but they'd bring it to me. So, we've been doing it at my house every Thursday from 6:00p to 9:00p. Thanks to Adrienne, my bar remains fully stocked and Faith and Krishna bring the food or have it delivered to the house while I'm in charge of the desserts.

Shortly after her arrival, I noticed Krishna wasn't engaged in our conversations the way she usually is. She was a bit withdrawn and distant and after the first 30 minutes or so we all noticed something was very different about her energy. Adrienne walked over to her, put her arm around her shoulders and gently whispered, "Just tell them Krish.

It's OK."

"Tell us what?" I asked.

"What's wrong?" Faith pressed.

As Krishna mustered up the courage to share with us what was weighing on her so heavily she began to cry and explained how deeply troubled her marriage is right now.

"I was so excited about the gala Frank and I were invited to attend last week. We were preparing to leave, the limo was on its way, Lauren was staying at a friend's house and as usual, I couldn't decide which gown to wear so I asked Frank for his input.

" 'Frank, look in my closet. There are two dresses hanging up on the left. Which one should I wear? The black cutout Balmain with the killer front split or the white silk Gucci with that crazy back out and drop dead split in the back?" I was on a mission to look my very best that night.

" 'I don't know,' he said disinterestedly. 'Makes no difference to me. Just pick one, and make it quick. I don't want to be late because you can't choose between black and white.' You know how impatient Frank can get with my indecisiveness and he was eager to get the evening started."

"I was *so* over black and wanted to stand out. You know how much I hate looking like everyone else, so I chose the white Gucci. 'Do you remember it? I got it on our trip to Hong Kong a couple of years ago. I paired it with my extra long Mikimoto teardrop necklace, but I wore it backwards so it draped down my back. I felt so sexy!

"I was excited about attending this gala because as you know, our marriage is going through another rocky period and I thought an evening out would be good for us, both personally and professionally. Plus, it was on media mogul Francis Dunningham's estate and personally hosted by him. I know I'm good, but every now and then I have had a hard time believing we were actually on the guest list. We were both looking forward to networking with people on that level; folks we'd only dreamed of meeting and, you know me, I'm a sucker for a black tie event.

"I ordered one of our favorite champagnes for the limo and was looking forward to having Frank to myself for at least forty-five minutes there and back. Spending time alone with him had become a novelty and I thought the limo ride would give us time to simply enjoy each other."

This was so like Krish. Ever the optimist and rightfully so with her company but I'm not sure I feel the same way about Frank.

Frank Fitzgerald, her husband, is an Executive VP at DMTG, which has recently expanded into international markets. As a result, their brand recognition is exploding. Frank is the "face" of the company – responsible for business development and marketing. He oversees the sales and marketing teams and most importantly, brings in business - *lots* of business. He's extremely personable and has the gift of gab. He can talk you out of your last dollar and then turn that dollar into five dollars with an award-winning smile. Krishna loves him more than anything and is extremely proud of what they've built together.

As for her part in the business, as President and *sole owner*, Krishna takes care of all of the operations and oversees much of the technical implementation on large and highly visible projects. While Frank may bring in the money, she makes sure they operationalize and keep it; pay their bills, maintain the wealth of talent they have in the form of their two hundred and fifty employees and invest the profits. Frank may be the "face" of the outfit but Krishna is definitely the "brains" and the visionary.

Krishna was smitten with Frank the first time she actually laid eyes on him. They were both attending a frat party -- she a freshman and he a junior. He was a football player and boy, was he *fine*. He had a smile that could melt the panties right off your ass and, trust me, there were a lot of girls walking around campus with no panties on at all thanks to Frank

Fitzgerald. He was incredibly charming and a bit of a sweet talker but didn't come across as arrogant. He was simply confident with his looks and charm and realized he didn't have to do much to get girls to drop their drawers. They just wanted to be with him.

"Oh my God, Dre, there he is!" she exclaimed to Adrienne when she spotted him for the first time from across the room.

"Who?" Adrienne asked.

"Frank. Frank Fitzgerald!"

"Are you sure? It's too dark in here. I can't tell."

"I'd recognize that smile a million miles away. Plus, I just peeped him in that football directory, remember?"

"Oh yeah, that's right," Adrienne responded. "He *IS* a cutie!"

"He's mine, girl. I claimed him first!" Krishna shot back.

Dre was Krishna's freshman roommate and they met on move in day. It was immediately apparent to Krish Adrienne *loves* having a good time. She's a ball of energy and loads of fun. Unlike Krishna, she's a free spirit and has always dated gorgeous guys. A beautiful, curvaceous girl, she could use those assets to her advantage when she wanted to get the upper hand when she set her sights on a man, but she was always loyal to her girlfriends and never posed a threat to any of us. However, if you were a "mean girl" she'd have no problem taking your man! Believe it! She was living proof that men are weak in general and they are like putty when they think there's even a remote possibility a woman like Adrienne is interested in them. Dre has that "thing" about her that most women are jealous of, but also wishes they had – sex appeal!

Krishna is just the opposite. At 5'9" and just over 130 pounds, she's been tall and thin her entire life. Between her shapeless "stick figure" and the thick glasses she had to wear through most of K-12, she was very insecure about most everything pertaining to herself, which I'm sure plays a large part in her introversion. She was always told she had a pretty face but almost never believed those compliments, she just thought people were being polite. She rarely dated in high school ("no guy in his right mind wanted someone so much taller than him and who also couldn't see past the tip of their nose without glasses," she would say), so like many other brainy introverts, she did what came naturally -- buried her head in her studies, math and science in particular, and excelled academically.

Given all of this, Krishna was very excited about starting college, where no one would know about her awkwardness and thick glasses (over the summer she'd replaced those with contacts to enhance her hazel/green eyes) and where there would be men much taller than her. Krishna also decided to work on her shyness, which granted wasn't going to be easy, so she was more than thrilled when rich, gorgeous, outgoing Adrienne Moran turned out to be her roommate.

A lot of the women on their floor were either intimidated or jealous of Adrienne, but not Krishna. She adored her distinctly upper crust manners, overall graceful and polished disposition and subtle Southern accent (which was distinctively different from Krishna's Long Island, NY speech) and she was one of the few genuinely happy people Krishna ever met (not to say Adrienne didn't have bad moods or days like the rest of us). Most importantly, to Krishna and her goal of acquiring a semblance of a social life and maybe even a boyfriend, she benefited greatly from being Adrienne's roommate due to the non-stop invitations Dre received to every campus activity and party imaginable.

Admittedly, there were times when Krishna thought Adrienne was a bit of a snob because she'd often turned down things Krishna would have jumped at the chance to attend, but Adrienne's taste was spot on and Krish quickly learned that with each missed opportunity, two more that were even better were sure to follow and this frat party turned out to be one of those. "Never attend every party or event you're invited to, Krish. You don't want to be known as the girl who goes to *everything*. Remember, always be selective because every event is not worth your time. Oh, and that applies to guys, too!" Dre schooled her.

As the evening of the party wore on, Krishna lost track of Frank and his whereabouts. But when the DJ began to play a slow song, she felt someone gently tap her hand and a voice asking her to dance. As she turned to see who it was, she noticed that big beautiful smile beaming back at her. It was Frank! Krish agreed to his request and let him escort her through the crush of bodies already gathered on the dance floor. He introduced himself, asked her name and told her she looked nice. They danced for two songs, talking the entire time. As she scanned the room, she could see the scowling faces of some junior and senior women. He didn't seem to care and neither did she. Krishna had gotten his attention, even if it were for only ten minutes and she was over the moon.

That night Frank asked Krishna for her number and while she gave it to him, she was immediately suspicious of his intentions. Over the next several weeks, she ignored his telephone calls until they eventually stopped. As much as she had a crush on him, the realist in her knew he wouldn't give her the time of day unless he just wanted another notch on his belt. But her instincts told her if the relationship were meant to be, it would be, heck, she was a freshman and he was an upper classman! She convinced herself he'd never really want to be in a relationship with *her* so she kept her distance, admired him from afar and didn't make herself available to him at all. Dre thought she was crazy and did everything she could to convince Krishna to go out with him, but that was completely out of her comfort zone so instead, she played it safe and stayed away.

After graduating top of our class with a BS -- double majoring in computer science and business administration and a minor in communications, it seemed like every big IT company wanted to hire her, not only for her qualifications but also because many of them were under pressure to have more diversity in their work place and her race and gender just added to her cache. While Krishna was not entirely surprised by this, she didn't realize there would be so many competitors trying to hire her. Some days she had a hard time grappling with the fact that even though she fully expected to be better paid than her classmates with liberal arts degrees, she didn't anticipate receiving *starting* offers with salaries that maybe, just maybe, she thought she could achieve by the time she was thirty!

While all of this was very exciting, Krishna wanted none of it. She had known, even before starting college, she wanted to be her own boss and own her own company. By graduation, she didn't care if her business was small or large. She just wanted it to be *"hers"*. With that goal in mind, Krishna politely (and when times got really hard, sometimes highly regretfully) turned down those offers and went to the Wharton School of Business to earn an MBA and learn how to grow and run a business.

She started DMTG right after graduating from Wharton when a family friend needed IT and marketing help for his small cleaning supplies company. After modernizing his business with cutting edge technology, other small companies in the area learned about her services and because they had similar needs, she quickly built a strong client base. Before she knew it, she was in business.

As much as Krishna thought she was prepared for her company's early success, the truth is she wasn't. She was happy to leave basic secretarial and administrative things to someone else and almost immediately hired a part-time assistant, Sylvia Thibodaux, who eventually became her full time, right hand woman. Krishna also knew that growing her customer base was going to be absolutely essential if she had any hopes of expanding past her local market so she had to find a hot rod sales person. Unfortunately, while capable, she wasn't comfortable doing the sales end of the business herself. Don't get me wrong. Krishna loves speaking to friends and family about her work and her company, but when it comes to *selling* it to a potential client, she simply doesn't have the comfort level needed to be confident and convincing. She's very self-conscious about her insecurities and as a result, when it comes to trying to make a sale, the dominant, introverted part of her personality wants to run screaming into another room and slam the door in fear.

Krishna was grappling with this problem around a year into her business when she bumped into Frank at an alumni event and they started talking. He reminded her of their dance at that frat party and how he'd repeatedly tried to make contact but she never returned his calls. He said this intrigued him because he never had a girl completely ignore his advances. He also said he couldn't get the White Shoulders perfume she wore that evening out of his mind and he wanted to get to know her better but didn't want to appear as if he was chasing a freshman! They laughed about it and began dating soon after.

Frank was Krishna's "first" in every way. He was the first boy she really liked, her first real boyfriend and the first person she had sex with. Unlike most of us and the majority of women we know, Krishna was a virgin until she allowed herself to open up completely to Frank. She says she can't say, "I saved myself" for him because the reality is she never knew if she'd ever see him again after college but she's always loved everything about him and still does. Adrienne, Faith and I, however, never felt he truly valued their relationship the way Krishna did. And after observing their relationship for a couple of years, we concluded he didn't show her the respect she deserves because he spoke to her very disparagingly when they disagreed or argued and he had a pattern of breaking up with her, dating other women and then going back to her when he was through.

During these "off periods", we'd encouraged her to date other guys and sometimes she did, but each time Krishna would say it felt like she was cheating on Frank so those "relationships" never grew or even lasted more than a few weeks. She wanted only to be with *him*. Each time he broke things off with her and began dating someone else, she'd convince herself he just wanted to be sure he wanted to be with her since he kept going back to her when that other relationship didn't work out. We thought she was crazy to endure that foolishness and felt she was obviously "whipped" by the fact that she'd lost her virginity to him (and, therefore, her mind) because she couldn't even imagine her life without Frank Fitzgerald!

Frank started working for Krishna's company and became her first "real" employee during one of their lengthy periods of being "on again". That's right. As I said, she knew she needed a salesperson, so along with her assistant, Sylvia, Krishna had hired a few "temp to perm" people but although they did help keep the business going, they didn't work out long term for one reason or another.

About a year after they'd started dating, Frank left his job as a junior marketing and sales account executive for the mid-size media IT company where he'd been working for about three years and went to work for Krishna. Being her first full-time salesman was surely a labor of love on his part because while she could match, and even slightly beat his salary with his former employer, they were both well aware there were several "make it or break it" years ahead. But despite a few wobbles and a couple of offers to merge with other companies, Krishna held fast to her dreams of owning her own company and after hiring Frank, she *did* make it. After a few years, DMTG had gained a dozen or so employees, annual net profits in the millions and her first salesman became DMTG's Executive Vice President and her husband!

Seven long years after committing to her vision, Krishna had succeeded in owning her own business and, as she likes to point out, not a small mom and pop operation either, "a *real* business". Around this time, Frank began to heavily campaign to become an equity shareholder and partner in the business, but Krishna never gave in and stood firm. From the beginning, she chose not to make him a partner in DMTG because it was her "baby" and she wanted to maintain as much control as possible over its direction -- forever.

Frank eventually aborted his quest of becoming a shareholder in the company and didn't seem to mind maintaining his status as an employee as long as he was making the kind of money he felt he deserved. That's probably why he's opted to stay and work for DMTG all of these years. He's his own man except for the fact that he works for DMTG – *Krishna's* company.

In large part, she set up her company this way because of a promise she'd made to her grandfather years earlier.

"Promise me, KiKi, you'll never go into business with a person who doesn't share the same work ethic as you" he said to her. *"You're a hard worker with an entrepreneurial spirit. I believe you'll own your own business some day and you're going to do well because you know in your gut what it takes to build a business, however large or small. But remember, if you partner with someone who is lazy or a spender they'll drive your hard work right into the ground and you'll be left with nothing but bills, loans you'll have to pay back and bad credit. A bad*

partnership is a leaking ship!"

"That won't happen to me Pop-Pop. I can promise you that!" she promised.

Krishna made that promise to her paternal grandfather in her late teens and years before she even considered going into business for herself in a serious way. He was a hardworking man who owned his own hardware business for over forty years until he died. Her grandfather saw something in her she didn't even know she had at that time. This promise stuck with her and has been the driving force behind her building the successful business she has today.

When Krishna founded DMTG, she set it up in such a way that if she became incapacitated or unable to make sound decisions for any reason her parents would be the only other people authorized to act on her behalf. She never altered that requirement, even after marrying Frank.

Given its success and the fact that she has always stood firm on not making him partner or giving him equity shares in the company, there's a part of me that believes her marriage and relationship with Frank took a big hit. Personally, I believe Frank has always been secretly jealous of Krishna's success. So, while he's always had the gift of gab, doing the *hard work* once the contract is in place is far from his interests. He enjoys the freedoms that come with his position and the lifestyle it affords him – a little too much, if you ask me. Krishna could tell from the very beginning that the business work ethic her grandfather spoke of was *absolutely not* where it needed to be as it relates to Frank.

Although Frank was instrumental in bringing in many of the big accounts they now have, Krishna was the one who staffed them with people capable of getting the work done and keeping their customers happy. Through their collective contacts in the market and Frank's charm, DMTG has grown and is expanding well beyond Krishna's original expectations for her brainchild. Consequently, they've had longstanding contracts, which continue to grow.

Krishna has always been very savvy and fiscally conservative and that's primarily because she knows the ins and outs of every aspect of her business. As the years have passed, she remains very hands-on relative to company expenses and expense accounts, and that meant *everyone* on the payroll, including Frank. She regulates his salary and personally sees to his annual bonuses, just like any other employee, but he takes advantage of the additional perks he has access to like corporate lines of credit and credit cards. Managing Frank's expenses in this regard is an on-going battle for Krishna but it's a leeway she affords him in order to distract him from his quest to become an equity shareholder.

On several occasions, Krishna has said she keeps an eye on his spending because he has little to no fiscal discipline and would spend every penny they made if given the opportunity. Fortunately, she's been able to bring in many new accounts in the last several years herself which have helped offset his sometimes ridiculous spending sprees like overseas golf trips to the St. Andrews golf course in Scotland, Formula One races in Monaco, or ring side seats to heavy weight fights in Las Vegas, all of which he's traveled to first class and stayed in premium hotels.

Sadly, Krishna's quest for the fairy tale life lulled her into the belief that the ultimate proof of his career satisfaction and his love for her came when he asked her to marry him. Becoming Frank's wife made her fairy tale dream come true and, if you let her tell it, "I've been living happily ever after ever since". I don't believe that, but as her girlfriend, whenever she is happy, I am too, and when she isn't, I share her pain. Of course, like any other married couple they have their ups and downs but in their own way they appear to be committed to one another and to raising their track star daughter, Lauren. DMTG is thriving, their lifestyle is the envy of many (even a couple of our other friends) and they're "happy" (I think).

"The gala was absolutely spectacular." Krishna continued. "Frank and I met and socialized with dozens of powerful business owners, politicians and celebrities. We worked the room and made some incredible connections that are certain to further expand the business. All the way home, we talked about how successful the evening had been and fed off of each other's energy and excitement. We were in a good place as a couple and things felt normal again. The limo pulled up to the house and dropped us off.

"As I made my way inside and began ascending the grand staircase, I could hear Frank fixing himself a drink at the bar. I called to him to fix me a drink as well, expecting he'd join me in our bedroom soon after. As I took off my heels and slipped off my gown, I realized something was wrong. Instead of hearing Frank making his way up the stairs, what I heard was the sound of his voice on the phone, the jingling of keys and then the slam of the garage door. It was 2 o'clock in the morning.

" 'Where's he going at this time of night?' I wondered. I watched his black convertible Bentley make its way down the long driveway and then I frantically began calling his cell phone. He finally answered after my third attempt.

" 'What's up?' he muttered, as if my calling annoyed him.

" 'What do you mean, 'What's up?'" I asked. I was *so* irritated. " 'It's 2 o'clock in the morning, Frank. Where are you going?' I could feel fear winning and self-control losing, right then and there.

" 'Out,' he snapped.

" 'You promised me you wouldn't do this any more. I thought we were working on *us*?' I said as I screamed through my tears and started to lose control.

" 'I never *promised* you anything, Krishna. I told you we'd see what happens, that's it. You always read more into things than what's actually there,' he said nonchalantly.

" 'What do you mean? This isn't what we talked about in counseling. This isn't how we fix our relationship, Frank!' I screamed.

" 'Look, you got me to admit to cheating on you. What more do you want? It's all out now, so it's all good. You do you because I'm always gonna do me. I'm my own man. You don't control me. Remember that!' he shouted.

" 'Control you?' I've *never* tried to control you, Frank. You've always been your own man. I've never gotten in the way of anything you ever wanted to do. Please, don't do this. We can work on us. I need you. Why are you throwing everything away?" I sobbed as I begged him to come home.

" 'You're trippin'... I gotta go. Take a Xanax, wash it down with that drink I fixed you and go to bed. I'll see you later,' he barked at me and hung up the phone.

"I screamed his name into the phone and called his number every five minutes for the next half hour but he never answered. Eventually, my calls simply went straight to voicemail.

"I was mortified and hurt. I wanted to know who he'd left the house to go see at that time of night and why it felt as if he no longer cared about our marriage or family. I *had* to find out. So, and Adrienne knows this but you, E, and Faith will probably laugh at this, I threw on the closest thing in arms reach – the wide legged, blue and white striped Chanel jumper I had worn the day before and the lace up black Chanel sneakers I bought last week. I knew I looked "fashionably confused" but I didn't care at that moment. I tossed my hair up into a high messy ponytail and ran down the back staircase toward the kitchen, grabbed my driver's license and AmEx card out of the clutch bag I had carried at the gala, grabbed the keys to the Range Rover and drove away from the house.

"I didn't know where to begin looking for him and I didn't know why I was doing this except for the fact that I wanted answers. I deserved answers; *real* answers and Frank Fitzgerald was going to give them to me. As I exited the community gates and sped through the neighborhood, I made my way onto the main street toward the highway. I could feel my adrenaline pumping. I was crying and rage inside me blinded every sensible decision I was capable of making which included driving the speed limit and abiding by the traffic laws. I wrongly interpreted all traffic lights as green as I flew through them. Fortunately, no one else was on the road at that time of night except for the police car that had its sirens and lights blaring as it came up behind me and indicated to me to pull over."

Hearing this, the girls and I all groaned - even Adrienne, who clearly already knew the story.

"I brought the truck to a stop, and sat there and cried uncontrollably. The officer made his way to the driver's side, shone his flashlight inside, tapped on the glass and told me to lower my window. As I lowered the window, the light nearly blinded me and I knew he could clearly see I was distressed. I was prepared for him to chew me out or even drag me out of the truck given that I'd flown through two red lights and one stop sign," she told us. "But surprisingly, he didn't. He actually began his inquiry in a gentle fashion.

" 'Ma'am, are you OK? What's going on? Do you know why I pulled you over?' With my hands in plain view and wrapped around the top of the steering wheel, I dropped my head again, leaned on the steering wheel and just shook and sobbed uncontrollably.

"I told the officer I believed my husband was cheating on me *again* and I was trying to follow him because I needed to know where he was going and who he was going to see," Krishna explained.

"After I had calmed down a bit and seeing I was alone in the car, the patrolman let me stay in my truck but followed police protocol. He asked to see all my paperwork. Without hesitation, I retrieved everything he asked for and remained broken and crying in the car as he walked back to the patrol car to run my information. As I sat there and waited for the officer to return, I wondered how my 'perfect' life seemed to have spiraled out of control and why Frank was so unhappy in our marriage to the point where he was repeatedly cheating on me. It was too much to bear. I felt hopeless and alone and, for the first time ever, completely out of control of my life.

" 'Ma'am please step out of the car,' the officer instructed me after running my driver's license and returning to the truck.

" I was shocked," she confessed to us.

" 'Why?' I asked as I followed his instructions and got out of the car. Officer Winsome told me that after running my license he learned there was an outstanding warrant out for my arrest from a previous traffic case.

" 'What? I'm not aware of any warrants. I've lived in this area for almost twenty years. What are you talking about? There's gotta be a mistake,' I told him.

"I pleaded with him to run my license again but he refused.

" 'Sorry, Ma'am, you're under arrest,' he said. 'You have the right...,' the officer read me my Miranda Rights as he placed the handcuffs on my wrists and escorted me to his patrol car.

"Before he placed me inside however, he said, 'I'm sorry but I have no choice. I know you've been having a tough night and this doesn't help but this is my job and these are the rules.'

"I was terrified, angry, confused and embarrassed because I had never been arrested for any reason before and now *this* was happening. I couldn't believe it. In my mind I blamed Frank and yet he was the first person I wanted to call to get me out of this mess," she confessed as Faith and I stared at her in stunned silence and Adrienne shook her head.

"Officer Winsome was very kind. While we were in the car he told me what I should expect when we arrived at the police station– paperwork, fingerprinting, and mug shot – as well as what kind of people and scenarios I might see while there. He explained that once I was booked, I could call someone to pick me up and although he was scheduled to get off duty within the hour, he would stay to ensure I was OK. I instinctively knew this wasn't police protocol and deeply appreciated his interest in ensuring I made it through the process OK.

"I was quickly processed at the station just as he explained and luckily, it was quieter than I had braced myself for. While I was there, I learned that three years prior to my arrest that evening, I received a moving violation which resulted in several points and my license being suspended. The matter would have been resolved had I gone to court but because I didn't appear the judge issued a bench warrant for my arrest. Somehow, the matter fell through the cracks and the sheriff's department didn't follow through so I was never picked up. Thank God!"

Recalling the time period, Krishna remembered the incident. "I admit to driving well beyond the speed limit on that day because I was in a rush to get to the airport. After a seven-day business trip, though, I completely forgot about the ticket. When the document arrived in the mail informing me of the court date, it got buried under other mail and completely forgotten," she told us.

Adrienne squeezed her hand and said, "Tell them what happened next." Krishna took a sip of wine, sighed and continued.

"After the booking process was complete, Officer Winsome told me I could make my phone call.

" 'I want to call my husband,' I told him.

"Are you sure?' he asked. 'You said you've been through a lot with him already tonight. Most people call their lawyer or a good friend -- someone who's going to be supportive. But, it's your decision' he told me.

Honestly, I wasn't entirely surprised when I learned Krishna elected to call Frank but I admit I was disappointed.

" I dialed his number. The call connected and the phone rang repeatedly.

"I was praying with each ring. 'Come on, come on, Frank answer the phone. Please answer the phone,'' she said with her head down in a soft, desperate whisper.

"Finally, I got through. 'Hello?' he answered and I started to cry, feeling relieved over my impending rescue. 'Hello?' he said again.

" 'Frank, it's me. I've been arrested and I'm at the police station,' I said sobbing.

"Then, he asked me angrily, 'Arrested? For what?'

"I explained to him all that had happened after he left. 'Please come and get me. I'm so embarrassed,' I asked him.

"There was silence on the other end of the phone and I began to get concerned the call had been disconnected.

" 'Frank?' I asked, checking to make sure he was still there. 'Did you hear what I said? I need you to come and pick me up. The arresting officer, Officer Winsome, is standing right here. He can give you the address or directions to get here.'

"He snickered and then scolded me, 'I told you to go to bed. What the fuck were you doing trying to track me down? You're out of your mind if you think I'm going to the police station! Figure it out.'

"And with those words Frank hung up the phone, leaving me to fend for myself. I felt two inches tall and less than human as I was forced to confess to the officer, 'He hung up the phone. He's not coming to get me.'

" 'That was your *husband*? Officer Winsome said puzzled. 'I'm sorry that happened. Here, let's try again,' he said, 'but this time, I want you to call either a family member or your lawyer, OK?'"

"This was so embarrassing! Who was I going to call? I couldn't believe this was happening to me after all the shit I've tolerated from him. I've always been so concerned about *his* welfare I don't spend the time I should with Lauren and *this* is how he treats me?!

"Officer Winsome handed me more tissues and gently told me to dry my tears and call someone else so I could get home and into my own bed.

" 'Sometimes a pile of crap has to land in our face before we start to see the other crap it's piled on top of' he told me. 'Our wake up calls are not always delivered to us in pretty designer packages. Call someone else.'

"He handed me the phone and I called Dre. I was so scared. But, true to form Dre answered immediately," she said with a slight smile as she looked at Adrienne, who took the story over from there.

" Poor Krishna had explained to me as much as she could about her arrest and Frank's refusal to pick her up and within forty minutes I was there at the station. I tried not to bombard her with a ton of questions as the paperwork was processed for her release. When everything was done, I put my arm around her and walked her out to my car.

"Of course, I couldn't help but say, 'Krish, girl, you're the only chick I know who has ever taken a mug shot in head to toe Chanel and her makeup beat to the freakin' gods! You're a DESIGNER GANGSTA bitch!!'"

"Admit it Krish, that cracked you up."

"Yeah, it did," Krishna smiled a little.

Adrienne's words broke the seriousness of what had just happened and allowed Krishna a respite from the pain and embarrassment she was feeling and we burst out laughing.

"And let me tell you two something, that Officer Winsome is a cutie pie! There's something about a strong man in a uniform with a gun that's crazy sexy! 'Ooo, save me daddy!' Adrienne laughed.

Krishna shot her a look like "Are you serious?" and all Adrienne could say was, "I'm just sayin' Krish, he is *fine*, girl! After what Frank put you through, you need to get you some Officer Winsome!"

"I hate Frank, Adrienne."

"I know you do, honey, but I got your back that night and I will *always* have your back. Now let me finish the story," Adrienne replied.

"I told Krish she was going to be fine but I didn't think she should go home that night though because Frank was certain to make his way home at some point and things could get ugly.

"I took her to the Marriott instead of her house so she could have some privacy and peace of mind. (We've got corporate housing there.) I told her she should stay there for a couple of days or at least for the night until she had a chance to think some things through. It's spacious and comfortable and the staff is great.

"Krishna was calm until I asked about Lauren and then she freaked out! 'Oh my God, Lauren! I forgot all about her!' she shrieked. 'Oh, oh, she's at Ashley's house for the night. But tomorrow she's going to Alabama for a track meet. They'll be there for five days although she doesn't run until day three. I forgot all about it!'

"I told her, 'Don't worry about that. I'll pick her up. Her mom and I play golf on Wednesdays at the club so I know where she lives and I'll make up some excuse for you. I'll take her to the house so that she can get her things and then I'll drive her to the airport. I'll text her in the morning and tell her I'll be the one picking her up.'

"In spite of everything that had just happened to her, you know what K's first thoughts were?

" 'She's going to be so mad at me for not going on this trip. I promised I would go. I haven't been to any of her track meets this season! I wasn't even there when she broke the state indoor record in the 100!' That's our girl!

" I told her, 'Whether you go or not is up to you, Krish. It may not be a bad idea to go, though. It'll take your mind off of things for a while and you and Lauren can spend some time together.'"

Adrienne has always been the kind of a friend who thinks clearly during a crisis and can gently calm you down, while I tend to provide a calming spiritual voice to a situation. Dre is great about giving practical guidance which makes you feel as if she's propping you up and has your back – much like a mom would do. I could see how this is exactly the type of strength Krishna needed at that time.

"Can you believe it, E? After I suggested she go to Lauren's track meet, Krishna said to me, 'Dre, I really don't have time to do that right now. I need to find out what the hell is going on. Going to that track meet now is going to get in the way of that.'

"I ignored her ass and we checked in and made our way to the corporate suite. For what it is, it's very warm and inviting and it was a much needed sanctuary at 5:00a after all of the drama Krishna had been through in the previous three hours. We both agreed it was perfect.

"Once she was settled in Krishna said to me, 'I need to find out what Frank is doing and who he's been with. I need the name of that PI you're using.'"

Faith and I exchanged quick glances.

We both knew she asked Adrienne this because she had mentioned she had hired a PI when *her* marital problems arose. She had had nothing but good things to say about Mr. Snyder's ability to get all the information she needed about Chris.

Krishna felt she needed a PI to do the work she simply wasn't prepared for or capable of doing. She was certain Frank wasn't stealing from her company because she kept a close grip on the finances and all of the accounts. But she was obsessed with knowing *everything* about the other woman and their relationship and she was willing to pay top dollar for it.

"I told her I'd give her his name and number later," Adrienne said, "But I also told her rest was a priority. I did everything I could think of to get Krishna to relax and to take her mind off of the situation, but she was focused on getting to the bottom of it so she persisted.

" 'Adrienne, I need to know how to get in touch with your guy immediately,'' she said. " I want to know who she is, where she lives, the type of work she does, if she has kids, all of it. Home wreckers need to be dealt with, Dre. Doesn't she know he's married with a child? You know this kind of pressure doesn't sit well with me."

Indeed I did know and I was certain Krishna had gotten annoyed with Adrienne's obvious unwillingness to share her information and her lame attempts at putting her off. The PI's information was important to her and she wanted the information. But Krishna can't let things go and that agitates Adrienne, especially at times like this when being practical is a necessity.

"She was really beginning to piss me off so I just told it to her straight," Adrienne said. "I didn't mince any words because she needed to hear the

truth, you guys. I said, 'OK, look, Krish, as your best friend of over
twenty-five years I'm going to be brutally honest with you right now
because I love you. *Get your head out of your ass!* Your husband just left
you to ROT in a fucking jail! There is no reason for you to waste your
money on a PI for information you already have. Frank *is*, and *has been*,
cheating on you for *years* and *you know it*! That's the truth! You know it
and so does everyone else. He doesn't respect you or your marriage. He's
public with his cheating now and could care less about who knows or
sees him these days. It's like he's lost all discretion with his shit and
respect for you and Lauren ever since he admitted to it.

" 'He's having the proverbial cake *you* made for him, eating it, and
smashing it in your face now! I love you with all of my heart and you
know I do, but my heart is breaking for you because you don't want to
see the pain he's caused you and how this toxic relationship between the
two of you affects Lauren.

" '*She* needs you, Krishna. *She* needs to be your priority right now, not
Frank. He's going to do what he's going to do; and you and Lauren be
damned. So instead of you wasting your precious time, money, and
energy on hiring a PI, focus your attention on accepting what has
happened here tonight and getting *yourself* strong so you can make some
serious decisions, *please*.

" 'I know this is hard to hear and I'm *really* sorry to have to tell you this,
but right now I'm trying to be the very best friend I can be to you. I love
you and I *hate* that this has happened.'"

Wiping away her tears, Adrienne told us she picked up her purse and
keys from the sofa and reminded Krishna, "'Don't worry about Lauren.
I'll follow-up on my promise to take care of her tomorrow. You stay here
and just think about what happened and what I've said. *Please*, Krish,
take time to think about what the hell has been going on. I'm here for
you and I will *always* be here for you, but no one can help you if you
don't want to help yourself. I love you, girl. Now, please get some rest.'"

Krishna confirmed to Faith and me she sat there in stunned silence,
listening to everything Adrienne said. If Dre wasn't her oldest and best

friend, she would have told her she didn't know what she was talking about or to kiss her ass and stay the hell out of her business. But Adrienne is Krishna's *ride or die* best friend and she knew everything Dre was telling her was true and coming from a loving place. Besides, she had no energy left to combat anything Adrienne was telling her so she just took it. It was without a doubt the worst day of her life.

Adrienne excused herself for a minute, "Us Southern girls always need more ice," and Krishna continued the story.

"Before Adrienne left, she gave me a big hug and told me she loved me again, but I was so exhausted I couldn't even hug her back. I curled up into a ball on the chaise lounge and wondered, 'Does *everyone* know that Frank has been cheating on me? Am I the laughing stock of this city and among everyone I know?'

"I realized my perfect life was in a complete shambles and I couldn't see my way out of it.

"I tried praying for myself for the first time in years but the words wouldn't come.

"I even felt alone in my prayers because I didn't know what exactly to say or how to say it.

"I wanted God's mercy and guidance but at the same time, I didn't feel I was worthy of receiving it because I didn't have a relationship with Him any more. I tried calling you, E, for spiritual counseling and to hear a calming voice, but forgot you were away on a long weekend family vacation and off the grid.

"I'd had it. I'd been through enough in the past eight hours and I didn't want to *feel* anything any more. So I turned to two things that seldom let me down, my Xanax (I keep a few in my wallet for emergencies) and Perseco and almost immediately, I began to feel better because I didn't *feel* anything any more."

Hearing this broke my heart. My girlfriend had turned away from her Maker and certain strength, relief, and guidance and turned toward the two falsehoods that would not make her feel better but would only magnify her suffering. She numbed her pain with drugs and drink in order to escape her reality -- a habit she'd acquired over the years and one that never served her well.

When she was done with her story, Krishna told us she spent the next 48 hours thinking about what happened at the jail and did her best to figure out how she and Frank had gotten to this place in their marriage and more importantly, how to repair her struggling relationship with Lauren. She was in pain. Her entire life was turned upside down in an instant but I am so happy we were all there to help her figure it all out.

PART 2

Section 2 - I Will Love You Until the End (or not)!

Choices: *Sometimes we must make some difficult ones and at other times they're made for us. Either way, the ripples they cause can be tremendous.*

CHAPTER 5

FAITH – "ENOUGH IS ENOUGH!"

On my last day of treatment, I went alone. I'd asked Mrs. Samuels to pick up a few things and after she'd left, I drove myself to the hospital. From the beginning, I'd purposefully mislead my girlfriends and Mrs. Samuels about the date of my final treatment because I wanted to give this demon her last official goodbye alone and on my own terms. I'd battled her for over a decade but when it came time for this final counter attack, I decided to do it by myself with only my God as my teammate and Comforter. I knew He'd see me through it and I would be fine.

With my eyes closed and ear buds in, I spoke with God throughout the treatment and this time I *know* I heard Him speak to me. For the first time since my initial diagnosis nearly a decade ago, I actually *heard* God tell me, *"No more cancer. You will never have to endure **any** of this again."*

Almost immediately, I felt as if my entire body was being elevated; I was floating and no longer surrounded by darkness but embraced by the most beautiful and indescribable light.

I felt whole again. I felt no pain or discomfort anywhere in my body. The entire experience was so incredible, so warm and so comforting I didn't want to open my eyes at the end because that meant I would have to face the reality of no longer being in the presence of God. But God was with me. He heard my prayers, felt my suffering and my pain and He healed me. I *know* He did!

Within minutes of arriving home and climbing into bed, my phone rang. When I answered it, I could hear the voices of my dear friends Faith, Adrienne and Krishna. They were all excited and talking over each other anticipating my last treatment was tomorrow. I felt badly knowing I would have to tell them I had finished it without them only because I knew they wanted to be there to support me and they'd likely be upset or feel as if they'd let me down or something. But I also knew they'd understand. I've been so blessed to have these three amazing women in my life because I'm an only child and most of my family still lives in the Caribbean. My girlfriends have truly been like "family" to me since I arrived in America over twenty-five years ago.

"Hey, Evey!! Tomorrow's the day, girl! Adrienne squealed in excitement. "We're going in there with guns blazing!"

Then they broke into a rendition of a famous Ray Charles road song and hearing them hack their way through it made me smile as it warmed my heart. I hated to have to tell them it was finally all over because they were so riled up, but at that very moment, I realized that if you're going to go into battle for any reason, these are the kind of women you want standing at your side and I thank God for them every day.

Faith was still reeling from the encounter she'd had with Van and consequently, D. When she first told me about this incident, she also told me how incredibly helpful Adrienne had been to her, even when she was in Switzerland on a business trip. "As soon as Dre landed, she called me immediately. God bless her. I was sobbing and on the verge of hyperventilating so I'm sure it wasn't easy to understand me after my conversation with Van."

Faith and Adrienne are similar in that they're both the "straight, no chaser" type of chicks. When things happen, they know they can always count on each other to be honest and brutally frank but never malicious. According to Faith, the most important piece of advice she received came from Adrienne during that call. Adrienne shared a story about a colleague of hers who had recently gone through something similar. This story helped Faith put things in perspective almost immediately. It was exactly what she needed to hear at that time and it was one of the best pieces of advice she said she'd received when it came to the DiMarco situation. Adrienne told her,

"Faith, I know you're deeply hurt, but based on how D reacted to what Van told you, you can believe he probably won't tell you *anything* – especially the truth. So, and I know this is going to sound really harsh but I gotta say it… it's time to wipe your tears and get busy," and then added lovingly but sternly, " Just like my colleague, you have to *think smart* and *move fast*! Open every piece of mail in your house, go online and check all bank accounts, check his email accounts, look for receipts and anything else you can get your hands on and make copies of everything! Be vigilant because when he's confronted, he's going to lie about *all* of it. You're gonna have to find out for yourself what the hell has been going on because he is not going to tell you everything – *if* he tells you *anything* at all. Once you've learned as much as you can on your own, and from whatever it is he does tell you, THEN and ONLY then do you begin making decisions– not before! Whatever decisions are coming are yours to make and to live with. So don't worry about what other people may think or may say once word really gets out."

"When she said that, I panicked, E," Faith said. "Once 'word gets out'? What do you mean? Nobody can find out about this! My reputation… It's embarrassing! It's humiliating! What will people think? What will they say?"

Adrienne calmly responded, "Faith, if he's been cheating on you with that woman for *ten years,* other people already know about it. Heck, Van and Clyde knew about it all of this time, so I'm sure a lot more people know about it. You already know he was introducing her to some of your other friends. Unfortunately, you, like the rest of us, are just the last one to find out."

"I was so distraught, Evey, I even asked her if *she* knew about it!"

Hearing that, I knew *that* question didn't go over well with Dre and I anxiously waited to hear how she responded.

" 'Faith, if I knew about it, it wouldn't have lasted for ten seconds after I found out! I can't believe you asked me that bullshit. You know I would have told you about whatever I knew as soon as I knew,'" Adrienne scolded me, but I didn't really listen and said,

" 'I know, but you've always said you wouldn't get in the middle of anyone's marriage so I just assumed...'" but before I could finish and justify my question, Adrienne interrupted.

" 'Yeah, but you're my girl first and foremost and I've known you for over twenty years. My loyalty is to *you* first. I wouldn't sit on the sidelines and not say anything while knowing your husband is cheating on you, Faith.'"

"I felt so badly because I knew she was right so I just apologized for doubting her and her loyalty. I was just so confused and hurt. I didn't know what to believe any more – and still don't," Faith admitted.

"After we hung up the phone I felt terrible about questioning her friendship and loyalty to me. I've *never* doubted any of you or your loyalty to me and I hope you've never doubted mine," she told me. "I called Adrienne back immediately and apologized again. I was an emotional wreck and obviously attempting to sabotage even the good things in my life. But the good news is, almost immediately, I realized I had to get a handle on myself and on the situation."

After this revelation, life at home quickly became unbearable for Faith most of the time. For the next ten months, she and DiMarco argued nearly every day. The tension in the house was thick and affecting everything in their lives. Daily routines requiring communication and coordination around the girls at school or their activities were almost impossible, so Faith did most of it herself which was difficult, but made it easier to avoid him.

Faith wasn't thinking straight during that time because she became consumed with learning everything she could about what had happened to their marriage. When she wasn't helping me, she was in constant pursuit of the truth and it became evident DiMarco was in constant cover up mode. He didn't want to address any of the issues surrounding his infidelity and instead was on a quest to deny all of it, even though she confronted him with numerous questions about it over and over again. Faith knew she was making his life a living Hell, but she didn't care because she was already living one herself, thanks to him.

Denial was just part of DiMarco's arsenal to make this all go away and try to preserve his life of "having his cake and eating it too".

His lies were never ending and he quickly spread them to people other than her when he felt he wasn't getting any traction. He began with lobbying friends and family to support his cause and through deception, lies and flattery, encouraged us (and others) to speak to her on his behalf. Neither Adrienne nor Krishna would have any of it. Our allegiance was to Faith – PERIOD! I tried to keep an open mind and hoped they'd work things out. I encouraged him to seek counseling on his own and try to prove to her he was trying to make the necessary changes to make their marriage work and he assured me he would.

During this time, Faith told me he'd even resorted to futile attempts at "buying her back" with a series of lavish gifts. For Mother's Day, for example, he bought her a beautiful three quarter length chinchilla swing coat, one month later a three carat diamond station necklace and on Christmas morning, he told her to go to one of the bedroom windows overlooking the driveway. As she peered out of the window, there, parked in the driveway, topped with a big fat red bow, was a brand new platinum colored Mercedes G550 SUV. Kennedi and Harper were screaming with excitement but all Faith could bring herself to say was an unemotional "Thanks." That Christmas day, he received nothing from her. Faith couldn't fake it and therefore, chose not to.

He proposed a two-week trip to South America for Valentine's Day the following year but Faith told him she wasn't going to go on any trips with him until he told her the complete truth. Needless to say, they never took that trip.

When it was clear she wasn't going to get the truth, Faith decided she wanted him out of the house but he wouldn't leave. She put him out twice and after a few days he'd return claiming either he had nowhere to go or that she had no grounds to remove him as both of their names were on the house title.

"Go back to wherever you've been!" she'd tell him repeatedly, but I think D believed it was in his best interest to remain in the house so he could maintain some proximity to her in order to know what she was up to. His was the old "keep your friends close and enemies closer" approach. The problem was it was driving Faith crazy because the relationship was going nowhere and it was affecting everyone.

Faith's choices in dealing with the issue were limited to either moving out of their home with Kennedi and Harper or enduring his presence for the girl's sake. Initially, she considered moving out in order to reestablish peace in her life, but as time went on, she realized the best thing for her daughters was for them to remain in the only home they've ever known. Faith rightfully concluded it was imperative some portion of the girl's lives remain constant, even though their entire family unit was being annihilated by their father. This made sense; keeping the girls in the family home enabled them to maintain a sense of normalcy relative to their daily routines, activities and friends. Without question, it was a nightmare for Faith, but a sacrifice worth making for her girls.

The decision to stay in the family house really took its toll on her. She felt mentally and physically imprisoned by DiMarco because like it or not, he was still a part of her life even though she wanted nothing more than to escape. Everything about him incensed her; even knowing he'd be home from work at some point in the evening would alter her entire mood and make her angry. When she spent time with me and realized it was time for her to go home her cheery disposition would completely dissipate. Sadly, once home, she'd retreat to her room or leave the house entirely after taking care of the girls and not return for hours. Faith wanted D *gone.* Her anger was quickly turning to sheer rage and all of this was adversely impacting how, and when, she engaged with Kennedi and Harper. I was growing concerned because her anger was palatable and my fear was she might carry out one of her many vengeful thoughts.

On one occasion, Faith told me that after D arrived home from work and changed his clothes, he was walking down the stairs in front of her and as he neared the bottom of the staircase, she visualized herself kicking him in the middle of his back as hard as her body would allow and watching him sail down the stairs, through the window and onto the front lawn.

"It took all I had not to do it, Evey! I've plotted his death multiple times in my head but always get hung up on how to go about disposing of the body and remembering the web of lies I'd have to tell to ensure the cover up. I couldn't bring myself to do it," she confessed to me.

Realizing that ultimately the murder would be solved, she would be found out and her children would be left with no parents, Faith repeatedly talked herself out of this type of vengeance. "Think of your beautiful gifts from God, Faye," I told her on more than one occasion. "You can't keep having those thoughts because at some point you just may carry one of them out! Either get out of there and maybe work on your marriage from a distance or figure out another way to live under the same roof with him until you decide what you're going to do." I told her. "He's not worth the *severe* consequences acting out what's in your mind will bring. As soon as those thoughts come, think of those beautiful girls – Kennedi and Harper – because they *need you* and the devil is trying to trick you into believing murder is the best way to deal with your situation. Don't become a victim to his game," I'd tell her.

Infidelity, lies and the arrogance some men have when their deceits are exposed can cause a reasonable woman like Faith to completely lose her mind. Over time and with counseling, Faith realized he was making her lose her senses with vengeful and murderous thoughts. Fortunately, Faith ultimately realized he wasn't worth any of it and her children needed her more than anything.

Honestly, Faith's children kept her alive and while she harbored passing thoughts of murdering D, her children and her growing faith kept her sane. "I thank God for them and most importantly, for His mercy and grace because at any time during this seemingly insurmountable road block, I could have made a life altering decision which would have assured me a life sentence where orange most certainly would have become my new black," Faith revealed to me one afternoon.

In hindsight, I know it was God's favor and grace that prevented her from following through and acting on those thoughts. *All* of our lives would have been negatively altered forever I thank God for guiding her and her girls out of that terrible period.

Sharing a bed with him was out of the question immediately. "I don't want him touching me. Seeing his face repulses me. In fact, everything he does repulses me – even hearing him breathe!" she'd say.

In addition, she quickly made an appointment with her OB/GYN and had her run just about every medical test known to man in order to ensure she was still healthy. Thankfully, all of the tests came back negative. Adrienne and Krishna did the same thing when they became practical and accepting of their husband's infidelities.

It didn't take long before the entire ordeal and the pressure to "keep up appearances" begun taking its toll on Faith. She couldn't eat or sleep for weeks after learning about DiMarco's cheating; eventually losing twenty-five pounds in ten months and while her thick shoulder length hair started breaking off in various sections of her scalp. Her health was declining and she began experiencing anxiety attacks that mimicked heart attacks. During that time, Faith had to be hospitalized three times for nervous exhaustion and anxiety attacks.

Her relationship with her girls was becoming negatively impacted because she was no longer present for them in a meaningful way and everything they did irritated her. Faith had become consumed with DiMarco: the issues that brought them to this place in her marriage and her incessant quest for the truth in order to rebuild their lives and somehow turn the clock back. The entire situation was slowly killing her and her marriage was getting worse and much more volatile.

As her friend, I prayed to God daily for strength and wisdom and repeatedly asked Him to reveal to me what exactly I should do to help her. Although I was dealing with my own health issues and the unfathomable situation between Len and I on top of it, I did my best to always be there to pray with her, cry with her and encourage her. I also advised her to fight for her marriage because until such time as it changes, "DiMarco is *your husband* and fighting for the survival of your family is worth everything you can do to save it, if that is what you want," I told Faith repeatedly.

Faith says it's because of me she didn't run to the courthouse immediately after learning of D's infidelity and instead made the conscious effort to try to save her marriage. "It was through, and because of, your examples of strength, fortitude and impenetrable faith in God, that my own faith strengthened. As a result, my ability to deal with the issues I was now aware of became tolerable and to some degree, manageable," Faith admitted.

In addition, all of the murmurings throughout the city about her marriage no longer affected her. Because of the spiritual strength she was building, she no longer cared about what others thought and that, in and of itself, was liberating and a blessing.

For the first few months after learning about DiMarco's infidelity, Faith agonized over whether or not to tell her parents and Luke about her marital problems because she thought she would work through it and didn't want them to worry about her and the girls or, worse, change their overall positive opinions about D. But as things got progressively worse, she had no choice but to tell them what was going on. When Luke found out, he was out of his skin with anger. The following day, he made the ninety-minute drive from Richmond, VA to her house and confronted DiMarco about his behavior, man-to-man. He got little out of him in the way of a real explanation and instead got a bunch of excuses and empty promises about making things right with Faith and their family.

"I swear, Evey, during their conversation, Luke said he saw something in DiMarco I didn't see or want to admit to until everything unraveled: DiMarco is a pathological narcissistic liar who cares only about himself and whatever affects him," she told me. Luke spoke matter of factly and told me, 'You'll never get the truth or a straight answer out of him Fee... D's in extreme denial and just trying to cover his ass. It's your decision in the end but I know you and trust is big for you. Until you get that back

– and it won't happen overnight – your marriage will suffer. He's not ready to be 100% honest with you and I don't know if he will ever be.'

" 'Listen… the decision is yours, but I guarantee you'll never be able to trust him completely again. He's going to say whatever it is he thinks you need to hear so you don't throw him out of the house and divorce him. I'm not trying to tell you what to do, but you're my sister and I don't want to see you suffer over this fool. Either way I'll support you but I'm just going to give it to you straight, baby girl, he's not worth it. Cut your losses and you and the girls move on. I got your back, whatever you need."

"Hearing Luke say that, E, was the hardest thing ever," Faith said to me. "I told him I still love D but he's making me hate him because of all of the lies he's told to cover up his shit. I don't understand why he isn't trying to fix what he *alone* destroyed? And all of his cover-ups and lies are only making matters worse. I can't believe he did this to us… to our family!" she wailed as the anger inside of her grew.

"And then Luke called him 'a bitch' and told me he wasn't worth the tears I was shedding! The saddest part of it all was that as much as I wanted to defend my husband, I knew Luke was right. What he said about DiMarco's character *really* hurt in a way that felt like humiliation because as his wife, on some level I still wanted to protect him and deny this ever happened. But I didn't. Honestly, I *couldn't* because deep down inside, I knew Luke was right and I needed to listen." Faith was visibly upset and shaken by what was going on in her life.

Faith insisted they go to counseling but DiMarco refused initially. When he *did* concede, he attended only three sessions and made virtually no effort to participate. She was frustrated but kept at it.

"We don't need anybody in our business. We're fine. We can work this out ourselves. We're talking to each other and that's all that matters," he'd say repeatedly, but they weren't "fine" and they weren't "talking *to* each other" in fact, they were only talking *at* each other and getting absolutely nowhere. Furthermore, Faith commented that if he said anything about his cheating while in the counseling sessions, it was all complete nonsense, talking in circles and repeatedly getting caught in one lie after the next and *never* actually admitting to anything. His mission was for her to "Get over it" and "Move on" but she simply couldn't let any of it go because there was *never* any purity or honesty in his words. They were all just a bunch of lies.

When DiMarco quit therapy, I insisted Faith continue with Dr. Buckingham; switch gears and move to individual counseling. Therapy allowed Faith to openly express her feelings to Dr. Buckingham, an objective third party whose concerns were about Faith's mental and overall health.

Fortunately, she listened and followed my advice because she and her doctor spent their time making her healthy and whole again. Those weekly therapy sessions were a blessing and helped Faith set her feet on more solid emotional ground and enabled her to see her way ahead more clearly. Faith and Dr. Buckingham decided that taking time off from work was imperative while she got her bearings and adjusted to her new circumstances.

"I can't think or concentrate so I've decided to take a hiatus from my jobs. It is definitely what I need," Faith told us during one of our "What's the tea?" Thursday talks. We knew her ability to focus at work had become severely impaired as evidenced by her forgetting and/or missing deadlines and assignments more and more frequently and she frequently had to reschedule appearances on radio and television shows because she simply couldn't pull herself together to go out into public. Colleagues filled in for her on air and taught her classes. "My bosses have started to notice both physical and performance changes in me and finally, one by one, began calling me into their offices to inquire about what was going on. I told them I was dealing with a personal family matter which was affecting my health and my doctor recommended I take a medical leave of absence for six seeks." This was a break she desperately needed to get things right again in her marriage and her life. Fortunately, her employers were all very understanding, extended themselves and any resources she needed, granted her requests and wished her well.

During that six-week hiatus from work, Faith still made herself available to me and although I insisted she focus on herself and her family, she refused. She continued to drive me to the doctor's office on the days that were her turn and kept a constant check on me via Adrienne, Krishna or Mrs. Samuels.

Adrienne told me Faith had followed her advice and opened and read every piece of mail that came to her house. She checked phone records, bank statements, email messages, online travel accounts and more. Because she had the passwords to almost all of his accounts, finding the information was easy. She learned DiMarco had basically cheated in plain sight. Everything she found was at her fingertips and it really didn't require much of an effort to prove it.

"I guess you can say I made it easy for him because I was never the type of woman who snooped around. I always felt if I had to do that in *any* relationship I didn't need to be in *that* relationship," she told Adrienne. With this amount of free time, more and more information regarding DiMarco's cheating came to her attention. What Faith found out was shocking.

She learned her husband had been having *countless* affairs with *numerous* women over the course of their marriage. The number had jumped from the one Van told her about to over *seven* women during the fourteen years they had been married! (And that's just based on what she was able to find out on her own!) His initial unwillingness to talk about "The Hostess" after being exposed made sense now because it was obvious he was concerned further exposure would reveal the full extent of his cheating. The more she learned about the trips he'd taken and the money he'd spent on gifts, dinners, lunches and whatnot for those other women, the more sick and then enraged Faith became.

I returned home from my mid morning walk one Saturday and Faith was sitting on my front step.

"Hey girl, what are you doing out here? You know Mrs. Samuels would have let you in." I asked as I got closer. "I'm filing for divorce, E. I'm done," she said flatly. The news of her decision stopped me in my tracks for a moment and then I sat down next to her and put my arm around her.

"I didn't rush to this decision, Evey. I weighed all of the evidence I'd gathered as well as every piece of advice I had been given, both practical and emotional, as to how this is going to work for my children and me and while I don't know what the future holds for us, I just know I can't do *this* any more." With her head on my shoulder, Faith calmly spoke without tears. She was so exhausted by all she'd been through she couldn't even cry any more.

The practical was pretty easy. As Adrienne had predicted, there was a paper trail a mile long with supporting evidence of his numerous affairs. Taking time off from work, as Dr. Buckingham suggested, was also a perfect solution for her. Since she had time to work with as she collected evidence, she took a lot of time for herself as well: she spent weekends with one or all of us, and partook in day spas and golf. Faith also made a conscious effort to eat better and she began to regain her physical health and vitality. She also increased her sessions with Dr. Buckingham so they could continue working on getting her mentally and emotionally prepared for whatever decisions she would necessarily have to make.

"Luke was right, Evey," she continued. " Deep down I know I can never trust D 100% again, and I can't live in a marriage without that deal breaking crucial element. I meditated and prayed on your advice to fight for and work on our marriage and I did before arriving at my decision. I must admit counseling saved me. It helped me open my eyes to things and to listen more intently when he spoke. The endless one-on-one conversations with D, hoping he'd come clean, become contrite and come back to me proved to be a waste of time because none of it worked. I compared all of the information I had collected (which he knew nothing about) and consistently found the discrepancies in his stories. He told lies on top of lies with ease.

"It's sad, because I came to realize DiMarco Rathers was *not* going to change for me or for our children's sake. Salvaging what was left of our marriage was not a priority for him – protecting himself, however, was! As a result, I had to begin thinking about protecting my children and myself and coming to grips with what was abundantly obvious – my marriage is over." And with that Faith got up, gave me a big hug, told me to continue praying for her and the girls and said goodbye.

The way she described how she'd arrived at her decision coupled with her stoic delivery made me certain Faith had cleared a major emotional hurdle and was resolute about her decision to end her marriage. The next step would be deciding how to go about it, which meant dealing with a whole new set of choices and variables, but for now she was comfortable with her decision, despite the long road she had to take to get there.

On the verge of officially filing the paperwork (and perhaps even harboring a bit of reservations about it) the final straw came when Faith was contacted by one of DiMarco's paramours. This was the very thing we all feared most and she had warned him about during several arguments, which always basically went the same way.

"You're a liar," she would tell him. "You've taken money out of our household to fund your trysts with these whores. I know all about it and you're a *liar!* You probably have these tricks thinking I'm in the way of them having 100% of you. There are only two things that haven't happened yet – a bitch calling me and someone ringing the doorbell with a baby on her hip telling me you're the baby's father," Faith would tell him.

Each time DiMarco would emphatically reply the same way, "No one is going to be contacting you about anything and I don't have any other children out there," he would say as if the possibility of such a thing happening was so remote it bordered on the ridiculous.

Just as his life and their marriage were spiraling out of control, so was his apparent control over his other women. I don't know which experience was truly the worst; Van telling Faith about his affair or her receiving strange phone calls which always resulted in spontaneous hang ups as well as several strange voice messages telling her that her husband had been cheating.

I'd just finished having an early dinner with my youngest son Isaiah when Faith, Adrienne, and Krishna conference called. I had had a good day and I was feeling well and energized. Faith got us all on the line and began,

" 'You're *never* going to believe what just happened to me.'

" ' I was pulling into the driveway when some bitch called and told me she knows D's been having an affair with a girlfriend of hers. Thank God the girls weren't in the car!"

We all were shocked and began hurling our first thoughts at her simultaneously.

"What?"

"You have the bitches *calling* you now, Faye? This is out of control."

What the hell is going on?"

"Oh my goodness, this is too much!" each of us sharing our shock and horror at what she had just told us.

"This woman claims to know about an affair D had been having with a friend of hers for over a year. She didn't identify herself other than that," Faith continued.

"She was able to describe DiMarco, his car and where he worked in enough detail to keep me on the line. After about fifteen minutes, she told me her girlfriend wanted to talk to me so she could personally apologize for everything that had transpired. Can you believe that? Given that D had been refusing to admit to anything, I jumped at the opportunity to talk to this woman.

" '*Please* give her my number and have her call me tonight at 8:30p. I welcome the opportunity to hear what she has to say,' " I told this anonymous woman.

What? The 'ho wants to *apologize?* Krishna blurted out.

"Damn! What do ya know! A 'ho with a conscience! I've *never heard* of such a thing." Adrienne added.

"Yeah," Faith replied. "That fool needs to get out of the pimp game because his 'hos are *out of control.* When your 'hos start calling your *wife* you need to turn in your pimp card because you've lost all control." While none of this was really funny, we all laughed after that remark.

"When is she supposed to call you?" Krishna asked. "We should be there."

"Tonight. 8:30p" Faith announced.

That evening we assembled in Faith's downtown office at 8:00p. The building was closed and there was no one working late in the office so we weren't concerned about others witnessing or overhearing anything. We agreed no one would speak except Faith although the phone was set on speaker mode and promised to only communicate with her by writing notes when the phone wasn't muted. At 8:35p her phone rang.

"Hello," she answered.

"Um… is this Faith?" a child-like voice whispered into the phone. I was appalled this woman called Faith by her first name as if they were friends or even remotely familiar with each other.

"You may be fucking my husband but trust me bitch *I* don't know you!" Faith later told us she thought as she could see us seething with anger as well.

Notes were flying back and forth.

"No! That bitch didn't just ask for you by *your* first name" Krishna wrote. "That trick's got some nerve! First name? Really? Too bad you can't punch her in her throat through the phone!" wrote Adrienne.

I observed, "She sounds like a child!"

Faith cleared her throat and spoke. "This is Dr. St. John. I understand you have something to say to me?" Wow! Faith really kept it together.

She calmly but sternly corrected her while acknowledging she was speaking to the proper person.

"Um… I just want you to know that I didn't know DiMarco was married when we started dating," the voice on the other line stated.

"Well, first of all what is your name and can you please speak up? I can barely hear a word you're saying," Faith instructed.

She was clearly irritated by the caller's near inaudible speech and took control of the conversation right away. It was obvious to me that this "woman" had self-esteem issues. She sounded meek and intimidated on the phone. Nerves? Perhaps, but I agreed with Faith the bitch needed to speak up!

I must admit her voice surprised all of us. We'd assumed she was a strong *woman* with some presence like the four of us. But the more she spoke, the more obvious it became she was only a cut above being juvenile relative to her mental capacity and perhaps even her age!

"Oh, sorry, my name is Chelsea."

"Chelsea what?" Faith demanded.

"Um… Chelsea Patterson. I just wanted to tell you I'm sorry about what's happened. At first, I didn't know he was married; he lied to me. I even asked him if he was married and he told me he was going through a divorce," she explained.

"You realize you can't 'date' a married man, right? By the way, how old are you, um, Chelsea Patterson?" Faith asked like the college professor she is.

"Um… 25," was the meek reply. With that, Faith muted the phone and dropped her head on her office desk. We were all in shock.

For the next forty-five minutes, "Chelsea" answered every question Faith flung at her. She said she was an aspiring model and she and D had met at the car wash and auto detailing shop where she works as a receptionist and he visits bi-weekly.

Turns out, DiMarco had driven Chelsea around in their family vehicles to sporting events, bars and restaurants and taken her on trips to Bermuda, New Orleans and Miami. He'd also bought her gifts and promised to introduce her to people he knows on the West Coast in order to help kick start her modeling career, but neither the promises nor the introductions panned out.

I *almost* began to feel sorry for this young woman because I felt he had taken advantage of her until she explained why she decided to contact Faith and spill the beans.

"He kept telling me that you guys were divorcing but you wouldn't compromise on the custody and visitation arrangement with the kids," she explained.

"You know about my *kids*?" I could see Faith's rage beginning to build at the mere mention of her children out of that woman's mouth.

"Yeah, he told me you guys have two girls but I've only seen pictures of them," she revealed. It sounded as if her confidence was rising and that bothered us, we wanted her to remain timid.

"He showed you pictures of my *children*?" Faith asked.

"Well, not exactly. I saw them when I was at the house one night," she revealed with a pinch of pride in her voice.

"You've been to my HOUSE? When the fuck did that happen?"

At this point, Faith completely lost it and I had to briefly hit the mute button. I told her to try to calm down while Adrienne and Krishna raged and paced the floor.

Once off mute, Chelsea continued, "I think you and the kids were away visiting your parents or something and he and I had gone out to this nice lounge downtown. We had been drinking a lot so when I got in the car, I fell asleep. When I woke up, we were pulling into the garage. I asked him where we were, he told me his house but we'd have to leave really early in the morning before the neighbors saw us. We opened a bottle of champagne and went to bed. That's when I saw the pictures of the girls."

"You went to bed where?" Oh my goodness! I know Faith's blood had reached the boiling point because she calmly yet deliberately asked that question and when Faith gets *that* calm, trouble is around the corner!

"In the master bedroom. We left really early in the morning though," she replied.

I muted the phone again and just in time because at that point Faith screamed, "The bitch was in my fucking *bed*! He fucked her in *our bed* you guys!" Honestly, none of us could respond. Faith gathered herself and calmly returned to the call.

"OK. Is there anything else you'd like to say before I hang up?" she said, attempting to regain control of the conversation.

"No, I just wanted to apologize because I didn't know you were still married to him. He's a liar. I figured out after I left your house there might be something still there between the two of you because something seemed out of whack. Your closet and bathroom still had your stuff in it and that got me thinking ..."

"You used my bathroom? You looked in my closets? OK, I've heard enough." And with that, Faith hung up the phone.

For the next four hours, we dissected every detail of that conversation. I had taped it on my phone so Faith could use it as evidence for her divorce if she chose, so we were able to listen to her confession over and over again.

Faith told us she wanted DiMarco out of the house immediately and we were in full agreement. According to Faith, DiMarco was scheduled to leave for a four-day golf tournament in Puerto Rico the following day, so she immediately called Sheryl and arranged for her to pick up the girls for the weekend while Faith, with the help of all of us, took action.

When I arrived home late that night, everyone was asleep. I climbed into bed and cried. My tears were fueled by the sadness I felt for Faith and the drama we had all witnessed that had now become her life. Deep down I prayed my life and my marriage wouldn't follow suit and fall victim to that sort of destruction because I knew it would kill me. But, while I was able to eventually get a descent night's rest, Faith was not, as I later learned.

When she arrived home, the house was quiet, but when she entered the master bedroom and turned on the light, she was incensed to see DiMarco in *her* room, lying in *her* bed. I don't know why he was in there because for months, he had been sleeping in one of their guest rooms. After everything that happened earlier in the evening, D's timing could not have been any worse. Krishna later told me Faith yelled at him to get out of the bed and accused him of bringing whores into the house. As she walked around to her side of the bed, she snatched the covers off of him and told him to leave. He apparently jumped out of the bed, grabbed her arms and in the struggle, ripped Faith's blouse and wrestled her to the ground. "They were in a full out brawl, E!" Krishna exclaimed, and then continued her recap.

"Faith said he sat on top of her and did his best to hold her arms down over her head as he yelled at her to stop because she was screaming at him to get off of her. At one point, he *was* able to pin her arms over her head with one hand and with the other hand now clinched into a ball he yelled, '*Shut Up!*' And what's worse, she said she was terrified by the look in his eyes and what looked like his intent to punch her so she screamed at the top of her lungs, '*God HELP me! Get off of me devil! Only God can help you now! You better pray He'll have mercy on you,*' and with that he paused, unclenched his fist and stood straight up. He climbed back into her bed and pulled the covers over himself. Can you believe the nerve of him?!

"She ran out of the room and down the stairs, grabbed her keys and purse and drove to the police station. She nervously filled out the paperwork for a Protective Order and waited to see the hearing examiner on duty. After explaining what happened, and citing that was the second time he'd put his hands on her, she showed the bruising on both arms from where he grabbed her—her left shoulder (in excruciating pain) and her blouse, clearly and visibly torn, the Order was granted," Krishna's voice quivered as she told me what occurred. She continued,

"Faith explained to the hearing examiner DiMarco would be leaving the house for a golf trip in a few hours and she would only return once she knew he was gone. She called me, told me everything, and spent the night at my house. He sent her text message after text message telling her he was sorry and they needed to talk when he returned, but Faye refused to respond.

The limo arrived at 6:00a to pick up D and Faith returned to her house around 6:30a. Sheryl was at the house promptly at 8:00a to take the kids to her house for the weekend as planned.

Faith went into the basement and pulled out DiMarco's other set of luggage. Before we arrived to help her, she had already packed the cheapest suit and shirt she could find in his closet and other "bare necessity" items. She also grabbed his laptop and put it and the suitcases aside temporarily. Faith removed every article of clothing D owned and piled them on the bed. The U-Haul truck and one-day dumpster she ordered arrived by 10:00a. Faith's "Action Plan" was in full effect. When Adrienne, Krishna, and I arrived at 10:30a, we packed the truck with as much of his personal items as possible and transported it to the men's shelter downtown. Faith is a firm believer in donating unwanted items to shelters instead of throwing them out. After all, one person's trash is another person's treasure, right?!

When Adrienne and Krishna got down to the men's shelter, they pulled into the parking lot. There was no formal announcement of a donation, per se. Once the back of the truck was opened, they just asked the homeless guys they saw hanging out there to form a single line. They told them everyone could take at least two items/outfits and then they let the guys help themselves. Everything was gone in approximately fifteen minutes.

Back at the house, we were busy putting the dumpster to good use. An avid golfer, DiMarco's treasured Callaway and Taylor Made golf clubs he didn't take on this golf trip were thrown into it along with all his ski gear and every piece of furniture and items in that "man cave" of his. By the end of the day, the dumpster was nearly full and everything in it was hauled away.

For my part, I took charge of all of the textbooks and any other professional books in the library belonging to him. I moved his diplomas and all of his files into file boxes. The books were driven to a used bookstore and donated, while his diplomas, certificates and files remained with the luggage and laptop Faith had packed earlier. She had a locksmith come to the house and change all of the locks and had him add a better one on the back patio door. Once she got the alarm company on the phone, she had Adrienne oversee changing the alarm code while Faith took a ride to the banks.

Faith visited the three banks where they have joint accounts. She made withdrawals from all of them and had the money placed into certified checks and had those checks placed into her mother's safety deposit box.

Lastly, since all of the cell phones are in Faith's name and she pays all of the phone bills, she contacted their carrier and told them to terminate his cell phone number on the day he was scheduled to return home. She also had the home landline number changed to a new unpublished number.

The next day, Faith had the classic Jaguar roadster she bought him for his birthday five years prior removed from their storage garage and stored at a friend's house. (The only name on that title was hers. A technical mistake made at the dealership she never got around to correcting, so it's definitely hers!) Faith drove to her attorney's office and gave her a check for the retainer and instructed her to move ahead with filing the divorce papers.

By day three, Faith made arrangements with a friend who is a Deputy Chief of Police in the county to have an unmarked police car with a patrol officer inside park in front of her house upon DiMarco's return. The morning of his anticipated arrival, she pulled the car title on the Porsche and placed it in an envelope. The Porsche is the only vehicle not jointly owned by both of them and so it is D's. He had purchased that car for himself for his birthday two years ago and as far as Faith was concerned, he could have it. She placed the luggage, laptop, file boxes and car title in the trunk of the car and parked it on the street. She locked the vehicle and left the keys in the mailbox for the officer to hand to him upon his arrival and then drove to Luke's house in Richmond, VA.

Faith was told that two police officers met D as his limo arrived and the driver unloaded his bags. They served him with the protective order and told him he is *not* allowed on the premises and therefore cannot enter the house. Further, he is *not* permitted to be within 500 feet of Faith and that everything he needed was in the trunk of his car. When he opened the trunk and saw the luggage, laptop, two file boxes and the envelope with the words "Car Title" written on it, he became irate. After fumbling through the suitcase and realizing less than a fraction of his belongings were inside he apparently yelled, "That fucking bitch! Where's all my shit?" D is a clotheshorse so I'm certain he was in a state of shock!

DiMarco told the officers that was *his* house, *his* belongings were still inside and he *needed* to get them. He apparently pleaded with them but all of that "noise" fell on deaf ears. The officers explained that allowing him access to the home was not an option given the protective order and instead, encouraged him to leave. They told him that should he insist on entering the house it would be a violation of the protective order and they would be forced to arrest him. Enraged and nearly frothing at the mouth like a rabid dog, DiMarco packed up the car with the luggage and golf clubs from his trip and sped away.

After the dust had settled a bit, Faith shared with me a journal entry she wrote after she decided to file for divorce.

"Given everything that transpired, I'm comfortable with the decision I made to walk away from my marriage and divorce my husband. I was faithful to DiMarco during our entire marriage and would have continued to be his wife, lover and confidant "until death do us part". But D squandered my love for him and took advantage of my loyalty. I've done what I had to do for my sanity, health and peace of mind and for the sake of my children. As a result, I harbor *absolutely no regrets* about the choices I have made. My only real concern is the impact the divorce will have on my girls."

CHAPTER 6

ADRIENNE – MORE THAN A NOTION!

"Ladies and gentlemen we are now boarding flight 4598 nonstop service to London Heathrow. Please have your boarding passes ready." I could hear the background voice on the loud speaker at Dulles Airport announcing Adrienne's flight as she spoke on a conference call with Krishna and me.

"Oh, they're calling my flight. I gotta go soon. I swear, this is one trip I can't wait to take because after I close the deal in London and tie up some business in Rome I look forward to spending an extra three days there relaxing and hanging out with Symphony – Lord knows I need it! Krish, I'll call you when Symph and I connect. E, I'll still keep in touch to check on you, as much as possible notwithstanding the time difference and our schedules. I'll even send you a few lovely pics from Rome since that's one of your favorite places on earth! Love you guys. I gotta go. Bye."

I'm sure hearing the flight announcement was like music to Adrienne's ears this go round and she couldn't wait to board and get the hell out of D.C. Over the years, she's taken her business trips in stride because she couldn't wait to get back home even before leaving. Like the rest of us, home brings her peace and it's where she's the happiest but this time was different.

Adrienne will miss her kids for sure, but she wants absolutely nothing to do with Chris. Since finding out about his affair and the secret overseas accounts, Adrienne has been avoiding him at all costs. Fortunately, given their busy schedules, it's been easy for them *not* to spend time together.

Personally, I can't wait for all of this madness in everyone's lives to settle down. It feels like it's just been one thing after the next for each of us and sadly, I don't get the sense that it's quite over yet. We need a break from it all so I'm happy that Adrienne will get a bit of a respite in Rome after her business trip to London.

I've started planning a girl's week for the four of us at my beach house in Nags Head, NC after school lets out and all the graduations are over. I just want us to decompress together, hang out, get some much-needed rest and forget about this crazy stuff for a good week. Lord knows we need it. My fabulous friend, Ken Henderson, is "on the job" helping me plan and I'm really excited about it.

Outside of my sister-girlfriends, Ken is one of my dearest friends and I'm confident he will help me plan a magnificent week. He's gay, fabulous, and an award winning event designer. He knows that sunflowers and birds of paradise are my two favorite flowers so he made sure that throughout my recent treatments flowers with at least one of those were always delivered to me. Those flowers brightened my days and made me smile. Since doctor's orders keep me from traveling to wonderful places like Italy right now — planning this summer get away gives me something else to do beyond training for the triathlon when I'm not consumed with green smoothies, blood tests and CAT scans!

This change of scenery in Rome will also give Adrienne the opportunity to think some things through. Her less than adventurous sex life and boring interactions with Chris have become small problems compared to what she found in the *Deb Horton* file and based on what she's told me, Chris is probably happy he doesn't have to hear her complaining about how little time he's spending with her and the kids any way. She says that since their sex life has been so intermittent over the years – *maybe* two times per week, Wednesday evenings and Saturday *or* Sunday mornings – not having relations now due to "schedules" comes easy.

How pitiful is that?! I know Adrienne she has no patience for nonsense. The reality is she's just waiting for the report from the PI to tell her what she already knows and probably more – Chris has been having an affair with a former client's ex-wife.

But worse than that, he may also be embezzling money from his employer, Braithwaite Fielder. I pray this isn't true, because if it is, I *know* for a fact Adrienne Morris will stop at nothing to completely disassociate herself and their children from him in order to easily exit from her sexless, disengaged marriage.

Unexpectedly, I received a text from Dre after she boarded her flight. "On board and all settled in – First Class, Row 3, right next to window! U know I prefer the aisle but this is perfect! Can't wait to hang out & shop w/Symphony! Stay well… UR smoothies will b delivered every day! Luv ya. I'll text when I land."

I love my girlfriend! She'll be out of the country on business for well over a week and is still doing her part to "take care of me" in her absence! This kind of support always brings tears to my eyes because the reality is she/they don't have to do any of this. My cancer is not *their* problem, but my battle for my life and subsequent recovery has my warrior sister-girlfriends engaged 110%. They promised me I wouldn't have to fight this demon alone and they meant it.

While I like London and enjoy Paris, I absolutely *love* Italy. For some reason I feel very much at home there, almost like I've lived there before. I'm very comfortable there and, like Adrienne, I'm almost fluent in Italian after all my visits. For a brief period in my nursing career, when I was between jobs and trying to figure out what my next move would be, I did some consulting work for Dre's company which required me to do some international travelling and as a result, she and I were able to travel back and forth to Italy together. It was tons of fun and over the years, she and I have made a few friends there and I can't wait to go back.

One good friend there is Symphony Walton, Krishna's former classmate from Business School. Symphony is living in Italy yet again, this time on a five-year work detail and now as a finance consultant with the World Bank in Rome. Whenever Krishna, Adrienne or I are in Italy, we always try to get together with her; she's a lot of fun and her personality is a lot like Adrienne's so they get along great and share impeccable taste in clothing, art and men.

Had she not taken that overseas assignment, I'm certain Symphony would have also been part of our *sister-girlfriend* crew. She's a beautiful person and we absolutely adore her.

Symphony is single and has no children. She was married several years ago to Mateo, the man she always referred to as "my soul mate and the love of my life" but a drunk driver killed him one night after he left their house on an errand for her. Married only three years and pregnant with their first child, the news and shock of the accident caused Symphony to go into premature labor. She had lost her husband and her unborn baby, a son, within three days of each other. Needless to say, she was devastated and we were all devastated for her.

Five years after the tragedy, while in Rome, she met her fiancé, Emile Fontaine. Emile is a very handsome French movie executive who had also suffered the sudden and devastating loss of his pregnant wife in a plane crash around the same time Mateo was killed. Neither of them have other children, so they invest all of themselves in each other. They're a beautiful couple and deserve the happiness they've finally found.

Adrienne finished her meetings in London and went on to Rome. According to her, the timing for a mini-vacation was perfect. Symphony had just returned from a month long business trip to Germany and decided to take a few days off as well, so they had a few days to be foot loose and fancy free together. It was a perfect plan and she was excited about returning to her favorite five star hotel; the only one she stays at when she is in Rome where the décor and services are second to none. Now that most of the staff knows her, they spoil her and she loves it.

This time, Symphony arrived shortly after Adrienne and after she got settled in, they caught a taxi and headed deep into the heart of the city and had dinner in an adorable restaurant just outside of The Pantheon. With great weather on their side, they sat outside in the piazza and delighted themselves in Italian cuisine, great wine and cocktails, all the while sending me silly photos, which I loved.

They caught up on things happening in both their lives and Adrienne told Symphony everything about Chris' cheating and how she found out about it, but she purposefully left out the part about the overseas accounts – at least for now. As always, Symphony was a great listener, very supportive and deeply comforting. It was just what Dre needed.

They watched tourists and locals stroll by and enjoyed a talented musician playing classical music on the violin. After dinner, they went back to the hotel and like two teenagers, just hung out and talked about everything under the sun until 3 a.m.!

Per tradition, at 8:30 a.m. they woke up just in time to change into their yoga clothes and treat themselves to the spa day Adrienne had planned in advance. After stretching and contorting themselves for forty-five minutes, they were practically begging for a massage after long work hours and a late night of "first day of vacation" drinking.

Relaxed and satisfied, they jumped in a taxi and headed toward one of our favorite shopping areas near the Spanish Steps – Piazza del Popolo. We all refer to it as "shopping heaven". The area is very popular and always heavily trafficked by tourists. We love it because every designer store you can imagine is there as well as other not so expensive shops, novelty stores and artsy places. When you need to take a break from all of the walking and, of course, shopping, the wine shops, restaurants, and cafes in the district are wonderful and great fun as well. They sent me the cutest pictures of them from some of the noteworthy locales in Rome.

Between all the high-end stores Adrienne told me she racked up quite a few items including several pieces of lingerie bought at one of them. Thirty-five hundred dollars later, on intimate apparel alone, she felt no remorse. "It feels good, actually, to be able to spend *my money* the way I want to again. The chains of Chris and his so-called 'frugal spending' guilt trips – except if it is money being spent on him, of course – has been broken. I've promised myself I won't completely lose my mind shopping on this trip, but after dropping $12,000 in a couple of hours, I feel I've done enough damage – especially since I've mentally limited myself to $15,000 for the time I'm here," Adrienne confessed to me in a phone call before having another day of fun and adventure.

"Symphony and I walked up the street and plopped ourselves down on a couple of chairs at an outdoor café on the corner. We were exhausted and did not want to carry our bags around Rome so we called the hotel and asked them to have someone pick up our bags and take them back there.

"As we were waiting, Symphony teased me, 'I hope Chris doesn't beat your butt when you get home after the damage you just did!' and I could only retort,

" 'Actually, if he *was* smacking my ass I might not mind him being upset. At least I'd get something out of it,' and of course she replied,

" 'Well, that garter and bustier you just bought may get a reaction assuming you decide to keep him around.'

" I had to work on not saying, *'Girl, please…That stuff isn't for Chris! I'm not going to spend $3,500 on lingerie that won't even get noticed or worse, criticized for the price tag! This stuff is for that special someone when I meet him – not for some little fling I might have from time to time now,"* she shared with me.

"Instead, I just said to Symphony, 'After everything I found out about his cheating, Christopher Morris can *kiss my ass*. How about *that?!'*. We high fived each other and laughed.

" 'Yeah, we have zero tolerance for cheaters!' Symphony said.

" 'I'm not budgeting the Chris Morris way any more, I told her. 'I don't have to. I'm going to start living my life again and begin spending *my* money the way I want to from now on."

" 'Good girl. But, we still have two more days before you leave!' Symphony said to me as she burst out laughing.

" 'While that's true…' I admitted, 'It won't break me.'"

"Now, *that's* for sure!" I thought, as Adrienne continued.

"Symphony and I clinked champagne glasses and enjoyed a variety of Mediterranean tapas and mini pizzas. With the bags on their way to the hotel, we decided to act like tourists and just walk around the city." The next time we spoke, she told me about the rest of her trip.

"Symphony and I hung out like college co-eds for the next two days. After our shopping spree we went to one of the newest and hottest nightclubs in Rome and when we got back, she hired a car to drive us to Naples the following day so we could attend a dinner party hosted by a friend of hers."

As Adrienne continued her story, I had a feeling she was reaching an important part.

"We made our way out of Rome and through some of the many winding roads toward Naples, I received a surprising and thoughtful text message that made me smile," she said.

" It read, 'Hi Adrienne, it was my pleasure meeting and speaking with you on the flight from DC to London. It was the first time the flight didn't seem so long! I hope your trip was successful and productive. I'll be back in DC in a few weeks on business. If you're available I'd like to take you to dinner. Marcel.'"

"Now E, remember when just before my flight took off, I told you a cute guy sat next to me? Guess who *Marcel* is?" she laughed, and I did too. "Truthfully, his text made me smile as I gazed out of the car window. I thought back to the flight and how Marcel immediately caught my eye when he boarded the plane.

"You know I'm a stickler for being on time, so I'd arrived early enough to make my way to the British Airways First Class Lounge and while I waited there, I got a pretty good idea of who the other First Class passengers were on that flight. Once the flight was called, I found my seat and settled in. I was so relieved none of the other passengers I'd seen in the lounge were assigned to the seat next to mine. I just didn't have the energy to be chatty and just wanted to be left alone. After I sent you the first text, I put on my headphones and closed my eyes. I casually opened them at one point and saw what appeared to be the last passenger dash onto the aircraft just before the doors were about to close. He and the flight attendant smiled at one another as she checked his boarding pass.

"I thought, 'Wow! That was close. He's cute… Beautiful smile… Looks good…He probably smells good… Hmm… Probably great in bed too!' as I looked out the window again and smiled. With my headphones on and my attention fixated on the choreography of the crew below who were weaving in and out of luggage carts and parked planes, I didn't realize 'Mr. Fashionably Late' was preparing to sit in the empty seat next to me.

"Once he got settled in, he smiled, said hello and introduced himself as Marcel Davis. As it turned out, he had gotten a late start, got caught in traffic, then was further delayed at security due to the crowds and had to run to the gate, barely making the flight.

"By the end of our flight, I learned that *Chef Marcel Davis* is a divorced Canadian restaurateur and trained sommelier with two children. He owns two restaurants in Montreal, Canada and had been in DC to scout locations for a new one. He was on his way to London for a chef's conference he was co-hosting and co-sponsoring. He's fluent in French, loves his kids, skiing, working out, travel, and photography and collects classic roadsters. And, oh my goodness, E, is he *fiiinnnneeee… Gurl!!!!!!!!!!!!*

"Marcel has a deep baritone voice which kept my attention over the drone of the airplane noise and the clean fresh scent of his cologne made me curious and I found him *sexy*! His conversation and his physique piqued my interest immediately. His hands were soft, yet firm, and his smile beneath his shadowy chiseled beard lit up his entire face. The way he spoke about his teenage daughters and how much they meant to him made me smile and think of him positively. He explained his marriage of ten years didn't work out because they just simply grew apart. They parted as friends after realizing they were better at that than they were being a couple. They co-parent their kids and communicate well. I can only pray for that type of relationship with Chris should he become my ex at some point," Adrienne shared.

"Oh, I forgot to mention that when we landed in Heathrow, we walked to the baggage claim together and after collecting our bags, he walked with me to the transportation desk where I had to wait for the hotel limo and he waited for some business associates to pick him up from the airport. Since we had already exchanged contact information during the flight, the only thing left to do was to say goodbye. He gave me a big hug that was a little long given we'd only just met, but I didn't mind. I felt a connection with him. There was a *truth* about him that was endearing and made me curious. He was strong yet gentle, smelled good (even after that long flight) and I felt safe in his arms. Honestly, I didn't want him to let me go.

" 'Mmmm… You feel good,' he whispered in that deep sexy voice as he held me. As he slowly released me from his arms he kissed my cheek and said, 'Your ride is here.' The limo pulled up and as the driver jumped out to retrieve my bags and placed them in the trunk, Marcel said, 'I'll be in touch' as he grabbed my hand and kissed me on the cheek and said, 'Stay beautiful.' I said goodbye and hopped into the limo.

"On the flight, Marcel told me he would be slammed with work at the conference. He lamented we wouldn't be able to see each other in London before I left for Rome, but said he wanted to make it up to me. So receiving the text message from him while I was in Italy was a pleasant surprise because I wasn't expecting to hear from him before I got back home to DC.

"His text definitely made me smile. I kept my response simple but showed a little bit of interest, 'Hi Chef, it was a pleasure meeting you as well. My stop in London was very productive. Now it's time for me to get in some 'me time' so I'm spending three days in Rome hanging out with a girlfriend. Having a great time! Definitely give me a call when you get back to DC. I'd love to go to dinner. Have a safe trip home.'

"He responded almost immediately, 'Great! I look forward to it. And, please call me Marcel... Everyone calls me 'Chef' but I like the way you say my name! ;-) I'll be in touch. Stay beautiful. MD'

" 'Whoa! Did he just flirt with me?'" I asked myself and of course, I had to take the bait.

" 'Marcel, are you flirting with me?' " I texted back.

" 'Yes,' he shot back immediately.

" 'Hmmm? Do you think you'd prefer hearing me say your name in a soft whisper or scream?'"

Dre knew she was venturing down a slippery slope but she didn't care. He was so gorgeous and strong with a beautiful smile all she could do was let her wild imagination take over – and so she did, even if only briefly.

"He texted back immediately saying,

" 'BOTH! Just as long as it feels good to you.'

" 'It'? What's the 'IT' you're referring to?" I asked. "'Feels good to me? Oooo!! You're fresh!' "

" 'What are *you* talking about? I just want to know that whenever you say my name, it makes you feel good. What were you thinking about, Miss Adrienne?' " he not so innocently replied back.

" It was obvious he was teasing me and trying to shame me all at the same time. After sending that last text, he immediately followed up with another.

" "Don't answer that. I want you to REALLY think about it and when I see you again, you can tell me exactly what was on your mind. Trust me, I won't forget to ask you! I want to see your beautiful face when you tell me what makes YOU feel good, OK?'

" 'You got it." I told him. 'But, make sure you're prepared to tell me what makes YOU feel good too, OK?'

" 'Meeting you!' he responded immediately.

" 'But don't worry, I'll have more to say when I see you" he added. "I gotta go. My break is over and I have to get back to the conference. Enjoy your trip but be safe. Stay beautiful."

" Hmmm…!" I thought and then Adrienne continued, "I really like the way he flirts. It's obvious, but not over the top to the point where I'd find him rude and offensive. He's brainy and clever. Very cute. I like him. He has definitely captured my attention and interest," she concluded and I knew she was smitten.

"I like the way he ends his texts with 'Stay beautiful' because it reminds me of what he told me on the flight, 'You have a beautiful spirit, Adrienne. Don't ever let anyone rob you of that or allow any situation to dim that beautiful light shining through you. It's a rare quality and I find it very attractive. I know what you're going through is really hard and you may not believe it right now, but you're going to be fine. Stay faithful to yourself. And don't allow the process to poison your beautiful spirit. You'll get through it. Stay beautiful.'"

Marcel's words of encouragement and expression of interest in Adrienne was exactly what she needed. He didn't realize how much he had elevated her spirit in that short period of time. It was like a shot of adrenalin for her and she felt sexy and alive again.

Adrienne, while very pragmatic in business, can be quite the romantic so when she describes encounters with romantic undertones – like a chance meeting with a very attractive and single chef/restaurateur on an overseas flight – she tends to use very flowery prose. That's how I know she really likes someone. It's the artsy side of her personality I suppose.

It appears he really captured her attention when he showed interest in her, the kids and some of the challenges she's facing in her own marriage now, because in one of her emails to Faith, Krishna and me she wrote,

"I found Marcel incredibly sexy and very interesting. I could tell he was an affectionate guy because he had a tendency to touch my hand or tap the top of my wrist when he spoke or was emphasizing something. He listened intently as I spoke, and was oddly encouraging – at least initially, about my failing marriage – until he learned how long Chris had been cheating on me. I found his genuineness sexy, too. It's obvious Marcel was just being himself and that is *so* attractive. Given what I'd told him about my marriage, I expected him to go in for the kill once he learned it was falling apart and how unhappy I was, but he did just the opposite; he was empathetic, compassionate and gave me good, solid, objective advice. That alone would have made him really stand out but being sexy and gorgeous too? I am intrigued by *Chef Marcel* and I've decided I want to learn more about him so I accepted his invitation to dinner the next time he is in DC!" she wrote.

From what I gathered, there is definitely a mutual "like" on both parts and from what Dre shared with me, he's very comfortable flirting with her too.

Meeting him was exactly what she needed especially after she saw Mr. Snyder's preliminary report on Chris shortly after she arrived in London. After reading it, she was certain her marriage was over and Chris could very well be heading for big trouble with the Feds. Distancing herself from Chris in every way was no doubt the best route for her and the children. Marcel was a breath of fresh air and Adrienne welcomed it. He was different and absolutely *nothing* like Chris. She *needed* to meet Marcel when she did and I thank God she did.

Symphony and Dre didn't do a lot of talking on the trip to Naples. As they wound their way to dinner, busy on their smart phones and in Dre's case, texting back and forth with a gorgeous French Canadian chef she'd only just met a few days ago she was enthralled. The girl's original plan was to spend the day in Naples and have dinner with some of Symphony's friends at the home of Francesco Esposito, another friend and former client of hers, before heading back to Rome. But Symphony and Dre got a late start so they decided to forego going into Naples proper because of the congestion there.

They did take time to stop and gaze at the breathtaking views of Sorrento and the Amalfi Coast below and send me a video of it. The panoramic view of the sapphire blue water sprinkled with a few large cruise ships in port was a sight to see. They resumed their ride but instead of going into the city, their driver drove them to one of the highest points on the outskirts of the city so they could stretch their legs, absorb the view from above and make another video for the girls and me.

This footage gave me a real appreciation for the significant amount of congestion within Naples. I could see the orange-red rooftops packed one on top of the other. When viewed from the mountainside road above, the densely populated city appeared like a sea of buildings interconnected by narrow veins of streets barely visible from where they were. It was impossible to see people or even cars threading their way through the city limits. While Adrienne videotaped, Franco, their driver and impromptu tour guide, did a good job of pointing out the city of Naples below. He drew our attention to the commerce district with its tall buildings in the distance, Mt. Vesuvius to the south and the lost city of Pompeii, which lies at the base of the infamous volcano. I really felt as if I was standing atop that hill with them.

Symphony called Francesco and told him they would be arriving early.

"The dinner party was lavish and very intimate – only twenty guests,"– Adrienne told me via Face Time once she got back to the hotel later that evening. "Francesco specializes in consulting to the EU nations on the petroleum trade. During our visit, we learned he had just embarked on a new venture in the clean and sustainable energy market and wants Symphony to advise him and his team.

"His wife, Antonia, and I hit it off immediately because she owns two successful art galleries in Italy. She told me she opened them after retiring from her career as a registered nurse and understood my desire to pursue my passion and open my own gallery and artist studio. Antonia assured me when I'm ready to get started, she'll make herself available to me as an advisor and maybe Francesco would invest in my venture.

"Over the course of the evening, I met a very eclectic group of incredibly fun and entertaining guests. We had a five-course meal on the patio overlooking a beautiful view of the Gulf of Naples and live entertainment. By 11:00p Symphony and I said goodbye to our hosts and a few of the remaining guests and made the ninety-minute drive back to Rome. It felt like we were pulling up to my hotel in no time because we talked the entire ride back," Adrienne said.

I was so happy Adrienne and Symphony were able to spend a wonderful few days together and I felt as if I had been part of most of it. The tons of pictures and handful of videos they sent helped me "escape" as well. I loved their thoughtfulness in that regard and appreciated their efforts to help me virtually "travel" to one of my favorite countries for a while and leave cancer behind.

As her trip was ending, Adrienne was excited to come home because this meant seeing her kids and catching up with them. Chris had left on business the day before her arrival so she didn't have to interact with him and that was a welcome relief. He was traveling to Asia and was scheduled to be away for two weeks. He would be in Hong Kong for five days and then on to Japan for the remainder of the trip. At least that's what he told her and that's what she told Mr. Snyder, the PI.

To their credit, since the beginning of their marriage and as their careers began to take off, the two of them agreed they would do their very best to ensure they are never on travel at the same time so as not to leave their children in the care of anyone – including family or Juliza—for more than one day. They've always kept their word on that and over the years it has worked for them and the children because they know at least one of them will be at home at any given time.

Dre told us she met with her dad and Mr. Snyder at her dad's house the day after returning from her trip in order to find out the magnitude of the problems Chris had created for himself and quite possibly, she and the kids. She also wanted to discuss her options for dodging and/or shielding them and her from the impending consequences coming *his* way.

Adrienne told us that as soon as she told her dad about the post cards and other files she had found they agreed on several covert ways of communication. Talking to him on the phone daily was never out of the ordinary for Adrienne and, as a result, Chris didn't find anything unusual about that. They agreed they would primarily communicate about the investigation via email through a secure email account he created for her through his foundation. Mr. Snyder also used the foundation's server to send Adrienne the preliminary report she received in London. Adrienne and her dad also agreed to *never* text anything about the matter.

As the weeks slipped into months "going through the motions" with Chris became easier because they really didn't interact much; Dre blamed it on work and he was fine with that. His domestic and international travel schedule picked up considerably as a result of a new account he was managing and wherever possible, she managed to slip in a couple of trips on her own or kept busy with the kid's activities in an effort to limit any real time spent in his company. It was the best way for Adrienne to deal with the situation, wrap her mind around her next move and begin the initial process of emotionally divorcing him.

" 'Adrienne, Chris is in big trouble. Here's the report as it stands now,' Mr. Snyder told me in a serious tone as he handed me the documents. 'Everything I'm about to tell you is in the written report and I've given your dad a copy of it as well.' " Adrienne explained to the girls and me over lunch one afternoon.

"I started flipping through the sixty or so pages he gave me and felt an overwhelming sense of doom come over me. Instead of attempting to glance through the papers as he spoke, I put them down next to me and just listened.

" 'While I'm sorry you found out about Chris cheating on you, quite frankly, that may have been a blessing in disguise. In fact, if you hadn't stumbled across that information, you probably would have never found out about all of the other things he's been up to until it was too late,' Mr. Snyder told me.

" 'First, as my preliminary report indicated, I was able to confirm your husband Chris has been having an affair with Ms. Deb Horton. The affair appears to have begun around the time of her divorce from one of his former clients, C. Patrick Horton.

"You now have more details about this affair, along with photographs and copies of financials and whatnot in the report I just gave you and you can read all of it at your convenience. But there is much more to Chris than just his affair and I'll just summarize that for you right now," Mr. Snyder said and then continued,

" 'Chris has had a gambling problem since he was in college. He found himself in some pretty hot water with a bookie just before you two met but he was able to pay his debt and make the problem go away. After you married, his gambling habits escalated, as you know. However, because he was making good money, he was able to pay his debts. From your perspective, once he got the job with B&F, it appeared all was well and he had either stopped gambling or curbed it significantly. The problem, however, was he just graduated to a bigger, more sophisticated level of gambling and this time it's been with *other people's money.*

" 'The truth is Chris has been embezzling money from Braithwaite Fielder via a few select clients, C. Patrick Horton being one of them. Horton has been with B&F for about seven years and Chris' stealing started about a year and half in. Initially, the amounts were small, I think he was testing the waters to see if he could get away with it and probably figured if he got caught, he'd be able to talk his way out of the situation and replace the money from his personal account. As time went on though, he was able to embezzle more and more and compared to what he was taking initially, the amount of money he ultimately graduated to made him millions.

" 'Thanks to his affair with Horton's wife, he was able to set up the Swiss accounts. Given the timeline, it appears the Belize account was the starter account and he opened it when he was with his previous company—this account, by the way, is the *only* overseas account where your name actually *does* appear as a co-owner and for whatever reason, he's been dumping nearly half of his salary from B&F into that account since the beginning.

" 'You should consider that account as *your* retirement account. Since it has your name on it, you have unlimited and direct access to everything in it. You can make deposits and *withdrawals* without his permission or approval. Currently, it has almost $3 million dollars in it. Honestly, I was surprised your name was still on it. I think as time went on, he probably just forgot all about it. Based on what I was able to find out, the amount of money laundered into that account might have come from one of his old accounts (clients) at his previous company. The laundered amount is approximately $500,000.00 because after the few initial deposits, he stopped. Once he moved to his current firm, the only deposits made into that account came directly from his salary so the rest of the money in there is not from client money.

" ' The Swiss accounts, however, are completely laundered and fortunately, they don't have your name on them at all. Three of the accounts are in the name of a fake company bearing only his and Deb Horton's names as officers but there are a total of *five accounts,* not three as you first thought based on what you first found. It looks like he and Deb Horton were working together to get at her ex-husband's money but Chris was cheating *her* too. The three accounts you found are the three she has access to based on the fake company they created. The other two are exclusively his. Those accounts are comprised of a combination of her money, her ex-husband's money and money from another client he's been helping himself to each quarter.

"The SEC audit conducted recently was unprecedented for B&F. It occurred because of the paper trail Chris left behind at his previous employer. Some of the same patterns of illegal activity which caused him to have to leave that position followed him to B&F. Apparently, the new CEO of his old firm and the CEO at his current firm know one another very well and in their conversations, Chris' name came up. By that time, the SEC investigators were already beginning to sniff around and the audit was scheduled. Chris was probably feeling very uncomfortable during this period because he likely feared they would find out what he'd been up to, but nothing negative has come back as of yet regarding that audit.

" 'All of this is serious and problematic for him and for *you.*

" 'First of all, I doubt Chris *really* knows what C. Patrick Horton is capable of. Horton made his initial millions in the trash business. That's a dirty pool to play in and there's a lot of illegal activity Horton was in the middle of at one point. He has some friends who have a history of serious criminal activity and he's not afraid to call on them when he needs things done or to get someone out of the way. As a general rule, people don't cross him and they *definitely* don't steal his money, screw his wife, *and* get away with it. Chris has done *all* of this. Horton's likely to cut him some slack over the wife, but stealing his money can cost Chris his life – literally, which means we must focus on you, the kids and your safety.

" 'Adrienne, you need to make some very serious decisions very soon. If you don't, and you choose to ignore what I've told you today, you put yourself and your children at risk because Chris *is* going to get caught. He's going to go to jail or worse, find himself at the bottom of the Potomac River if Horton gets to him before the SEC does. It is only a matter of time.'"

" Wow!" is all that would trickle out of my mouth. I was in shock and couldn't believe just how deep Chris was involved. It was also shocking to even *think* that "Mr. Upright Citizen" could be at the helm all of this stuff.

"What, if anything, did you say, Dre?" I asked her once my brain connected with my mouth.

"Evey, I sat motionless on my dad's leather couch in the library through the entire discussion. As I listened to Mr. Snyder's report my stomach did flips and I felt myself getting really angry. I felt like I had been betrayed by an emotional and economic thief. I wanted to run, but at the same time, I wanted to kill Chris. I realized, as Mr. Snyder spoke, I had married a *criminal* and my *children's father* was that criminal. He'd brought shame to our family, my parents and our name and reputation in our community. We'd plucked him out of nowhere and *this* is how we are repaid?" she wailed.

Seething with anger, she continued, "He's been a hustler his entire life and combined with his brilliance, he simply crossed over into a more sophisticated version of hustling. He hustled me into believing he was a hardworking guy who was able to pull himself up (with a little help from my family) by his bootstraps and make a great life for us. Instead, he is nothing more than a common criminal and someone I don't want to associate with," she admitted.

"Dre, this is just terrible," Krishna said. "What are you going to do?"

Adrienne responded, "Mr Snyder said to me, 'I know this is a lot of information, most of which is shocking and I'm sorry about that. But, if you don't ignore what you now know, we can hatch a strategy to get you and your kids on the right road and out of harms way. If you act quickly, you'll come out of this just fine.' He told me he would give me a few days to think about what he told me and said we should meet again later in the week. He also told me that depending on what I decided certain activities would have to take place almost immediately in order to properly address this matter.

"I felt like I was drinking water through a fire hose. I sat there and thought about how this would impact our children and the rage inside me grew. I shook my head, tilted it backwards, took a deep breath and stared at the pattern on the ceiling for a short while. Neither my dad nor Mr. Snyder said a word. They allowed me to take my time as I attempted to process all I had learned over the last hour. Everything seemed to move in slow motion.

"When I stood up from the couch, my dad and Mr. Snyder stood as well. They probably assumed I would thank Mr. Snyder for his time and tell him I'd be in touch as my dad escorted him to the door. Instead, I heard myself whisper, 'I can't keep living this lie.' I then said, 'Mr. Snyder, your report was very thorough and I appreciate all of it. You're right, this has been a lot to hear, learn and process. Some things, like Chris' gambling habit, for example, were known to me but the depth and magnitude of it is all very new and very troubling. I had no idea. His criminal activity is shocking to learn. I had no idea he would sink to such lows, that's just greed. But with all of what you have shared with me today, I cannot ignore it because the *only* thing I care about is the health and well being of my three children. That's all. I *must* protect them at all costs because he obviously couldn't give a damn. So, I would like very much to meet again soon.

" 'If your schedule is open, I'd like for the three of us to meet again at the end of the week because as you were speaking, I was starting to formulate my exit strategy. Before you leave, there are a few things I want you to know,' and with that, I explained my exit strategy and plan for divorcing Chris.

"I told Mr. Snyder and my dad I plan to file for divorce as soon as possible but certainly in a timeframe that would be best given all of the pieces of this puzzle and so as not to jeopardize anything. Second, I asked Mr. Snyder to prepare to clear out the account in Belize leaving only the $500,000.00 plus interest he believes came from client monies. I asked him to have the money he withdraws from there on my behalf placed into a certified check and I will decide from there where it will go.

"I also asked him to have all of the contact information on that account changed and told him I would provide him with that new information later this week. I assured him I realize timing is everything and he should expect to begin working closely with my attorney regarding the withdrawal from that account. Lastly, I told Mr. Snyder I want the SEC to be made aware of his findings but I do not want them to know its origins. All of the financial information regarding Chris and Deb Horton is to be shared with the investigators. I can only imagine that once the SEC finds out what they've been up to, C. Patrick Horton will also find out. Hmm…! Won't that be a damn shame? Any way, I asked him not to act on any of this until the three of us meet later this week. My mission and objectives are clearly laid out and Mr. Snyder is prepared to execute my plan.

"My dad walked Mr. Snyder out and I fell back onto the leather sofa – sickened by what I'd heard. I wept for my children – the helpless, innocent victims of their father's greed.'

CHAPTER 7

EVEY – WE NEED A BREAK!

All my cancer treatments have ended and although the state of my marriage hasn't changed, I'm beginning to feel like my old self again. My appetite is almost completely back and I'm working out again! The goal of participating in a triathlon next year now is clearly in my sights. I have more energy and I'm feeling great! My final interview for the nursing administrator position is scheduled in a few weeks and I'm really optimistic and excited about that and I'm looking forward to getting back to some sense of normalcy. I improved so quickly Mrs. Samuels decided to make the move to California to be with her children and grandchildren. Given everything she did for me during this period, I took the responsibility of coordinating her move.

I'd planned a send off reception for her but she would have none of that, so Faith, Adrienne, Krishna and I took her to brunch at the Four Seasons and I presented her with a beautiful two-carat diamond heart pendant/necklace as an expression of my adoration, gratitude and appreciation for everything she had done for me. A pillar of grace and strength, Mrs. Samuels wept as I placed the necklace around her neck and told her how much I loved her.

Thankfully, graduation season is over! Zeke graduated with a BS in Mechanical Engineering from Rensselaer Polytechnic Institute and will be starting his Biomedical engineering, Master/Ph.D. program at Duke in the fall. He wants to develop safer helmets for the NFL and has had one of his papers peer reviewed and published. Tim graduated from high school and will be attending the University of Miami in the fall. He received a full academic scholarship and will be playing football. He wants to go onto law school and become a sports agent. Isaiah starts high school in the fall. He's a competitive swimmer and given his times and accomplishments in the pool, he has a good opportunity to go to the Junior Olympics! As part of our arrangement, my parents will "escort" the boys down to Antigua for the summer after graduation and they are thrilled at the prospect of another summer there. I am thankful that the boys and Len are speaking again and that brings me joy although the communication between the two of us has improved only slightly.

I realize my life is transitioning now and I'm ready for it. In fact, I welcome it with open arms. It's been one hell of a year so far and now it's time to relax. I wanted to thank my closest girlfriends for everything they've done to get me through this last battle with cancer so I planned a seven day get away for the four of us at our beach house in Nags Head, NC. I've been planning the details for months and I can't wait. Ken Henderson and his amazing staff have been helping me plan a girlfriend's week of bliss and pampering, I immediately enlisted Ken and his amazing staff to help me pull it all together. I was clear and detailed in what I wanted for all of us each day but left the responsibility of the coordination and execution to him because I, too, wanted to be surprised by his brilliance.

I arrived at the house two days before the girls so I could open everything up and get ready for Ken and his staff. The house was immaculate because the property management company we retain keeps it clean and ensures renters don't damage anything. Ken and two of his staff arrived the next day and prepared the house.

They began with beautiful arrays of fresh flowers strategically placed throughout the house. The living room, dining room and kitchen tables all had magnificent arrangements of flowers on them. Freshly cut tulips in an assortment of spring colors were artfully arranged in short geometrically shaped glass vases with natural rocks at the base and accented every alcove and all of the bathrooms. Tightly bunched arrays of colorful flowers also lined portions of the wraparound deck and each bedroom had a different floral theme based on the tastes and personalities of each of my girlfriends. Faith's room had white orchids, Adrienne's, a colorful assortment of roses with greenery and baby's breath, Krishna's white water lilies, and I, of course, had the biggest sun flowers known to man.

Throughout the house, Ken placed silver picture frames surrounded by Swarovski crystals next to each vase, with black and white photographs of us over the years as an especially personal touch. These pictures were a chronology of our lives in a variety of settings – college parties, graduations, concerts, vacations, pre and post baby photos and many more. They were like a time capsule of our friendship and reflected *only* the happiest moments in each of our lives.

With my input and detailed lists of what to include, Ken brought to life amazing personalized gift baskets for each guest. The baskets contained a plush white monogrammed bath robe with matching slippers, fruits and gourmet chocolates, Pellegrino water, a miniature photo album that had copies of all the photos arranged throughout the house, an assortment of snacks, sunscreen, a big black floppy straw hat for the beach and a silk Hermes scarf in each of my girlfriend's favorite colors.

In separate individual gift bags, I added a two-carat channel set pink and white diamond eternity band set in platinum. The four alternating rows of pink and white diamonds in the ring represents the four of us: the pink rows of diamonds represents the challenges we've faced in our lives with beauty and grace, while the white rows represents the purity of our friendship. Each ring is inscribed *"Friends for a Lifetime: Faith, Adrienne, Krishna & Evelyn"* which I planned to give them individually.

When they arrived, they were greeted with a glass of Perseco (our favorite), and an ice cold citrus-dipped washcloth to refresh. Faith, Adrienne and Krishna were all dressed in the coolest of colorful summer linens, designer high-heeled sandals or wedges, and wearing big clustered necklaces and bracelets embellished with precious and semi-precious stones. Everyone was beautiful and looked ready for a week of relaxation and pampering.

I escorted them to the wraparound deck while Thaddeus, one of Ken's assistants, delivered their luggage to their rooms. After we hugged and kissed, we settled down on the plush deck furniture and enjoyed our food and drinks, as well as the beauty of the surf and sand below. Knowing they would be hungry after getting off the road, I had Stephan, our personal chef for the week, prepare a casual but elegant deck side buffet which ranged from a variety of delicious hors d'oeuvres like puffed gouda and blue cheese pastries and caviar along with other treats such as braised beef skewers with dollops of whipped garlic mashed potatoes drizzled with au jus gravy, jerked chicken fondue, grilled veggies with homemade breadcrumbs, and a variety of incredible miniature desserts which we chased down with edible chocolate shot glasses filled with Grand Marnier.

After we were done and the dishes were cleared away, I asked Thaddeus to bring out all the gift baskets. As they began to explore their baskets, I explained what was inside. There was a combination of laughter at the pictures and squeals of delight at the small gifts as a sense of relief began to set in with the realization that *we'd made it through my cancer together* and we were *all still here – ride or die.*

After the girls went through their gift baskets, I presented each one with a smaller beautifully decorated bag containing the ring and set one aside for Ken. I asked the girls not to open their bags until I presented Ken with his first because he was preparing to leave for an event he was hosting for a client in D.C. He was very moved and emotional when I explained what his ring signified and told him how much his friendship meant to me and how much better my life has been because of him and his life long partner, Julian.

His ring (and the one I had made for Julian as well) had three rows of blue and white pave diamonds, representing the friendship between him, Julian and me. The two blue rows anchoring the white row in the middle represented their strength for me. Inside of his ring the inscription read, *"Friends for a Lifetime: Ken, Julian & Evelyn."* We hugged, he thanked me and the girls applauded. As he walked out he said, "Evey, I'm gonna need your glam squad to set me straight. I can't go out with puffy bags under my eyes, girl!" We laughed and said goodbye.

After Ken left, I presented the girls their rings. I told them how much I loved them again and told them to open their bags. After explaining what the rings signified, I read the inscription. *"Friends for a Lifetime: Faith, Adrienne, Krishna & Evelyn,"* and continued, "What is inscribed in each of your rings and mine comes from the deepest part of my soul. I love you guys with all of my heart."

While I had planned to say some specific things about how much each of them meant to me, each time I tried, I couldn't hold back the tears and kept breaking down. In the end all I could say was,

"Thank you for being *my true friends and my sisters*. I am *alive* today because of each and every one of you. You have *never* given up on me or abandoned me in my time of need (and this is my third time dealing with this demon). And because of you, I was able to maintain my will to fight and my will to *live* and I thank each and every one of you for that. You ladies have been a real blessing to me and my family and I know I can never really repay you for all you've done for us so I hope this small token helps symbolize how I feel."

When I was finished, we were all crying, hugging and saying a thousand *"I love yous"*. Finally, Krishna lightened the moment with near uncontrollable laughter.

Faith asked, "What the hell are you laughing about, Krish? We're having a moment here!"

Krish's response was unpredictably hilarious, "I know and I'm sorry you guys, but my right eyelash is dangling off of my right breast and my left shoe heel is stuck in between the deck boards and I can't move!"

"Oh my God, girl, is that what that is? I thought it was a caterpillar crawling on your blouse but I didn't want to say anything because I thought you'd freak out!" Adrienne blurted out.

We all burst into laughter and Adrienne and Faith helped Krish extract her heel out from between the boards. It was a great start to what would become a week of laughter mixed in with some tears. We spent the rest of the afternoon and evening drinking, eating, laughing and reminiscing.

Chef Stephan prepared three daily meals. For breakfast, he made everything from smoked salmon and cream cheese on bagels or delicious omelets prepared any way we liked, to healthy chopped or spinach salads with grilled chicken or blackened salmon for lunch and a variety of dinners with things like southern style fried chicken, smothered pork chops with homemade macaroni and cheese, collard greens, and Crème Brule or homemade ice cream and raspberry bread pudding for desserts. We had fresh fruits and freshly squeezed juices each morning and always on hand were homemade lemonade and sweet berry teas, Bloody Mary's and a bar completely stocked with all of the top shelf liquor we could consume!

Our activities differed each day but the goal for the entire week was rest and relaxation. We were to leave all of our troubles behind, do as little work as possible and minimize the "tea" talk unless it was someone else's "tea"! There were yoga classes and meditation on the beach, a visit to a spa for mani-pedis and massages, bike riding, walking, jet skiing and shopping, of course. Using cell phones or checking email was strongly discouraged between the hours of 10:00 a.m. and 5:00 p.m. If you were caught, you had to drop $5.00 in the no cell phone / email jar and we ran a running tally of the offenders. Faith was the first to get sacked with the $5.00 levy. She claimed she thought the no cell phone policy started at 10:30 a.m. instead of 10:00 a.m. Hmmm? I can't say I believe that but she got pinged any way and had to pay up.

By day two, Krishna was already out $30.00 and Adrienne $15.00 and we still had five days left! By the end of the week, the no cell phone / email jar racked up a total of $250.00! I love these crazy hardworking, "go make that money" women but trying to get them to relax and unplug is not easy. We decided to give the money collected to Chef Stephan's assistant, Marcus, as an additional tip because he waited on us hand and foot without any prompting and he was a joy to have around.

By the end of the week, we were all relaxed and felt reconnected as friends and much more spiritually centered and grounded. We did violate the "no tea" rule because we depend on each other to be each other's sounding boards and "counselors" – but it's what we do, need and depend on each other for.

Toward the end of the week, Faith and I had a heated conversation.

We were in the kitchen candidly speaking about our individual situations while Adrienne and Krish relaxed on the patio downstairs. I began by strongly encouraging Faith to stay in her marriage and work it out. Even though she'd put DiMarco out and the divorce proceedings had already begun, I felt it wasn't too late to save her marriage. I realize now I may have over stepped my bounds by being so direct with my comments, but she's my best friend and I felt she should know exactly what I thought about her situation.

I told Faith people make mistakes but that everyone deserves a second chance, but she would hear nothing of it. (Admittedly, I didn't have a real appreciation for the lack of effort DiMarco was making to save his marriage! I took him at his word and that was a huge mistake.)

"Every time he cheated, E," she said, "he *was* getting a second, third, fourth, heck one hundred chances and he *never* thought it would make sense to stop?! It continued for *ten* years – and that's just with *one* woman! *Ten* years! That's NOT love, Evelyn, that's ABUSE! And I'm not going to voluntarily remain in a marriage where my husband cares so little about me that he's willing to put my health *and* my safety in jeopardy! I can't be in a loveless marriage. I *can't* fake it!

"D doesn't love me. That's obvious, because if he did he wouldn't have done this to me… to us, to our kids! He ONLY loves himself!

"As far as I'm concerned, with the exception of my children, my entire marriage has been nothing but a big fat lie and a complete *fraud!* I was living a lie and I won't do that any more – not by choice. If you want to continue to fool yourself about your situation and live in denial with that bullshit, E, go right ahead but I'm not doing it. I need my peace of mind. DiMarco can kiss my ass… I'm out!"

Honestly, I never thought DiMarco stood a chance after his initial remarks to Faith when she confronted him with what Van told her on the phone that day. Had he just admitted to it, perhaps she could have found a way to forgive him in time, but he took the cowardly approach, never owned up to his mess immediately and kept lying to her and everyone else too. He made matters exponentially worse by continuing to cheat even *after* being exposed!

The truth is a woman like Faith loves hard and doesn't give her heart, or her love, away to just any one, so the fact he had the *audacity* to cheat is hard for her to overlook or even forgive. In my case, I haven't had proof of Len cheating smack me in the face. I really don't know what he's doing and frankly I don't have the energy or the interest to snoop around and find out. If, perhaps, I get evidence similar to what Faith has had to come to grips with, I may view things differently, but either way, I strongly believe until it's officially over, you still have a chance and a responsibility to fight for your marriage. Of course, I realize it takes *both* people to be committed to doing that.

Although DiMarco may not have been her first choice to marry, when Faith made that commitment she gave it **everything** she had. She committed herself to him and their marriage, helped him build his career and was 100% supportive of everything he did. Therefore, it galls her that her tempered choice cheated on her when, in fact, she feels, she did him a favor by marrying *him* in the first place.

After Faith said her peace, I told her my feelings about my marriage, the vows that went with it and the possibility of Len having an affair.

"I *must* stay. I feel compelled to try to work things out," I told her.

"Wait a minute. I'm confused. What the hell are *you* working out, Evelyn?" Faith's voice elevated to a near perfect yell.

"*You* didn't abandon him during his greatest time of need. *He* abandoned *you*, did you forget? In fact, he's *still* not around. What about the part of the vows that talks about 'through sickness and in health'?" she swung her arms up to show air quotes. "He could care less. He was out sowing his oats and God only knows what else while you were at home puking your brains out or shivering under six blankets on your bed because you couldn't warm your body. You deserve better than that.

"I know he was there in the past during your other two battles with cancer and he *should* have been. He's your *husband*. And, honestly, Len took great care of you during those periods. I had mad respect for him for doing that – still do. But this was a new battle and a new fight. He took that vow but that doesn't give him a pass *now!* He should've been there. Period."

And with that she began to shed tears only a sister-girlfriend could shed for you.

She continued, "You're a good person, a wonderful God-fearing woman who didn't deserve any of that – not the cancer *again* or him abandoning you. He should be ashamed of himself and *he* should be the one *begging* you to come back and *begging* for your forgiveness…. Not *you* trying to 'work it out'" she air quoted again. It was obvious my dearest friend was pleading with me to understand her position on how Len was treating me but I was steadfast.

"Faith, Len didn't ask for cancer to creep into our lives and systematically eat away at us. He'd endured two previous bouts with this demon and me and he was there for me each time. I think this time was just too much for him and this is his way of dealing with it right now. I don't agree with *how* he's chosen to handle it because if he is cheating it's adultery, but I *do* understand how he got there," I told her. "And, honestly, I don't know for sure he *is* cheating on me but *something or someone* is definitely occupying all of his time." I said softly in a contemplative tone.

In a sober tone Faith asked me a pointedly serious question, "So, tell me this then, what if he decides that this new found life of his is easier and better than the one with you and he decides he doesn't want to be married any more? Then what?"

"He's just going through something right now, Faith. That's all. It's temporary. He just needs time to figure it all out," I responded. "I won't give up on us… Len won't give up on us. I know he won't," I told her as I tried to convince her and perhaps even myself that Len and I would survive this situation.

I could tell she didn't agree with what I said or how I'm handling my situation but I don't need her approval or endorsement for any of it. Right now, I just need her to be a non-judgmental friend and to stop her relentless attempts to force her opinions down my throat!

At the end of our conversation, Faith said, "I hope you're right, E. I *really, really* do. I just want you to be happy and healthy in every part of your life. I think Len's a good guy, but he sure screwed up this time. But if you can forgive him, I'll learn to over time as well, I guess. Either way, you know I got your back – even though I think you're crazy!"

She got up from her seat and leaned over me and gave me a huge hug as I remained seated at the table.

"I know you do, Faith, I know you do and I know you mean well but he's *my* husband and this is *my* marriage and *my* life", I told her. "The way you are dealing with your situation may work for you, but that's not my choice. You got smacked in the face with D's shit. I didn't. *You* don't have to forgive Len, as his wife that's for *me* to do. I just need you to be my friend and to continue to be there for *me*."

"I can respect that, E, and I'm sorry. I apologize if I was too forceful or too personal," she responded. "I don't want to add to your pain, frustrations or stress. I just want you to be complete and whole again. You deserve it. You don't need any additional stress in your life and I'm sorry if I added to it by even talking about all of this stuff. We've had a fantastic week thanks to you, and it should end on a positive note. So, please, remember I love you and I will *always* be here for you – no matter what. OK?"

It bothers me how deeply hurt and consequently bitter, Faith has become through this entire ordeal but that's what infidelity, lies and betrayal does to a person – male or female. It's toxic and destructive. It changes good people and forgiveness doesn't always come easy for many people. Although therapy is beginning to help her overcome those toxic emotions and it's teaching her how to deal with them, Faith still has a long way to go but I'm sure she'll get there. The reality is I imagine we *all*, in some way, have a long way to go but at least we have each other to help us through it.

As we hugged and I listened to her impassioned apology I cried, nodded my head in agreement and whispered, "It's OK, I love you too, Faye. Thank you."

We released ourselves from each other's arms and started laughing. Our laughter was a collective reaction to the relief we both felt to this discussion that finally had been had. Everything we'd wanted to say, but for whatever reason hadn't said, was now out in the open and we survived it because we're still the best of friends. It truly was a relief.

"Ahhhhh!!! I need a drink and some of that good medical weed you have stashed in here some place!" Faith practically screamed as she reached for more tissues.

"Shit, we all do!" yelled Adrienne from the downstairs patio and with that, we all burst out laughing.

"You guys can keep the weed. Just give me a stiff drink. I gotta protect my security clearance," added Krishna.

"What do you guys want?" Faith responded as she began pulling glasses out of the cabinet.

"I don't care what it is at this point. After that cat fight, I need the strongest thing you can find though!" Adrienne shouted.

"Oh, whatever!" Faith yelled back.

"We heard most of your conversation," Krishna confessed as Faith and I joined her and Adrienne on the patio. "I'm glad we stayed down here. Dre was all in favor of going up and refereeing, but I said with my luck, the tide would shift somehow and the next thing I know *I'd* be the one staring down the shaft of Faith's shotgun! Nope, we're safer down here!"

"Yeah, you were right," Adrienne laughed and agreed. "I figured eventually you two would realize we were here and would come looking for us in order for one of you to get one of us to co-sign your side of this argument."

"Yeah, that's true, but I think I kind of agree with E, on this one Dre," Krishna added.

"What? You're just as crazy as Evey is, except you'd stay for a different reason – cause you love that fool's dirty drawers," Adrienne snapped back. "Evelyn is deeply committed to her faith and she takes her marriage vows damn near literally. I don't get it, but that's her and I'm not going to judge her for those reasons. Plus, Len is having a really hard time with her cancer this time around and I honestly don't believe he's cheating on her. He can't help her and make it go away, so he's checked out. I don't agree with his approach because he did abandon her when she needed him but he's in pain too and hurting *a lot!* He *really* loves E and I think there's still a chance he can fix the problems he's caused in their marriage.

"But *YOU*, you, Krish my dear, will endure hell fire to stay with your cheatin' man! I *definitely* don't understand that shit. But, like I said about E, I'm not going to judge your crazy ass either. I'll just be sure to be there to catch you guys or to *bail you out* when things go haywire!" Adrienne laughed uncontrollably.

"Oh, shut the hell up! You know too damn much! And, any way as *my best friend* you're *supposed* to be there for me. We're supposed to be there for each other, remember that, chick! That's what friends are for! Uh oh, Dre, I feel a Dionne Warwick moment coming on."

"Oh no! Krishna don't! You know you can't sing." Adrienne begged her not to sing because she is completely tone deaf. Krishna did anyway because she absolutely *loves* to sing any song that stirs an emotion and she *always* sings it at the top of her lungs!

She started singing that popular Dionne Warwick hit and wouldn't stop.

"All together now…" she begged.

"Oh Lord! Please *stop!*" Adrienne covered her ears in a futile attempt to mute Krishna's awful singing and as she tried to get up from her deck chair, Krishna jumped on her lap and tried to pull her hands off of her ears as she kept singing and hugging her best friend.

"Tell me you love me," she kept singing and pulling Adrienne's hands away from her ears.

"What? No, you're crazy and tone deaf! Get off of me you creep!" Adrienne begged.

Krishna's singing got louder and then she stopped and said, "I'll get up and I'll stop singing if you tell me you *love me* and that I'll be *your best friend for the rest of your life*! Now say it!"

"Okay, okay... I love you, argh!" Adrienne finally gave into Krishna's demands. "You'll be my best friend for the rest of my life. Now get the hell off of me and stop singing, *please*! Oh my goodness. The dogs are howling... You're disturbing the peace! Do you hear those sirens? I know someone called the police! Hearing you sing hurts! How do *you* even stand it?"

As Krishna peeled herself off of Adrienne's lap she responded and laughed hysterically, "I can't *hear* myself, remember?! And, any way, I'm not *that* bad!"

"Oh my God, you have no idea how really bad you are. Don't ever do that again, I swear!" Adrienne immediately said while shaking her head and we all burst out laughing.

As the week drew to an end, we agreed it was the best girls' get away we'd spent together as a group in a long time and we committed to making it an annual event.

The day before we were scheduled to leave, the group decided to go into town and browse the local shops. We were gone for several hours but returned in time to enjoy a late lunch. After lunch, we were sitting around the bar in the kitchen drinking margaritas when the doorbell rang. I made my way to the door, opened it and after a middle aged gentleman confirmed I was *Evelyn Montague*, he handed me a large manila envelope and told me to have a good day. After closing the door, I made my way back to the kitchen to join the conversation and began opening the envelope as I took my seat.

What was inside literally took my breath away and Faith, noticing my reaction, immediately asked, *"E, what's wrong? What is that?"*

With my heart nearly pounding out of my chest I stammered, *"Len filed for divorce."*

CHAPTER 8

KRISHNA – "SHOW SOME DAMN RESPECT!"

"Oh my goodness! Mom, you're here! Did you see my race?" Lauren screamed as she saw me walking toward her after her 200-meter race. She ran towards me and practically leapt into my arms as if she were five years old again," Krishna wrote in a group email to all of us.

This was the first track meet she had attended since the season started and it was a big one.

"I loved it when she used to do that. I'd pick her up from kindergarten and she was always so happy to see me, she would literally run at top speed into my arms and I'd swing her around and around. It seems like only yesterday she was that little girl. Now, she's a senior in high school. I can't believe how quickly time flies! I'm so proud of her!" Krishna's email continued, sounding so positive.

She was obviously happy she flew down to Alabama for the track meet Dre convinced her to go to after her night in jail. Lauren was thrilled to see her there and Krishna wisely kept her in the dark about the events the night before. Of course, we were elated Krishna finally seemed to get the message we'd been trying to get through to her over the last year or two – "Spend more time with Lauren. You won't be able to get these years back once they're gone."

I thought about flying down to Alabama to attend the meet and just get away but Isaiah was in a qualifying swim meet for the Junior Olympic team and I wouldn't miss it for the world! Faith made the trip and brought her girls and Juliza brought Adrienne's kids because Dre was in Miami on business.

I can only hope that Krishna realizes the long-term implications of Frank not coming to her aid the night she was jailed. While I pray she and Frank can create a better marriage, I believe with all my heart Lauren is a crucial part of their family triangle and it will fall apart if all the parts are not connected. I hope now Krishna realizes the importance of re-prioritizing Lauren in her life and that means putting her first.

" 'I'm so glad you're here Mom!' she told me. And, I gave her the biggest hug imaginable and held her as tight as I could and told her I saw the whole thing! She was *amazing*! I am so proud of her!" Krishna's email continued.

"I can't believe she broke the record *here*. It hasn't been broken in *ten years,* and I'm so glad I saw it in person!

"I had almost managed to talk myself out of going to this meet, but I kept hearing Adrienne's voice, '*She* needs you, Krishna. *She* needs to be your priority right now, not Frank,' repeating inside my head over and over again and that compelled me to go.

"The look on Lauren's face when she saw me was absolutely priceless. I'd forgotten how important my presence at her events is to her. I'm so glad I went," she confessed in her email.

Over the next two days, Lauren and her teammates went on to break several more indoor track records. It was an exciting week for those girls and Krishna was thrilled to be a part of it. The more time she spent with Lauren and her friends, the more she began to realize how much she had missed of Lauren's high school years and that saddened her, but by the end of the track meet, she made a full personal commitment to change course and make Lauren her number one priority, (as she should have been all along).

It wasn't long after Krish and Lauren returned home from the track meet things there began going downhill. While Lauren and Krish were spending more quality time together, Frank was spending less and less time at home. As if leaving Krish at the police station to fend for herself wasn't bad enough, he further expressed his distain for her by limiting their interactions whether it was home or at the office to solely about work. Any topic pertaining to their relationship was off the table and this irritated Krishna to no end.

Frank's interactions with Lauren (when he was home) were limited to superficial questions about school or track, which he would quickly get disinterested in. If her answers got too detailed for his limited attention span, he'd switch the topic to himself.

When Lauren asked him why he didn't attend her meets, Frank always had the same excuse, "Daddy's gotta work, baby girl. I gotta bring home the bacon so your mother can try to cook it. Maybe one day she'll learn how to cook something we can all actually eat!" he'd say and then laugh.

That's just one of the constant verbal jabs he took at Krishna. He always seemed to go out of his way to make her feel inadequate, then he'd laugh about it and the cumulative effect began to take its toll on her. She rarely said anything to defend herself against his verbal barrages because she didn't want to incite an argument with him, especially in front of Lauren, so she took his abuse and internalized her feelings.

The only time he doesn't criticize Krishna is at, or about, work. DMTG is the *one* place where Frank shows her the respect she deserves. And it's the only part of her life where she *never* wavers on a decision.

Krishna's therapist, Dr. Buckingham, showed her how the pattern of Frank's verbal abuse is part of his morbid attempt to even the playing field between them. She also helped Krishna realize Frank has been verbally and mentally abusive throughout their entire relationship (which is what the girls and I have always thought).

She has told us his bullying started with her weight. "As you guys know,

I've never had a weight problem, but Frank makes me feel as if every morsel I place in my mouth puts me in jeopardy of gaining fifty pounds and becoming fat," she lamented.

" 'I can't be with any woman who can't wear a string bikini. Anything over a size 6 and 135 pounds is a problem. Don't get fat, because that'll be grounds for divorce,' he says to me even sometimes within earshot of Lauren."

Fortunately, Krish has always been thin but hearing him say these things almost on a daily basis was very upsetting for her.

Next, he moved on to criticizing how she wore her hair. Krishna has always had healthy, longer than shoulder length hair but because of Frank's constant comments about loving very long hair, she felt compelled to put in a weave to appease him. She hates it, but did it any way.

Over the years, it became obvious to us sister/girlfriends that more and more of Krishna's self-esteem was being chipped away. She somewhat acknowledged this and would often lament she didn't recognize herself any more.

There were many things about Frank Krishna was willing to overlook like his selfish spending, his lack of attention to Lauren, his laissez-faire attitude toward his job and DMTG in general and the affairs she knew about but never addressed directly. That all changed the night he left her to fend for herself in jail. Even Officer Winsome, who did not know her at all, intuitively said, "Sometimes a pile of crap has to land in our face before we start to see the other crap it's piled on top of."

For months prior to the incident at the jail, Krishna nagged Frank constantly about his numerous infidelities and was only met with his repeated lies and denials. She kept her attacks up and was eventually able to coax him to return to marital counseling. It took until the fifth session when his heap of lies was finally against the wall. He finally admitted to the affair that was the impetus for Krishna's arrest. She thought they had made a breakthrough during that session and it was going to be a foundation for a course of healing, but Frank stormed out of the session and never went to counseling with her again. The consequence of his admission on their relationship that day was dramatic. The lack of substantive, positive, and effective communication between them worsened and the overall climate in the home progressively deteriorated and the girls and I all noticed.

While Krishna and Frank's joint sessions didn't last long, Krish learned a couple of things during them as well as afterward as she continued seeing Dr. Buckingham one-on-one.

She learned her self-esteem issues began long before she and Frank ever met and as a result she became co-dependent on him for her identity and self-worth, despite his emotional and mental abuse of her throughout their entire relationship. Dr. Buckingham encouraged her to have a mental evaluation done in order to ascertain and/or eliminate the possibility of any mental illness caused by a chemical imbalance or biological disorder, but unfortunately, both pride and fear her job's security clearance might be jeopardized wouldn't allow Krishna to do that, so she didn't follow through.

After their final joint session, Frank became increasingly verbally abusive toward Krishna and living with him under these conditions became unbearable.

Krish was loathe to admit this to *any* of us initially, especially Faith. (I can *hear* Faith saying, "I hate to say 'I told you so' but I told you so. A leopard doesn't change his spots,' K told me.) Faith's "straight, no chaser" delivery is hard to hear at times and for fragile Krishna, this is one of those times.

Frank has reached the point where he no longer cares about how he speaks to her or whether or not he damages her emotionally. Traditional male-female roles in their household don't seem to matter to him any more either. He could care less about personal matters that are important to Krishna their impact on their relationship and the poor example he's setting for Lauren. "It's as if he's living two completely separate lives – one married and the other single," Krishna consistently complains.

As months past after the jail incident, Krishna did her best to focus less on Frank and more on Lauren, but DMTG's biggest government contract was up for renewal and things at the office were heating up. She had no choice but to put more time into DMTG as it was in the throes of proposal development and the stress level there was mounting.

Krishna admitted she was concerned about this contract primarily because it seemed to her Frank was having interpersonal issues with the new government program manager overseeing it. "I don't understand why she and Frank are suddenly at odds. I thought they got along. When I try to get him to explain the problem to me so I can follow up and maybe smooth things over, nothing he says seems to make any sense," she confided. Her calls requesting to meet with Ms. Donaldson, the government program manager, went unanswered for weeks, and when she finally *did* return them, the conversation between her and Krishna was brief and Ms. Donaldson showed absolutely no interest in meeting.

Despite putting in countless hours of work and over a hundred thousand dollars worth of man-hours and other resources over a period of several months on this multi-million dollar renewal proposal, DMTG received the bad news they did not win. As the incumbent, it was a major blow and after having had that account for ten years, it hit Krishna especially hard. She was angry and felt defeated because while she had no real proof, Krishna was convinced Frank had somehow screwed up the relationship with their long-term customer.

The result of this contract loss was twenty-five employees were at risk of losing their jobs and Krishna was beside herself. She was able to move eighteen of them onto other contracts or in supporting roles for other projects, but seven had to be placed onto overhead; a huge expense for the company. After three months, she was able to reassign five of them to other parts of the company, one resigned in order to go to graduate school and the other took a position as a government employee.

It was, without question, the most stressful period in the history of her company and an experience Krishna prayed she'd never have to face again although she was thankful she didn't have to lay off anyone. Through it all, Frank offered little assistance or support either at the office or home. It was as if he didn't care about DTMG losing the contract and, to make maters worse, he'd left her to clean up the mess she felt he had some role in creating.

Thanks to the rest of her senior staff, DMTG got through it. Instead of making any effort to help with the company's challenges, Frank was making plans for a trip to Dubai – one of the many places in the world he has dreamed of playing golf. Krish was incensed!

"I'm all for capturing the best life has to offer and living it to the fullest, but not at the expense of the livelihood of others. We just lost a $200 million government contract because of some *bullshit* he did, said, or didn't do and he's planning to go to Dubai anyway? Who *does* that? What type of message does that send to the rest of the staff?" she screamed into the phone as Faith, Dre and I listened.

I couldn't understand it either, but honestly, I wasn't entirely surprised. I mean let's face it; Frank Fitzgerald is selfish and self-centered. He cares about no one other than himself. He left his wife to fend for herself in jail and never addressed that matter. And any attempts Krishna made to reason with him about the Dubai golf trip and get him to change his plans were either completely ignored or dismissed.

The truth is, Krishna's marriage was rapidly disintegrating. She was in denial, her business had taken a huge financial hit and she was rapidly falling into a state of depression. As a result of all the stress, she had not spoken to her mother in any meaningful way in weeks and she was fast becoming a wreck. Our daily conversations and weekly "What's the tea" gatherings with her became more and more infrequent and when she was there and spoke, she purposefully kept conversations that veered toward her short.

She seldom returned our frequent phone calls and when she did, she never had much time to talk. Adrienne was out of town on another business trip so she wasn't able to pop over and check on her the way she normally does when Krishna goes dormant. Adrienne is the only one of us who knows how to break her out of these funks when they occasionally creep in. She's been doing it since college and I think there is a deep layer of security Krish feels with Dre than either Faith or myself. I respect that, but there was something different about this time. Faith and I stopped by a few times but we couldn't get her to open up and tell us everything and we were growing increasingly concerned. "Honestly, she seems unstable to me Faye," I observed after I had a brief lunch with Krish. "Yeah, I'm going to text Dre and tell her about it," Faith replied.

Although Krishna has never been formally diagnosed, I'm beginning to think she suffers from some type of depression. Adrienne has told me that over the years Krishna has told her there are times when stress takes her to very dark places in her spirit and finding the strength to come out of it is difficult. When these "episodes" occur, Adrienne told me Krishna confided she finds herself going through the motions at work and not being very productive. Then, she tends to isolate herself from friends and family all the while blaming it on being busy at work and slipping deeper and deeper into a state of sadness and despair. It worries me that while Krish is aware of these episodes and acknowledges them, she has yet to have herself properly evaluated.

Between the issues in her marriage and the knowledge she's not fully present and available to Lauren only adds to the weight Krishna is already carrying at work and all of this is stressing her out. I'm sure she's convinced herself she's been managing things pretty well on her own anyway, even despite losing the government contract. But, clearly she hasn't because she's an emotional wreck and seems to be teetering on the verge of a nervous breakdown!

Krishna was raised Catholic, but when I asked why she doesn't attend her church more regularly she says, "I appreciate the rituals because they're consistent and I know what to expect, but I don't really find myself being *moved* by the priest's homily. Once I left for college, I put my faith aside and never really practiced it as an adult." She says she enjoys the sermons and choirs at my church, but she's yet to make church going a part of her life. "I know I need to strengthen my faith and lean on it when times get hard but I haven't."

We've all tried to encourage her to try to make a connection with God and center herself. But her excuse is always the same, "My conversations with God seem fruitless and the answers I'm looking for don't seem to come. As a result, I decided a long time ago there's no point of wasting *His* time and *mine* with prayers—He's too busy to answer them any way. It's easier for me to take care of *my* problems *myself, my* way. It's worked for me all of these years and I'm fine." In my opinion, that's arguable!

While her religious routines are sparse and inconsistent, there is one aspect of Krishna's Catholic faith she *does* believe in and adheres to without question. *Divorce is not an option.* While the Bible says adultery is the exception, Krishna definitely chooses not to exercise this option. "I believe that *anything* can be worked out. No marriage is perfect and mine is no different, and I will continue to work at it. When I decided to get married, I chose to never divorce. I don't believe in it and I certainly don't believe you should divorce simply because you're unhappy in your marriage - things will turn around in time, you just have to be patient. My marriage vows are a covenant worth fighting for and I've decided no matter how difficult things get, I must try to save my marriage. I will *never* divorce Frank," she has adamantly stated time and time again.

Graduation season could not have been busier. Most of our children were having landmark graduations from middle and high school and for over a month, it seemed like every weekend was a joyful celebration of caps and gowns, as we collectively celebrated our children's achievements. Lauren, Krishna's little track star - was recognized during her graduation ceremony for her academic and athletic achievements. We were all very proud of her but Krishna and Frank especially, their faces beaming with pride. Lauren graduated with honors and received full academic and athletic scholarship offers from some of the best track programs in the country and eventually decided to attend a California university in the fall. As part of Lauren's graduation gift from Krishna, she received first class airline tickets to Italy and France for her and her best friend, Ashley.

The weeks leading up to Lauren's departure to Europe were crazy. She and Krishna were busy buying things for the trip and doing all the other prep work needed for the three week European vacation. If the timing were better, Krishna probably would have gone with them, even only for a week, but she arranged for Lauren and Ashley to stay with Symphony for their trip and felt comfortable leaving them in her charge.

Lauren was so excited. Symphony will be taking them to France with her when she sees Emile for two weeks and vacations on that beautiful southern coast. She has tons of other amazing things planned for the girls, which will definitely make this a trip of a lifetime and a wonderful graduation present.

"Of course, they'll visit all of the notable places in Rome including the Coliseum, the Vatican and the Sistine Chapel but Symphony has also planned for them to travel north via the Eurostar bullet train and spend two days in Florence, three days in Milan, and two days in Venice the following week before their time on the French Riviera," Krishna shared with us as we talked about Lauren's trip over stuffed crepes one morning.

"I know Symphony is going to show them an amazing time. It'll be a wonderful and memorable experience for Lauren and Ashley and it's so great they'll be able to do it together. This will deepen their bond for sure although I miss them already!" Krish lamented.

After seeing the girls off at the airport, Frank vanished for three days. Adrienne mentioned Krish told her he's been calling into the office for his messages but hadn't been there either. Frank is fundamentally passive aggressive and typically doesn't like confrontation, so this cat and mouse game he seems to be playing in order not to discuss the problems in their marriage didn't surprise Krishna. Like so many other verbal cowards, Frank has no problem making snide remarks to make her feel inadequate, but when confronted with issues which directly point to his own shortcomings, he purposefully makes himself scarce.

We all know keeping up appearances is of critical importance to Krishna

– sometimes too much, as she's learning in therapy – so Frank's absences from work bother her tremendously because the staff notices and they're beginning to talk. As a consequence, she has reduced herself to making excuses for him in order to maintain the impression she's still in control of the company and knows the whereabouts of her husband.

Adrienne also told me that during that conversation, Krishna opened up and told her she's really having a difficult time dealing with Lauren's absence. She told Adrienne she doesn't regret sending Lauren on the trip, but it saddens her because she knows that shortly after Lauren returns, she'll be leaving for college. Krish was just beginning to make in-roads with Lauren when she was living at home and is worried about the challenges in continuing to strengthen their relationship when Lauren is truly on her own and starting her own life. The realization Lauren is no longer a baby and Krish has spent most of her time worrying about a man who disrespects her is beginning to hit home now.

Krishna wasn't at all happy about her first couple of days alone because for many years she, like the rest of us, has defined and identified herself as either someone's wife and/or mother. Now, she didn't feel like either of those things any more and she was having a very hard time dealing with it.

"Faye, E, and your mom have been really worried about you, Krish. You barely talk when they call to check on you and when we visit, you just don't seem like yourself. What you're going through is normal. It's a classic case of 'empty nest syndrome', girl. But you'll get over it and you'll be fine," Adrienne told her, while we were having lunch at a local Korean barbeque restaurant a couple of days after Lauren went on her trip.

"I know, but I'm not doing it on purpose, Dre. I just don't want to admit to Faye she was right," Krishna replied. "I also don't want to upset, *you,* Evey, now. You're doing great and you're in a good place with your health finally. I don't want to burden you even more with my crap. And, on top of all of that, Frank has been gone since Lauren left. How do I explain *that* to anyone – especially my best friends *and* my mother? It's friggin' embarrassing, you guys!" Krishna confessed.

"I hear you, girl, but if you can't be honest with your *best friends* and *your* mom (who you are closer to than all of us) who *can* you be open and honest with?" Dre replied. " You can't keep all of this stuff bottled up inside of you Krish! You used to do that when we were in college and over the years you've gotten a thousand times better, but you're reverting back to those old ways again and that's *not* good for you. Frank's gotten in your head and you're going to explode! If you can't be honest with your friends then you're not a friend at all, you're a FAKE!

"Remember when we were in college and we got the nickname "F.A.K.E.s" because whenever we walked together, we always seemed to walk in the order of the word when it's written out. So a girl in one of our history classes started calling us "the FAKEs"? The name stuck because some of the 'haters' thought we were being fake toward them. But we didn't care. We knew she and the rest of them were just jealous of us and there was *never* anything fake about our friendship. *Nothing* has changed, Krish. We're still as REAL as we've ever been when it comes to the four of us and after twenty plus years we're *still* here for one another and we will *always* be, so don't shut us out now that another milestone has been reached in Lauren's life or a shift has occurred in your relationship with your husband. We're here for you – always!" Adrienne reminded her.

When we walked into the hospital room Krishna was laying motionless on her bed, looking out of the window, her eyes fixed on the beauty of the flowers that had blossomed on the huge Magnolia tree outside. No one said anything until she did, "I used to think I was as beautiful and strong as the Magnolia but now…" her soft voice fading. Her mom and the three of us moved in to cover Krishna from head to toe in a blanket of loving arms and collectively told her, "You still are, Krish. We love you."

Prior to entering her room we were advised by her doctor she was in a very fragile emotional state and we should only offer our presence as comfort, do our best not to ask her questions but be willing to listen should she decide to speak about the events that led her to become hospitalized.

Mrs. Williams, Krishna's mom, curled up next to her in the bed and held her closely while the rest of us took up positions either on her bed or in the chairs next to the window. "I'm so sorry I just wanted peace and I wanted the voices to stop," Krishna said softly.

"We're here for you Krish – all of us – and we'll *always* be here for you." Adrienne told her and we all echoed her sentiments. And then, while still looking out of the window, Krishna took a deep breath, softly spoke and with little to no expression in her voice told us exactly what happened that afternoon.

"I got up early, went to the gym and headed back home to shower and start my day. I left the house and drove to the office, worked for a couple of hours and then left to run a few errands. By mid afternoon, I had done everything I'd planned to do and grabbed a take out salad for lunch. I made my way home around 3:30p and heard the voice mails from you and Faith about going to dinner at 7:00p. I wasn't sure if I felt like going, but I had some time to eat lunch and relax for a bit before I had to decide.

"After I ate, I poured myself a glass of wine, curled up on the sofa and just gazed out at the pool and pool house through the family room window. I could hear the faint sounds of lawn mowers in the neighborhood as the landscapers trimmed someone's yard. Suddenly, in the distance, I heard the sound of Bob Marley music getting louder as it got closer to the house as Frank pulled up in his convertible and backed into the garage. Given how quiet the neighborhood is generally, anything louder than the sound of lawn mowers seems to ring loudly. Frank can always be heard *before* he's seen because he constantly blasts his music when he's alone in the car.

"The music stopped and I heard the garage door open and then slam shut. Once inside, he put his things down in the kitchen and made his way up the back staircase toward the master bedroom. I knew he'd seen my car in the driveway but he made no effort to call out my name or look around to see if I was even in the house.

"About twenty minutes later, after changing his clothes and piddling around upstairs, Frank made his way back downstairs and into the kitchen. He opened the refrigerator, grabbed a couple of slices of left over pizza and placed them in the microwave.

" 'Oh, you're here. Why didn't you speak when I came in? I didn't know you were even in the house,' he said, sounding both surprised and startled when he finally noticed me at my window seat.

" 'I was always taught that when you enter a room and someone is there, *you're* supposed speak – not the other way around,' I solemnly responded.

" 'What?' " he said, surprised.

"But before I could repeat my comment, he dismissed the possibility of a response from me by saying, 'Never mind... Listen, I leave for Dubai for that golf trip in about a week. Shelby made all of the reservations but I don't like the hotel Sylvia booked. I want to stay at that top hotel your buddy runs so I need you to get in touch with him so I can get the hook up. I want the *Arabian King* treatment when I land. First time in Dubai, I gotta do it up *BIG*! You know what I like, so make it happen for daddy!' he dismissively demanded.

" 'Make it happen for daddy?!' I must have repeated his words in my head at least three times and each time I did, I felt rage growing inside of me. I sat quietly on the sofa, glaring out of the window while he went on and on about this upcoming trip and all the fun things he was planning to do. He didn't say one word about the night he left me at the police station, let alone address the larger issues at work or in our marriage. Never once did he offer an explanation or an apology for his absence over the last three days and now he had the *nerve* to ask me to do him a favor and call my contact in Dubai so that he can impress his buddies?" she recalled with a tinge of anger.

"As these thoughts raced through my mind, I talked to myself in a low voice, quietly expressing my disgust with the entire situation.

" 'He's got the nerve to ask me to do something for him when he hasn't been here or in the office for *three days*? He thinks he's just going to come and go as he pleases? Who the *hell* does he think he is? I'm not his secretary, I'm his wife. I don't work for *him*... If anything, he works for *me*! He hasn't shown his face in the office for three days and nobody knows where he's been or if he's coming in... and now he has the nerve to ask me to call Mohammed and get him to hook him up... treat him like an '*Arabian King*'? I should fire his sorry ass right now!'

"As I sat there, I made the decision not to respond to him directly or to leave the room. Hurt, pain, anger and disappointment filled my spirit but I felt glued to the sofa. I didn't want to turn around to see him because I didn't want to find myself begging him for answers again, so I remained seated and continued looking out of the window.

"I heard the microwave stop and the cabinet doors opening and closing. He got a glass from the cabinet and began fixing himself a drink as he scarfed down the pizza," Krishna continued, "My senses seemed incredibly heightened because when he pressed the button for the icemaker, the cubes of ice landing in his glass sounded magnified, like the crumbling of concrete.

"As he mixed and poured the drink and went through his mail, the annoyingly loud and slurping noise of the sips he was taking enraged me. Everything he did and every move he made was loud and annoying. With each sound, I found myself getting increasingly more agitated because everything was amplified. As much as I had thought I wanted him home, now I couldn't stand to see or hear him moving around.

" 'What'd you say? There you go again, talking to yourself. Only crazy people do that. Are *you* crazy, Krishna?' Frank said to me, in an attempt to provoke me. He also startled me because he leaned in behind my left ear and invaded my space when he said that. As he backed away, he shook his head disappointedly, smirked and walked over to the wet bar to refresh his drink.

" 'You're acting crazy, you know. Why don't you call one of your yapping friends so you can stop talking to your damn self? Where are those two know-it-alls, Faith and Adrienne any way? Or better yet, what about Evelyn? I bet that tree hugging, Bible thumper can give you some bible verses to read or take you to a yoga class or something.' I'm so sorry he said that about you, guys, you know how thoughtless he can be," she said apologetically.

"Krish, don't you dare worry about my feelings or apologize for him. You're the person who needs care and attention right now," I said.

"You don't have to talk anymore if you don't want to. It's totally OK if you just want to get some rest," Faith said.

"No, I'm OK", Krishna replied softly. "It feels good to talk about it and try to make some sense out of everything," and continued,

"This was the lowest Frank had ever sunk with his verbal abuse. 'Heck, call your crazy ass mother. You talk to her every day, all day long any way. That's where you get that shit—from her side of the family. She talks to herself too. I've heard her. I hate that shit. They're all crazy on her side. Hell, didn't her father blow his brains out? I hope Lauren doesn't end up like that – talking to herself all the time.'

"Momma, I'm so sorry," Krishna said to her mom as the tears flowed down her face. "Shhh… don't you worry about that." Mrs. Williams said as she pulled her daughter closer and Krishna continued,

" 'If you have something to say, 'Say it!' You don't see me talking to myself. I talk to PEOPLE, Krishna, because I have a LIFE!' Frank just went on, making me feel worse by the minute.

" 'And by the way, you need to get your hair done. You look like shit and you're letting yourself go. Remember, you represent *ME* when you're out there, so get it together. I can't have you out there acting *and* looking crazy.'

"As I sat there and listened to him chide and berate me, and make disparaging remarks about the people who matter to me most outside of Lauren, and throwing my family's history of mental illness in my face – a topic he *knows* is extremely sensitive and painful to me, I could hear the voices in my head getting louder and louder. They told me to stop feeling sorry for him and to stop making excuses for him. They told me he didn't deserve my compassion any more because of how poorly he's been treating me and how he's been ignoring Lauren as well. They told me to shut him up.

"I couldn't control these thoughts which danced around in my head without my consent. Like choreographed steps, they connected with the feelings of sadness that had been brewing inside of me and eventually I began to feel numb.

"I wanted the voices in my head to stop and the pain inside to end," she said, crying a little.

"Sadness turned to anger and then anger turned to sheer rage. I was a ticking time bomb with no off switch. In a calm and calculating tone, I made one last attempt to make him understand how much I was hurting and how everything he was doing had been affecting me, but it was obvious Frank didn't care.

I said to him," 'After everything we've been through together, trying to get pregnant after Lauren and the four miscarriages, building the business that *you're* now fucking up... *this* is how you treat me? I've suffered because of you, Frank. That night you left me in that jail to rot and you didn't care what happened to me... what kind of man *does* that to his *wife*?" I said to him.

" 'My family doesn't come around any more, I've disconnected from my friends, I don't know who I am any more, what's the point of this marriage? There's *nothing* healthy about it... And it's all because of *you*. You have the nerve to call *me* crazy? After everything I've done for you? You're where you are today because of me! You spend *my* money on those whores...'

"But before I could finish my plea, I heard him snicker. As I slowly turned around, I could hear him laughing and saw a smile on his face as he shook his head and took a sip of his drink.

" 'Helloooo... I'm over here,' he said sarcastically as he waved his hands above his head as if to get my attention.

" 'Who are you talking to, Krishna? I'm right behind you in the kitchen, not outside the window at the pool!' He refreshed his drink one last time before leaving. As he walked away and made his way up the stairs, I heard him announce, 'I'm taking a nap. I'm not going to stay down here and talk to a crazy person!'

"I could hear him laughing and mimicking me '*My family doesn't come around any more...I've disconnected from my friends,*'" he chided. '*Blah, blah, blah... Whatever. I wouldn't come around your crazy ass either... sitting there talking to yourself.*' The laughter only stopped when the bedroom door closed.

"I was blinded with rage and lost all sense of time. I suddenly realized it was dusk and I had been pacing the kitchen floor for nearly two hours. Frank's laughter and mimicking enraged me. I wanted him to know I wasn't going to sit idly by and take his shit any longer. I paced the floor and cried, pulling and yanking at this damn weave I never wanted in the first place. I was furious he had the nerve to 'take a nap' after everything he'd just said to me.

"I didn't realize I'd missed dozens of phone calls and messages from Faith and you, Evey, about dinner plans as well as several from Adrienne telling me she was back a day early from her business trip. Mom had also called to simply check on me as she does daily, but when I didn't answer or call her back ..."

"Oh, that's what happened, " Faith said. "You know I adore your mom but I was surprised when she called and asked me to swing by the house to check on you because she said she felt strange and just wanted to be certain everything was OK. She also said, 'It's not like Krishna to not return *any* of my phone calls. You know Krish is a creature of habit and reliable. If she tells you she'll return your call, she always does and it's been since this morning that I called her and she said she'd call me back. I've yet to hear from her. Something isn't right. I'll try to swing by the house later myself,' your mom told me.

It was like what Faith had just said didn't register with Krishna as she continued (I shot Faith a look because I was annoyed she had interrupted

K and as a result she might stop talking),

"I can't believe he *said* those things to me... I'm his *wife!*" Krishna continued. "How dare he speak to me that way? ...Talking about my mother and my grandfather... after everything my family has done for him and his family. *My* parents gave us the down payment on our first house. *My* parents paid off *both* of our student loans as a one year anniversary gift so that we wouldn't have all of that debt starting out – *one hundred fifty thousand dollars worth of student loans between the two of us!* I helped his cousin get into graduate school... it was *my* friend who got him in when he was wait listed. How *dare* he speak to me like that?"

At that point, I knew the voices in her head had gotten louder and louder, continuing to tempt her, but despite everything she had been through, she continued to tell us what had happened a couple of hours ago.

"I paced the kitchen floor and banged my hand on the island every time I thought about how rude and disrespectful Frank had been to me. As I turned the corner on the island for probably the twentieth time, the cuff on my blouse got caught on the utility drawer handle and pulled the drawer open. What was inside caught my attention," she continued, "After pausing, I picked up the cordless house phone and dialed 911.

" I calmly reported, 'There's been an accident. Please send an ambulance to 25897 Chamberlain Street. In Overbrook... in the Windsor gated community. The gate is open and the front door is unlocked.'

" 'Ma'am, what is your name? What type of accident?', asked the dispatcher.

"I hung up the phone, walked over to the master key pad on the wall and electronically unlocked the front gate and front door. I grabbed the item from the drawer and slowly walked up the stairs. I made my way down the hall to the master bedroom, opened the door and saw Frank in the bed asleep on his back. The drink he'd made was on the nightstand between the clock and his cell phone. I approached the bed. He didn't know I was standing over him, and without hesitation and before he felt my presence, I raised up the hammer I'd taken from the utility drawer and with one blow and all the force I could muster, slammed it down onto his mouth.

" 'Next time you speak to me, show some damn respect,' I told him calmly as he lay there convulsing and gurgling in his own blood. I could hear the faint sound of sirens in the distance. The hammer fell from my right hand onto the floor next to the bed. I slowly walked out of the room, down the hall, walked down the stairs, sat at the bottom of them and waited for the police and ambulance to arrive.

"As police officers and EMTs entered through the front door, they asked if I was OK and if anyone else was in the house or needed help. I pointed upstairs and at that very moment you guys and mom came running through the door," Krishna said and broke down crying.

That explained the scene that greeted Faith and I when we arrived at Krishna's house.

We had gone over there planning to check on her and bring her dinner. Instead, when we arrived we saw police cars, an ambulance and emergency personnel swarming in and out of the house. Krishna's mother grabbed hold of her and tried to get her to explain what happened, but she couldn't speak. All she could do was cry and rock back and forth in her mother's arms.

As the EMTs carried Frank's near lifeless body down the stairs on the stretcher, a police officer walked behind it, carrying a plastic bag with a bloody hammer inside. Krishna buried her head in her hands. We could hear one of the EMTs telling another police officer, "He's still breathing but most of his teeth were smashed and his jaw bone is crushed. Getting the tube in was almost impossible because when the hammer was drawn back, it ripped through the entire top of his mouth, tearing through the back of his throat, palate, and base of his nose. It looks like whoever did this only hit him once but that one blow did a lot of damage. He's lucky to be alive. If she didn't call us he would have asphyxiated on his own blood, teeth and bones for sure."

After hearing that news, Krishna said to us, "I felt relieved and doomed all at once. I'm relieved he's still alive but what's going to happen to *me* now?" then she added, in a near quiet whisper as a tear streamed down her face, "God help me, please." Her mother held her closer and whispered, "Shh… It's OK, baby, you're safe now."

"Oh God, Krishna, we're here for you." Adrienne said. "And I know it was a relief to you that Officer Winsome was there as well. He was so nice to you during that other situation," she added sincerely.

"He told me I'm going to be fine and I believe him," she said. "Just as I did that night at the jail. I trust him although I don't even know him. I felt as if God actually showed up for *me* this time and I'm thankful." And with that Krishna closed her eyes. The sedative she had been administered finally kicked in and she was at rest. I held her hand, and along with Faith, Adrienne and her mom, we all prayed for her as she drifted off to sleep.

PART 3

Section 3 – Live Your Truth!

Re·demp·tion - the action of saving or being saved from sin, error, or evil.

CHAPTER 9

KRISHNA – HONESTY IS EVERYTHING!

Krishna's breakdown and subsequent assault on Frank had very serious medical and legal consequences. Once the police determined she alone was the perpetrator, she was immediately arrested charged with attempted murder, felony assault, assault with a deadly weapon and placed under psychiatric observation. Due to the severity of the pending charges and her fragile mental state, it wasn't difficult for her attorney, Sylvia Millwood, to convince the District Attorney to allow her to be transported and immediately committed to a Georgetown hospital where her therapist is on staff and I'm a rotational nurse. Krishna's arraignment was postponed until she was well enough to be released from the hospital. Attorney Millwood then used Krishna's phone to text her assistant, Shelby, to tell her she'd be taking a couple of days off and would not be in the office beginning Monday of that week.

When Frank wasn't in the office on Monday, no one thought anything of it. Between his already sporadic appearances there and his relentless bragging about his upcoming golf trip when he *was* there, no one missed him. Frank's absences were clearly becoming a relief to his co-workers who undoubtedly resented his "Arabian King" vacation plans while they were still cleaning up the mess after the company had lost that multi-million dollar government contract.

In reality, after the assault Frank was rushed to a trauma hospital in critical condition. Due to the severity of his injuries, there was justifiable concern brain damage could occur and between that and the excruciating pain he was in, he was placed in a medically induced coma for two weeks. This permitted his body to heal and stabilize as he went through multiple surgeries to correct the tremendous amount of damage that was done to his face with that one blow. Once out of the coma, he remained in the hospital for months for reconstructive and cosmetic procedures. He also required many months of rehabilitative speech therapy and psychiatric out patient care. I could keep track of his progress thanks to updates I received from several colleagues on staff at the hospital.

While Krishna's name and the fact she had been arrested on multiple charges had to be entered into the police blotter and was therefore a matter of public record, Faith used her media connections to squash the story. As a result, Krishna's arrest never got the attention of any police reporters and therefore, there was no news coverage. Damage control was immediate and each of us did our respective parts to protect our fragile friend.

With the help of Adrienne's father, a top-notch legal team was quickly assembled in order to minimize any possible damage to Krishna, Lauren and to DMTG's reputation, brand and image. With Frank "on vacation" and Krishna "out of the office" for a few days (at least initially), this legal team started floating rumors around the office she had decided to file for divorce. Understandably, the staff assumed this action was directly linked to the loss of the government contract along with other swirling rumors of Frank's rampant infidelity.

A few days after the divorce rumor took hold and got stronger, it was formally announced Krishna had decided to take some time off and would not be in the office on a daily basis for several weeks, if not months, in order to address the complexities of the divorce and other family matters. A member of Krishna's management team was identified as the company's point of contact in her absence but all major decisions regarding the company would still be decided by her or temporarily placed on hold.

So much happened over the next three weeks it's still difficult for me to keep it all straight; especially during the time Krishna was hospitalized. Thank goodness for her legal team and our other girlfriends.

I helped coordinate the team of medical personnel involved in her case. The physicians and psychiatrists worked very closely together in the first week or so Krishna was hospitalized as they tried to get to the bottom of her breakdown. I ensured her therapist was instrumental in filling in the gaps and shared his clinical notes of her months of counseling sessions with her psychiatrist. To my amazement and theirs, what was initially thought to be bi-polar disorder turned out to be a Cortisol deficiency, stemming in large part from all the stress she was under, both from work and within her marriage. The Cortisol deficiency was an indicator Krishna's pituitary gland was malfunctioning and this malfunction often mimics the symptoms of bi-polar disorder; hence, the initial misdiagnosis.

The lack of Cortisol, a necessary, regulatory chemical of the nervous and endocrine systems can cause dizziness, fatigue, low blood sugar, generalized weakness and weight loss caused by digestive problems. I knew that patients with this condition often suffer from depression, memory loss, irritability and they're also unable to tolerate physical or mental stress.

This diagnosis was freeing for Krishna because it helped explain a host of things that had been plaguing her physically, mentally and emotionally over the years and consequently had been robbing her of the happiness and joy for life she should have been experiencing.

As tragic as her assault on Frank was, had it not occurred, Krishna probably would not have learned about her Cortisol deficiency. As a result of that incident and the physical and psychiatric evaluations that followed, she received proper treatment immediately.

After the divorce rumors effectively caught on, news of Frank's "accident" was publically revealed a couple of weeks later. The staff at DMTG and the friends he was scheduled to go to Dubai with were told he had been in a major car accident the night before Dubai. Notifying and explaining the circumstances of Frank's injuries to his immediate family wasn't a consideration as his only sibling and mother are deceased and his father is suffering from Alzheimer's in a senior citizens facility.

Krishna's attorney wasted no time taking advantage of Frank's coma and thus, his inability to make any progress against her legally.

On another front, Dr. Moran once again enlisted the services of Don Snyder, the private investigator, to conduct a thorough investigation into Frank's past in order to round out Krishna's defense strategy. To my shock and horror, Mr. Snyder unearthed three previous charges of domestic violence and one charge of attempted rape in Frank's past. As part of the inner circle tasked with protecting Krish, I felt privileged to learn this information but that didn't lessen my shock when I learned this.

The first two assaults happened while he was a freshman in college before he transferred to our school to escape his past. The third domestic violence charge occurred off campus his sophomore year and as a result, didn't affect his ability to stay at school. None of us knew about this because it happened a full year before we started there. The attempted rape charge occurred after he'd graduated and prior to him and Krish reconnecting after her graduation so none of these charges, or the incidents surrounding them, were known to any of us.

After Frank came out of his coma, it seemed like no time before he was mentally fully functional with guns blazing. He initially tried to play hardball and was adamant about pressing charges against Krishna and threatened to go to the media about the assault.

During the first round of negotiations from his hospital bed, he told the attorneys he wanted ownership of her company since he was "next in line" and he wanted her "crazy ass in jail where she belongs." When he was reminded he is, and has always been, strictly an employee of DMTG, he changed his tune almost immediately and attempted to go after money he thought he should be entitled to given his injuries.

It was rapidly apparent he could care less about DMTG and its employees and only wanted the equivalent of half its value in cash. He wanted to walk away with nearly $150 million based on his perceived value of the company *and* he wanted Krishna in jail. While he pressed for this large settlement and made many threats to have her "put away", Krishna's legal team did an excellent job of managing his obvious greed.

This became apparent during a video conference between Frank's lawyers and hers, which I sat in on with Krish. After his team presented their case, her legal team informed him of Mr. Snyder's investigation and his findings. Her attorneys explained to him that given his history, should he insist on bringing this to court, they would exercise their right for a jury trial and would seat as many female jurors and men sympathetic to domestic violence issues as possible. With a jury composition like this, they would be able to make a strong case Krishna's assault on him was self-defense. If this scenario played out, the likelihood of her spending even one day in jail was practically non-existent. Furthermore, should she have to endure the humiliation and embarrassment of a trial, he would walk away with absolutely nothing financially because legally, he was nothing more than an employee, *not* an officer in her company.

Forced to confront his past with the evidence provided by Mr. Snyder and the rest of her legal team, by the end of the meeting, Frank's attorneys advised him to sign the papers and start his life over.

Through his wired jaw and growing dependence on pain medication, Frank agreed to a sizeable settlement in lieu of pressing charges against her. The settlement included a mutual and amicable filing for divorce; continuous health insurance for five years as an employee of the company in order to have his on-going medical needs addressed; a $10 million dollar cash settlement, half of which would be deposited into his account within thirty days of his signing the agreement and the remaining portion paid out over the following five years; their six bedroom ski chalet in Taos, New Mexico; his two cars and all his personal possessions.

The terms of the agreement also had a clause stating that under no circumstances were the details of the "accident" or the specifics of the settlement could be revealed in any form to any person or entity by either party at any time, except to their daughter Lauren. Furthermore, if Frank breached this part of the settlement, he would have to repay any money that had already been paid to him, plus interest and all other portions of the settlement would immediately become null and void. As part of this settlement, there was also another clause that stipulated that whenever either of them was asked about his injuries, they had to stick to the script surrounding the car accident story.

Lauren's European vacation made Krishna's communication with her from the hospital exceptionally easy. Since Krish was now there voluntarily, she was able to speak to and text Lauren just as she would if her life was normal. The time difference worked to her advantage as well, making it easy to explain missed communications.

The prospect of telling Lauren of her tragic actions was by far the hardest thing Krishna ever had to do and for that reason alone, she dreaded Lauren's homecoming but she put those concerns aside as we went to get her at the airport. When we arrived, Lauren looked relaxed, happy and excited to see her grandmother, Krishna and I waiting for her when she disembarked the plane and exited the gate. During the short ride home, I could tell she had matured during this trip. She was noticeably more positive and upbeat and this was refreshing. Listening to Lauren's anecdotes affirmed Krishna's decision to keep her in the dark about what had happened between her and Frank while she was away.

Although Krishna's mother and I advised her not to tell Lauren everything immediately, she decided against this and planned to tell her all that had transpired in her absence once we got to the house and she was settled in.

I can only imagine this decision hinged on Krishna wanting to face what she'd done head on and tell her daughter. As part of her therapy, Krishna had to come to grips with nearly killing Lauren's father and destroying their family. She also had to admit to her battle with mental illness and just tell her daughter the truth. Lastly, she had to admit to herself to having placed her only child on the back burner for the sake of keeping a man.

Krishna was justifiably worried Lauren would want nothing to do with her and would choose to cling to her father out of sympathy. "I am afraid she won't love me and outright abandon me because I have destroyed our family," she thought out loud to me while she was in the hospital. Of course, I was concerned for Lauren and how she would react to the news but this was Krishna's decision and I had to respect her wishes.

These thoughts had preyed on her mind for days leading up to Lauren's return home and most likely on the drive home and while Krishna tried to be present and interested in the stories Lauren shared about her trip, she appeared nervous and worried.

When we pulled into the garage, Lauren immediately saw Frank's car.

"Oh, wow! Dad's home! That's a first. He's *never* home this early," Lauren commented as she sprang out of the car and made her way into the house.

"Mom, I'll get my bags in a minute. Dad, I'm back. What are you doing home so early?" We could hear her yelling to Frank as she made her way into the house.

As we made our way inside, Krishna's mom thanked me for going to the airport with them and for supporting her daughter but after we walked in, she decided to leave. I don't think she could watch Krishna relive that entire ordeal over again. It had been difficult for her to hear the first time at the hospital and she was comforted by the fact that I was going to be there with her.

"Bye, Lauren. Grandma's leaving. Welcome home, sweetie. It's so nice to have you back," her mom yelled to Lauren upstairs.

"Bye, grandma. Thanks for coming to the airport to pick me up," said Lauren as she made her way downstairs and gave her grandmother a big hug and a kiss on her cheek.

Once the door closed, Lauren immediately asked Krishna, "Where's dad? He's not back from Dubai yet? Why is his car in the garage?"

It was obvious these questions made Krishna anxious. I imagine her immediate instinct was to feed the same lie to Lauren about the car accident everyone else had been told. But, Lauren was a legal exception and through her attorneys, Frank had already been told Krishna would tell Lauren the truth upon her arrival. He was also told Lauren would visit him as soon as she wanted to after she was brought up to date on everything so he would know her reaction to the news first hand. Unsure of how Lauren would react to the news, however, Krishna's attorneys and her medical team advised against this but she insisted and moved ahead to bring everything that had transpired out in the open.

"He's not here," Krishna solemnly replied. "Have a seat. There's something I need to tell you, Lauren," and the three of us sat down at the kitchen table.

Lauren sighed and said "Oh God, mom, what is it? Did you guys *finally* decide to divorce while I was away?"

Her prodding yet conclusive question shocked us. Krishna's initial thoughts and somewhat prepared speech as to how she would break the news to her daughter were derailed and ended up taking a slightly different direction.

"A divorce? Why would you say that?" Krishna asked, obviously shocked.

"Mom, come on. I'm not blind and I'm definitely not deaf. You and dad haven't had the greatest marriage for *years*. You argue all the time. He's almost never here any more and you keep acting like everything is perfect. It's *not* and I know that. Personally, I don't know how you've stayed married to him as long as you have because you're not happy. I mean, you do *a lot* to *try* to make him happy but it's never enough and he doesn't seem to appreciate it. He just talks down to you and makes you feel bad and frankly, I hate it. He barely spends any time with me either because he's totally consumed with whatever it is he's doing these days. That's why I spend as much time as I can with my friends... plus, *you* work all the time," she said matter of factly.

Krishna was completely blown away by what Lauren said. All these years she thought she was protecting Lauren from the slow and painful dissolution of her marriage and their family unit. As she was clinging to what she felt was worth holding on to in order to preserve their family, *Lauren* could tell the marriage wasn't healthy and actually felt her parents should have divorced *years ago*! This was unbelievable. Krishna sat motionless for a while before the words sputtered out of her mouth. She began,

"While you were away, your father and I had an argument. While I was trying to get him to understand how hurt I was, he said some things to me that were very hurtful and made me very upset and angry."

"What things? What did he say to you, Mom?" Lauren asked empathetically. These questions appeared to make Krishna sad and caused her to relive the pain he'd verbally inflicted on her that evening all over again. She shook her head as if to say, "No, I don't want to repeat the horrible things he said to me," but Lauren insisted, "Mom, please tell me."

As a health care practitioner, this was my fear. I was very concerned Krishna was still too psychologically fragile to deal with the realities and magnitude of this situation and it was possible she would be setting herself back and require psychological care and observation all over again. But, she persevered and explained,

"He called me crazy and he talked about my Pop-pop and what he did to himself all those years ago. And he called grandma crazy. He laughed at me and showed no compassion whatsoever. It was awful, Lauren."

As Krishna struggled to tell her, I stood up and wrapped my arms around her. She completely broke down and as she did, Lauren grabbed her mom's hands.

"It's OK, Mom. I'm sorry that happened to you," she said with empathy and understanding. Krishna bravely continued with the story.

"He fixed himself a drink and went upstairs to take a nap," she told her.

Krishna paused and put her head in her hands, crying uncontrollably. It was obvious she was having a hard time continuing with the story, but she did.

She shook her head and cried out, "God, please forgive me."

"Oh my God, mom, what did you do?" even though her voice was cracking and stricken with panic, Lauren insisted on hearing the rest of it.

"Mom, tell me. What happened?"

"I, I hit him. I hit him in the mouth with a hammer while he was sleeping." Krishna confessed.

"You did *WHAT?*" Lauren asked rhetorically in a tone of simultaneous shock and comic relief until the magnitude of the act began to register.

"A hammer? Oh my God, did you kill him? Please tell me you didn't kill him, Mom," she begged.

"No, I didn't kill him but that one blow did *a lot* of damage to his mouth, nose, jaw, teeth - *everything*. I called the ambulance and they got here quickly," Krishna quickly explained.

I decided to help by jumping in and filling out the rest of the information. "Lauren, the ambulance rushed your dad to shock trauma. He's still there recovering. They had to remove all of his teeth so they could reconstruct his jaw; he just had his fifth surgery two days ago, I believe. His mouth is wired shut and they keep him heavily sedated most of the time so that he can rest and heal. He's gonna have to have more surgery and…"

Before I could finish, Lauren jumped out of her seat and blurted out to her mother, "Thank God you didn't kill him otherwise you'd be in jail for murder. Is he alert? Can he talk? Does he remember what happened to him? Oh my God, Mom, a hammer…Really?!"

Lauren sat back in her seat and had a strange look on her face. It was a combination of relief Krishna didn't kill him, disbelief at the method of punishment doled out and a juvenile smirk that spoke volumes of "he deserved it" written all over her face.

"Auntie Evey, Can I see him?" she asked.

"Yes, of course. He's out of ICU," I replied.

Krishna added, "Lauren, I have to tell you that outside of the lawyers, grandma, and your aunties, absolutely *no one* can know the truth about what happened. The staff at the office, his friends, the neighbors and anyone who asks has been told he was in a car accident. It's just better that way and it's part of a legally binding agreement we have. You only know because I insisted on it. I didn't want to lie to you.

"And, yes, we are divorcing," she added.

"Well, *yeah*! That's wild, though. But don't worry, Mom, our family secret is safe with me. I don't plan to tell any one how he got that way," Lauren assured Krishna as she grabbed the car keys and left for the hospital.

After Lauren left, Krishna told me how relieved and proud she was she mustered up the courage to tell Lauren what she had done. And I was proud of her too. An incredible weight had been lifted off her shoulders and a difficult and painful truth was out.

It has taken many months, but both Frank and Krishna are on the road to healing from that unfortunate episode which is now part of their shared past: him, physically, and she, mentally and emotionally. They are truly a broken family. Strangely, the person who appears to be the most stable and "put together" these days is the one for whom Krishna was most protective and worried about, Lauren. Physically, she's strong and healthy and mentally, she's stable and fully equipped to deal with anything the world is preparing to throw at her. We're all so proud of her. She is an amazing young lady and in many ways the reason Krishna is still here, still fighting and working toward 100% recovery and healing.

While one senseless act of violence nearly cost Frank his life and Krishna her freedom, it was a wake up call for *all* of us. Krishna thought everything she was or needed was wrapped up in him. *She* wasn't healthy, *he* wasn't healthy and consequently, their relationship wasn't either. But somehow they were able to raise a daughter who is healthy. Strangely, this tragic situation has brought Krishna closer than ever before to Lauren and she's thankful for that. It's the first time in years Krishna made the choice to be 100% honest with herself, her friends and Lauren about anything involving she and Frank. The fact she had to share her truth with her daughter, however, was a very hard pill to swallow but, as strange as it may sound, it paid off and we are all most thankful for it.

CHAPTER 10

ADRIENNE – THE PROOF WILL SET YOU FREE!

Once Adrienne, with her dad's assistance, devised a plan to extricate her and the kids from her marriage to Chris, she wasted no time organizing and assembling a team, consisting of her father, Mr. Snyder, her PI, Ann Marie Portsmouth, a powerhouse divorce attorney. The strategy meetings Dre had with this team were intense and initially, fairly frequent. Ms. Portsmouth was the tactician and coordinated all of the moving parts, which included covering every possible angle and hashing out every possible scenario to ensure Adrienne and the children were protected legally and financially.

On top of all of this, Adrienne had to hire a new financial team, because John Durell, her previous financial planner, was a long time friend of Chris' and they had consistently utilized him throughout their marriage. She felt John had to be replaced because as Chris' friend, she was convinced his ultimate loyalty would be to his friend and she couldn't risk him telling Chris what she was up to once she began the divorce process.

It was an incredibly intense period because Dre still had to be *Mommy* and manage her household, which was difficult and stressful. She couldn't eat and lost nearly 30 pounds but some how managed not to get sick. When she stopped by the house one day, I was floored. I hadn't really noticed her transformation until then but it was as if she'd lost that weight over night!

Adrienne's size 16 frame dropped to a size 12. "Oh my goodness, Dre! You're shrinking before my very eyes," I told her. "I know, right? I feel good, though! It's the stress, I know, but honestly I'm happy I lost the weight. I was annoyed I'd allowed myself to creep into that size to begin with; I'd gotten stuck there and was too lazy to do anything about it. I just wasn't healthy. Dropping back down to my normal size 12 is perfect. I've dug out clothes I haven't been able to even *look at* in a year!" Adrienne said excitedly.

"Honestly, I feel my best and, of course, look great when I'm in a solid 12. I don't need to be a "lollypop head" and starve myself. I love my curves," she said as she ran her hands up and down her curvaceous body.

Like most women, Adrienne does her best to prepare for swimsuit season so during the summer months she's usually in a size 12, but during the winter months, she packs on "winter weight" because, as she willingly admits, she's lazy and doesn't workout as she should. It's been her "little dance" for years and she's pretty much accepted it. Over the last year or so, however, she's gotten comfortably into a size 16 and usually only complains about it when something she wants to buy isn't in her size and designers don't make size 16s!

"Heck, I'm not built to be a size 6 any way and after the blessing of giving birth to three beautiful children, I'm quite happy with the body God has blessed me with – stretch marks and all." Adrienne always keeps it *real!*

"I do my best to stay healthy – although I admit I could do better. I do *most* things in moderation and that's how I live my life. My one prayer throughout this life-changing nightmare is not to get sick because my kids need me to be healthy for them. So, Lord, *please* keep me healthy through all of this so the kids and I can just move on with our lives and get out of this situation unscathed," she said as she took a sip of wine and picked at the cheese plate I put out.

"I have no desire to starve myself in order to wear a size 8. I think the last time I saw that size was in college! I believe a woman should look like a *woman* and not like some pre-teen little girl playing dress up; this has got to be confusing to men. Plus, I don't like feeling hungry all of the time!" she argued.

My girlfriends fight to keep their weight off in order to be proportional with their smaller frames and that's fine for them. Krishna's a size 4, Faith is a solid size 8 or sometimes 10 because she's bustier than the rest of us and when I'm healthy, I'm a size 6/8. "I think we all look fabulous, but Krish is so conscientious about every morsel of food she puts into her mouth, it sickens me at times," Adrienne confided.

"She is the absolute *worst*, E. She constantly counts calories and barely eats. Weight has never really been a problem for her – she's a natural waif – but Frank has her paranoid about it. He even threatened to divorce her if she got past a size 6! How shallow is that? I never did like that arrogant asshole. I just put up with his ass for her to be honest," she admitted.

As for me, my battle with cancer has had a huge impact on my weight and its maintenance. While I've fought this battle over the years, the medications I've had to take, and/or treatments I've endured, have directly impacted my weight both up and down. Consequently, when I'm in remission, I carefully watch my diet – green smoothies and mostly healthy foods. I've morphed into a vegetarian of sorts over the years. But very much the "Caribbean Queen", I do enjoy my "Salt fish and Choba" every Sunday. It's the one vice I won't give up. ("Salt fish and Choba" is a traditional Antiguan breakfast consisting of boiled codfish: chopped and sautéed in oil, tomatoes, garlic, onion, parsley and green pepper mixed together in a ketchup base and served with chopped, seasoned eggplant on the side. It's incredible and any one who has ever had it *loves* it!)

Faith is probably closest to the center of the "what's reasonable spectrum" and makes wise food choices but like Adrienne (and me from time to time), has no problem eating foods that'll "stick to your ribs" every now and then.

Eight months after learning about both her husband's infidelity *and* criminal activity, Adrienne finally had all of her ducks in a row and was prepared to formally file for divorce. Their rented, fully furnished, four level brownstone home in a gentrified area of the District had become vacant and she had it prepared for its next occupant, Christopher Morris. It's a spacious, beautiful property that's been completely gutted and remodeled. It has all new stainless steel appliances, new cabinetry and floors in the kitchen, incredible lighting throughout the entire space and new hardwood floors on all four levels. Chris decorated it himself so it's somewhere he should be quite comfortable in.

During a three week business trip of his to parts of Europe, as well as Qatar and Dubai, Adrienne suspended all of *her* business travel and worked exclusively from home. While the kids were in school, she had all of Chris' belongings (which she had no problems conceding to him as part of the impending divorce) moved out of the house and taken to the brownstone.

Preparing to tell her children she'd filed for divorce from their father was far more difficult than learning about his infidelity. "How are you going to tell the kids, Dre?" I asked her when I swung by her house one afternoon after doing some volunteer work at the hospital.

"Honestly, Evey, I don't know what to say. No time seems right because I feel like I have to prepare myself in case one of them breaks down or some other type of backlash I haven't anticipated occurs, even though I've been over this with my therapist enough times to be prepared," she said.

"Just be honest without being critical or judgmental of Chris. Madeline and Madison are old enough to understand that relationships sometimes don't work out. You'll have to decide how much more you share with them beyond that," I told her.

The girls are pretty close to their dad – Madeline more than Madison – and Dre feared the news would devastate them. After speaking with her own dad and sharing her concerns about how and when to tell the kids, Dre and her dad agreed it would be best for her to tell Chris she filed for divorce while he was traveling so he would know he couldn't come back to the house when he returned. She told me she would tell the kids the evening after she broke the news to him.

The day before Chris' scheduled return, Adrienne decided to inform him of her decision in a video conference and asked me to come over to her house for moral support. I stayed out of view as Adrienne told Chris she filed for divorce and the reasons why.

Telling him wasn't terribly difficult for her because a few days before, Mr. Snyder sent her an update and informed Adrienne that Deb Horton met Chris in Qatar and they appeared to have had a fantastic little vacation together and he had photographic evidence! Hearing that news more than likely erased any and all possible doubts or hopes for reconciliation she may have been flirting with.

Adrienne learned the Qatar trip wasn't part of the business trip at all and Chris had only told her that in order to extend his trip by an extra week after his meetings in Dubai. It's all part of the same region, so rendezvousing "next door" to where you've been meeting business associates made sense and didn't throw up any red flags. It was the perfect way to deceive Adrienne because she assumed the Qatar trip was part of the overall business trip.

"Hey you, how's everything going? How are the kids?" Chris inquired via their video call.

Before Adrienne could answer, we heard a knock on his hotel door.

"Hold on, someone is at the door," he said.

He walked away from the computer and we heard him opening the door and an exchange of male voices, "Good morning, Sir. Are you Mr. Morris?"

"Yes."

"I have a delivery for you, Sir."

"Thank you."

The door closed softly and Chris walked back to the computer while Adrienne watched him open the sealed manila envelope.

"I hope this is Robert's final version of the documents he said he'd send over. He's not a computer guy so we always have to accommodate him by getting his long hand changes and then inputting them for him. It's annoying as hell because we have to hold his hand through everything but given his account is so big, we just do it," he explained.

"Hmmm… OK," Adrienne replied. I'm sure she could feel her heart pumping.

She had enough of playing these stupid games and behaving as if she cared about anything regarding him any more. She was *over* it, *him* and the marriage. She wanted *out* and she wanted it *OVER* with.

"What the hell is this, Adrienne? Divorce?" he blurted out as he glanced at the stack of papers he pulled out of the envelope and looked at her via the computer monitor.

"I want a divorce, Chris. Those are the papers. I've filed," she told him directly.

There! It was finally out and I'm positive she felt relieved because I could hear an audible exhale as she sat back in her chair.

For the past eight months, Adrienne had been dodging and weaving him, faking interest in his life and faking orgasms during the limited and nearly scheduled and ritualistic sex sessions they had from time to time, but she never wanted to participate in. All of it was beginning to sicken her. She didn't want him touching her at all but, "I have to 'fake it until I make it' and in this instance, 'making it' is making my exit out of this joke of a marriage," she confided to me.

"But, *why?*" he asked as he flipped through the pages without really processing what was in them.

"I thought we were fine. What's going on, Adrienne? Is there someone else?" he asked in what appeared to be a combination of shock and anger. I thought I also heard a hint of relief in his voice, perhaps because she beat him to filing for divorce and therefore, his exit from the marriage to be with Deb Horton was made easier.

That was *my* initial impression. He seemed almost too calm and frankly, that was beginning to piss *me* off and he's not my husband!

"I know I've been traveling a lot but…"

Before he could finish, Adrienne responded and snickered at his last question.

"'Is there *someone else?*' "Yeah, muther fucker! Every guy I ever thought about every time you were *trying* to fuck me, you bastard!" she later told me she had thought to herself, but I just heard her calmly say,

"No, Chris, I haven't been sleeping with someone else. I wish the same were true for *you,* though."

It was best she responded that way instead of what was swimming around in her head. There was no need to give him false ammunition.

"What are you talking about? I haven't been cheating on you, Adrienne," he replied.

"Oh Lord," I thought. "Here comes a lie in the form of denial. So predictable."

"Of course you haven't, Chris. Isn't that the standard line all cheaters use?" she asked rhetorically. "I knew you'd deny it, so I made sure I was thorough," she told him.

"Open the other envelope and as you take in all of that shit, let me tell you how this is going to go down. "

What? Another envelope? *I* didn't even know what was coming! There was another envelope in the package? At this point I not only felt uncomfortable – like I shouldn't be witnessing this – but I also felt afraid for Chris, *very afraid.*

"I've moved you out of the house."

He looked up at her momentarily and then down at the second envelope as he started to open it.

"All of your shit -- clothes, shoes, jewelry, office files, desk, *everything* has been packed up and moved to the brownstone. I had your things moved there because that's the property I'm giving you as part of the divorce and so the kids have some place comfortable and safe to stay when they visit. Don't bother coming back to the house because there is absolutely nothing here any more that belongs to you. I've already had the locks and codes changed and your car is in the garage at the brownstone. As it relates to the kids, an every other weekend and every Wednesday for the girls and a Thursday visitation schedule for Marc-Anthony is best, but of course, if your travel schedule interferes with that for any reason we can make the necessary adjustments," she told him.

Wow! If I'm sitting here in shock over hearing all of this I could only imagine the thoughts that must be running through Chris' mind now – and I *knew* about the "move." But, what's in that damn second envelope? I assumed it was just the titles to the brownstone and his car.

As she spoke, I could just about make out his reaction to the contents of the envelope Adrienne instructed him to open. Inside were about ten 8x10 photographs of him and Deb Horton over an eight month period, some in a variety of compromising poses. Each labeled with subject, place, date and time.

The first four pictures were just typical, couple on a romantic vacation photos but the others were photos of them performing a range of sex acts on each other including oral sex, doggy style, standing and in a tub. Adrienne had told me Mr. Snyder had come up with some damning photographic evidence, but that did not prepare me for *this*!

Oh my goodness! Part of me wanted to jump up, high five her, and yell Boo-Yow -- just like the late Stuart Scott of ESPN fame used to do after watching an amazing play -- for being so freaking thorough in catching him red handed and putting to bed the ridiculous lies that were certain to continue without hard evidence to the contrary. But, honestly, the other side of me was sad because after all of these years of marriage and three absolutely beautiful children, their marriage was ending like this. There was nothing to celebrate or "high five" about! Another marriage had just been wiped out and I was witness to this one too! "I sure hope *Deb Horton* was worth it, Chris," I thought to myself.

I don't know how she managed to do it, but Adrienne stoically sat there and watched Chris squirm and become visibly uncomfortable. He placed both of his hands on top of his head and slumped as low as he could get in his chair. He then covered his mouth in shock - his eyes as large as bowling balls and his breathing elevated.

"Let's not drag this thing out by playing games. Sign the papers, Chris. There's no denying it or lying about it. It's all there in vivid color and I know *everything!* I've known all about Deb Horton for several months and the accounts in Switzerland and the one in Belize," she told him. "It's all in there so I don't expect you to contest *any* of what I've generously agreed to part with," Adrienne said calmly.

"I've made arrangements for someone to meet you at Dulles when you land to collect the originals documents with your signatures. Please don't be misled by what appears to be a limited number of pictures in that envelope either. There are many, many more photos of you and your whore in very compromising positions which are also in my possession, so I suspect that for once in your life, you'll do what's right and what's best by our children and not cause this whole thing to go public by contesting it. In fact, if you lose your sanity, decide *not* to sign the papers and choose to contest *any* portion of what is in those documents, I will make sure *everything* I have becomes public, and I do mean *everything*," she assured him.

"I told you a long time ago you *never* want to find yourself on the other side of a Moran. We'll *bury* you! You thought you were getting away with something and had me mistaken for 'Boo-Boo the Fool' and the truth is, you *did* for a very long time – which *really pisses me off* when I think about it, but that's neither here nor there now. Our marriage is over Chris and I want you out of my life *forever*. Frankly, I don't ever want to see your face *again* but given we have three beautiful children – who your selfish ass obviously thought nothing about when you were cheating on *us* – I don't have much of a choice," she lamented as she tried to keep her emotions in check.

"Can we talk about this, Dre? I mean… the accounts… Umm… What are you going to do, Adrienne?" he asked, concern and fear showing in his voice.

"You greedy, selfish son-of-a-bitch!" she screamed. "Is *that* all you care about – the money you stole from C. Patrick Horton and your other clients?

"After everything my family has done for you, the sacrifices I made by putting *my* dreams on hold trying to appease your fake, social climbing, grey boy ass, while you're out there stealing from clients and stashing money in overseas accounts, all you care about is what I'm going to do about the *'accounts'*?" FUCK YOU!! Stew in your own shit trying to figure out what I do next. I owe you absolutely NOTHING!" Adrienne screamed and truthfully, at this point I thought I was going to have to emerge from the shadows to rescue her because she looked as if she was about to jump through the computer monitor.

"Well, I just… it's just… I mean, the kids…" he stuttered.

"Shut up! Don't even think about using our children as some sort of pawn to get me to feel sorry for you. Sign the fucking papers and hand over the documents when you land. If you don't, *I promise you I will fucking bury you and your bitch* and then dance on your graves. I hope that cheap trick was worth it, you dumb ass."

And with that, Adrienne disconnected their video call.

She was shaking and upset and I jumped up from my chair to console my friend. I had my reservations about being there initially because I felt it was a private matter, but in the end I was glad I was there for her. She shouldn't have been alone at a time like this.

"Evey, can you believe this shit? I mean, initially, there was a part of me that wanted him to beg and plead for me to take him back and ask how I found out. But instead, he showed me what he really cared about – himself and that damn money," she said through her uncontrolled sobs and then she caught her breath. "Actually, in hindsight, I'm *glad* he didn't try to make a case for himself. He already looked like a complete ass; sitting there squirming in his chair like a bitch; own your shit now, *bitch*!" she screamed at the blank computer screen.

Based on what I witnessed, it was best that Chris *didn't* try begging her back during that conversation. Adrienne would have immediately seen through his crocodile tears, had he shed any, and she would have verbally annihilated him the way he annihilated their marriage.

As I was leaving, Adrienne said, "Thanks so much for being here tonight. I don't think I would have been able to keep my cool, had I not known that Calming Evelyn was near by, keeping an eye on me," and she and I both laughed before she said somberly, " Evey, you know I am going to tell the kids tomorrow night. I need closure and to focus on moving ahead. Do you think you could come over? I hate to impose on you two days in a row, but just knowing you're around calms me. I know exactly what I am going to say to them, so I don't need you around for that, but it would be nice to know I have a backup if there is a problem."

"Of course, Dre," I said. "We are friends for life. Have you forgotten that ring I gave you? It's a nice ring, but the words are far more important than the stones. I'll see you tomorrow."

After dinner at Adrienne's house the next day, I volunteered to clean up the kitchen while she spoke to her children. I could hear the entire conversation once she collected them all in the adjoining family room.

"Mom, what's up?" Madison inquired.

Once they got settled, she began. "Well, I don't know how else to tell you guys this so I'm just going to say it. Your dad and I are divorcing. I filed," she told them.

"Whoa, wait a minute, Mom! What happened?" Madeline responded.

"Why"? Madison asked.

"Your father and I have been having problems for a while. The truth is he simply hasn't been honest with me and some of the decisions he's made have only benefitted *him* – not our marriage or this family. I realized I can't live a lie in terms of pretending everything is OK when it's not, so I've done what's best for me and ultimately, *all* of us."

"He cheated didn't he?" Madison inquired with spot on accuracy.

"That explains those boxes I saw stacked up in the garage last night when we got home from the game," she observed with a sudden level of awareness. "We noticed them but I didn't think a whole lot about it because I just thought it was a shipment of art stuff. Is that *dad's* stuff, mom?" Madison queried.

"Um?" Adrienne couldn't bring herself to admitting Chris' indiscretion to their children so she simply paused and closed her eyes.

"Mom? You always said you would never stay in any relationship if the guy put his hands on you or cheated on you and you told us to never stand for anything like that either. I *know* dad wasn't crazy enough to hit you so he must have cheated," Madison concluded.

"Oh my goodness, Mom. Are you OK? Did he apologize?" Madeline's attempt to comfort Dre was surprising because *she's* the one closest to her father.

"That explains the text we got this morning," Madison recalled.

"What text?" Adrienne asked.

"I don't know. It was weird. Outta the blue we got this text from dad saying he was 'Sorry'. I didn't understand it and it was early," Madison explained.

Hearing that made me slow my pace in the kitchen so I could tune in to the conversation.

"When I asked him what he was sorry about, he never replied, so I just ignored it," Madeline added.

"He sent *both* of you a text saying he was 'sorry' without an explanation for *why* he was sorry?" Adrienne asked searching for clarity. She was seething and I could tell anger and jealousy started building inside because *she* hadn't received an apology from him.

"Yeah, the message said, 'I'm so sorry.' That was it. It was weird. But now it makes sense. He was apologizing for what he'd done to you," Madison concluded.

"But Mom, did Dad apologize to *you?*" Madeline persisted with her previous question.

"No. No, your father has never apologized to me," she quietly replied, trying not to show her pain and disgust. She looked at me as I stood there listening and as our eyes met, I signaled to her to try to remain calm.

"I mean, if he apologizes and you guys go to counseling then maybe you guys can work it out, right?" Madeline clung to the possibility of reconciliation because she's the type of kid who avoids conflict at all costs and just wants to see people get along. She's very much the Pollyanna of the house while her sister is the pragmatist.

"Mad, he cheated!" Madison explained. "How can you be trusted again when you cheat in your marriage? I mean, if you do it once you're probably going to do it again. That's how I see it. Dad's hardly ever here any more any way. He's traveling *all the time*. I mean maybe I just notice it more now because I'm older but dad travels *a lot*! And that can't be good for any relationship," Madison concluded and then continued,

"So what does this *mean*, Mom? If you filed for divorce, does that mean he has to move out or did you put him out already. That's his stuff in the garage, isn't it?" she pressed.

"Well, who moves out isn't directly linked to who filed for divorce. But yes, your father won't be living here any more and yes, that is what is left of his things. Everything else has already been moved to the brownstone," Adrienne explained.

At that point, Marc-Anthony became fully aware of what divorce actually means and its impact.

"Dad's not going to live here any more? Where is he going to live? Why didn't dad tell you the truth and say he's sorry? Will we be able to see him? I think we should have a family meeting. Dad's going to be mad he can't live here any more."

The innocence in Marc-Anthony's questions made me tear up.

He may be developmentally challenged but Marc-Anthony is no fool. He sees things in black and white and speaks his mind. Family is everything to him and learning their family unit won't be the same was very troubling to him.

"No, Dad won't be living here any more. He will be living in the city at the brownstone so you'll be able to see him as often as you'd like or as his schedule allows. We've worked out a schedule, that, at least for now, will hopefully work out for everyone," Adrienne answered in an attempt to reassure him.

"Regarding counseling and having a family meeting… Listen you guys, I'm past all of that. I have no intentions of going to counseling to resolve any thing between your father and me nor do I plan to sit down and have a 'family meeting' about it. If you guys want to sit down and try to get his perspective on this whole thing, you're more than welcome to, but I won't participate in any of that. This has been a *really* hard thing for me to come to grips with. I've been seeing a therapist for several months now and he has helped me through most of it already.

"Filing for divorce is not a decision I took lightly or made hastily because I knew it would impact *all* of us. But I've made my decision and I'm satisfied with it. I'm not turning back or changing my mind. I've come to grips with ending my marriage to your dad and it makes me sad to see it end like this, but I *cannot* and *will not* continue to live a lie. It's not the type of example I want to set for you – especially you girls – so I have to do what will be best for me and make you all happy too in the long run," Adrienne explained as she wiped tears away.

"But you didn't give him a chance to apologize!" Madeline snapped.

"Mad, what's the point? Dad apologized to *us* but didn't apologize to *Mom!* That's crazy! I can see why mom feels the way she does. Can't you?" Madison reasoned.

"You may feel comfortable with being a child of divorced parents but *I'm NOT! Everybody* deserves a second chance, Madison! Even *Dad!"* chided Madeline and with that, she got up and stormed out of the room.

Adrienne allowed Madeline to leave because she knew this was difficult for her and she needed time to process it. After Madeline left the room, Madison and Marc-Anthony got up and sat down next to their mother. They hugged her as she did her best to assure them they would be fine and she would make sure nothing in their daily routines would change.

When Madeline left the room, I motioned to Dre I would go and speak to her but she came over and said, "This is a lot to process and she just needs a little time right now," she said. I respected her wishes and left her alone. Adrienne told the other two it would be an adjustment at first but over time they would iron out the kinks and get through everything *together*. She reminded them she will always be there for them, the lines of communication will always run both ways and they can still talk to her about anything, at any time. She encouraged them to speak to their father if they felt the need to do so and to try not to take sides because no matter what, the end of their marriage didn't mean their love for them was ending.

By the end of the night, Madeline came back downstairs. Since I was the first person she saw, she grabbed me and I hugged her. I told her everyone is going to get through this and that whenever she needed to talk, I would always be there for her. Madison and Marc-Anthony spoke with Madeline and Adrienne spoke with her too. Adrienne told her how sorry she was that their family couldn't remain intact and I told Madeline I understood her pain, anger and frustration and she was entitled to every one of those emotions. Adrienne encouraged her to talk to her father as well and tried to reassure her that divorce didn't mean that they – her parents – were abandoning her or her siblings. This was simply the best decision for them and she *had* to make it. I was relieved when they hugged and told each other "I love you".

After the kids went off to do their own things, Adrienne shared with me that, "Once I'd made my decision a few months ago, it was *final* and I've had some time to deal with the end of my marriage. But, while I feel a sense of relief after filing for divorce and speaking with Chris, my kids are now at the first stage of their grief so I have to be patient with each of them."

"Dre, I think you should seriously consider getting counseling for them as well so they can learn healthy ways to deal with the sense of loss they are experiencing, because this is tough for everyone." I told her.

"Yeah, E, you're right. I will," she agreed.

   "The reality is divorce is a death that doesn't have to kill you (or your kids) if all of you get the help you need. This won't be easy, Dre, but with time and God's grace you guys *will* get through it. I'm here for you, girl," I told her as I gave my friend the warmest hug a sister-girlfriend could offer to another.

CHAPTER 11

FAITH – "YOU'RE NOT BROKEN!"

All of the craziness surrounding me was obviously affecting Len as well. After being served with divorce papers, I gave him the space he needed and completely cut off all communication. While we continued to share our home, I chose to disengage from him completely. He wanted to sever our marriage and so it began, but I would decide how I would participate in it. My approach was something no one understood – not my parents, my girlfriends, my boys and most of all Len, I'm sure.

Over time, however, I noticed that he was spending less time away from home and our communication – albeit brief – had improved. When he engaged me, I responded but I had stopped initiating all communication. Basic cordial greetings such as "Good morning or Good night"; relaying verbal messages; and, matters dealing with the boys (I left to them to communicate directly to their father) all ceased on my part. If Len didn't initiate a conversation or ask a question I said nothing.

I began living my life more independently. My Saturday morning trips with Len to the farmers market had ended many months ago and I had stopped going because I associated those trips with "our time" but I enjoy that activity so I started going again, usually alone, but Faith joined me occasionally. I also started seeing the latest movies with my girlfriends or some friends from my triathlon club but if no one was available, I had no problems going alone.

Now that my health is progressively improving since *"The Bitch"* is being managed and is in remission, I'm making every effort to begin reducing my emotional dependence on Len. I feel doing this is best for my overall health for now. While I want to remain his wife and continue our lives together, I've sworn I will *never* allow anyone or anything to make me an emotional cripple again. If I can overcome cancer for a *third time* and not allow *that* demon to *kill me*, then I can certainly build up my emotional strength and rebuild that side of me as well. I'm strengthening my mind, body and spirit and as a result, I'm fully and completely making myself over and whole again. I think surrounding myself with strong women like Faith and Adrienne (and in her own way, Krishna) all of these years, has rubbed off on me in a good way.

Len made some halfhearted attempts to inquire about their marital problems in order to engage me I suppose but said nothing about ours. Honestly, that bothered me immensely. We didn't speak about the divorce papers he'd filed and after being served, I *never* brought it up to him. I just stopped talking to him. As a matter of pro forma, I retained an attorney, but gave her no authority to move forward beyond informing Len's lawyer I now had representation. Perhaps my approach was naïve and I was in denial, but it was a battle I didn't have the energy to take on, fathom, or partake in. My spirit told me to do nothing or say anything and I listened.

The energy in our home was not one of hate - it was simply stagnate. Together, we engaged the boys as we've always done, but the loving banter between Len and I ceased. I didn't feel bitter toward him - I just kept quiet. He was never mean toward me; he was just physically absent from the home and emotionally distant when he *was* there. We were in a voided space where neither of us seemed to know what to do. I knew I couldn't linger in that space for very long and that at some point, I would need to have closure – one way or the other – relative to the direction of our marriage. However, I needed to hear *only* God's voice and so I chose to be quiet and allow my spirit to listen.

With a protective order in place against DiMarco, Faith was finally able to get some peace of mind in her home. But taking that action didn't come without some consequences – at least for a short time. Shortly after the order was granted, Lisa Doughtery, a young rookie reporter on a mission to quickly make a name for herself at *The Washington Post,* got wind of it and decided to do some snooping around to find out more. Unsure of how to proceed, she approached Deidre Kressel, an influential senior writer and member of the news staff, for guidance assuming Deidre would help her build a story around it.

What the nosey Miss Doughtery didn't know was Deidre is a good friend of Faith's. So instead of developing a story, she was told this was a personal matter a member of the "Post family" was dealing with and she was to ensure *none* of it ever saw the light of day. "Are we clear?" Deidre asked rhetorically. "If it does, you will *never* work in this town again. We protect our own. Understand? Now delete it!"

In this town, relationships can either make or break you. The story never went public.

Given Faith's prominence in the media, keeping her personal life out of the limelight was an obvious concern but with Deidre's help, this was a hurdle she easily overcame. It certainly paled in comparison to her worries about how she would break the news to her children and the impact her decision would have on them. When she shared her concerns about this to me, I told her to be honest with the girls about the divorce but to never bash or bad mouth DiMarco. "Trust me, anything those girls will learn *about* or *from* their father *he* will reveal on his own and *you* won't have to say a word. Through his behavior and attitude, he will either end up as a prince or a scoundrel in their eyes and then they will decide the role they will want him to play in each of their lives," I told her and Faith agreed.

In hindsight, Faith realized there were two things that played in her favor relative to how the girls will adapt to the changes that are certain to permeate their lives.

First, as the years had past through their marriage, DiMarco's habit of going out after work grew both in scope and frequency. As a result, he was rarely at home and when you're not around, life goes on without you. Faith commented to me one day, "When we were first married, D seldom went out with the 'the boys 'and when he did, it was usually limited to a couple of times a month.

"After Kennedi's birth, I noticed a change. By the time she was about six months old, he'd increased his time with 'the boys' to about once a week and our bi-weekly date nights ceased. I didn't make a big deal out of it because I figured he needed a break from work. His nights out with the boys were usually limited to a Thursday or Friday night Happy Hour and he was typically home by 8:00p or 9:00p.

"Unfortunately, as time went on and he began building his business and client base, what I initially viewed as an understandable need to 'work late' or 'take potential clients out in order to build the business' became more frequent and less understandable because he was spending less time with us. Doubts about his whereabouts or his activities never crossed my mind because I thought he was doing what he said he was doing (working) to better our family while I did my part as well," Faith told me as she helped me sort through some of Timothy's old clothes I was donating to charity.

As a professional woman whose career was also on the rise, Faith understood that. She, like many of us however, chose to make sacrifices in her own career. Faith didn't take on additional assignments or make career moves that would have certainly propelled her professionally. "I thought it would be unfair for our daughters to be raised by a nanny and two workaholics. I made sure *I* was the one who was at home in the evenings and on weekends and I limited attending events I was invited to," she said.

"Then, when Harper was born, DiMarco's late nights increased to upwards of three to four nights per week and most Saturday evenings, you remember, I used to complain to you about it all the time! I also complained to him constantly about his absence but my concerns fell on deaf ears and I just got the same excuses about 'meeting with clients'.

When things went completely south in our marriage, it just got worse and he chose to stay away even more," she said with a sigh. "That's a long way of saying the girls are used to him not being around much," she added.

Faith's second reason for believing the girls would adjust well to the divorce made perfect sense as well. Faith's almost one year delay in filing for divorce while remaining in the family house with DiMarco still under the roof caused Kennedi and Harper to be first hand witnesses to their family unit unraveling. Even though the girls sometimes heard yelling and screaming and a few times even witnessed the raw emotions bubble up to the surface, this was rare for the most part but staying in the home ensured they had some sense of normalcy. When the fragile peace was occasionally broken, the girl's constant pleas were for things to be fixed so they could return to having a happy family.

Although Faith braced herself for the worst when she had to tell Kennedi and Harper she filed for divorced and kicked DiMarco out, the girls seemed relieved. Faith assured them the arguing would stop, they wouldn't have to move, they could remain in their schools and keep their friends and they will be able to see their father regularly. With these issues addressed, the questions stopped and peace again reigned in their house, hearts and minds.

To her credit, Faith took my advice and as a precautionary measure, made appointments for the girls to see my friend, Dr. Patricia Wilmott-Davis, a fantastic child psychologist, who specializes in divorce to ensure they got through this OK. When DiMarco was asked for his input and participation in these counseling sessions, he opted out from the very beginning.

I accompanied them to their last session. Dr. Wilmott-Davis told Faith to, "Keep doing what you're doing with them, they will be just fine," and Faith replied, "They're great girls and I know they love me as much as I love them and that love is the foundation of our relationship. Thank you so much for giving me some simple strategies to help them get to open up. I'll just continue to make sure we speak about our family situation as often as they need to and I'll keep close tabs on their overall behavior and performances in school. This isn't anything special in my book -- it's what I need to do as a mother and it's what my girls need in order to emerge from this horrible experience happy, healthy and whole."

"You'd be surprised how many parents don't put the time in like you do, Faith, so keep it up. You're doing a great job." Dr. Wilmott-Davis replied.

Almost immediately, Kennedi and Harper began seeing their father on a regular bi-weekly schedule and, while they're not as close to him as they are with Faith, the visits are enough for them to maintain a relationship with him and keep them balanced.

"I make sure the girls and I spend *a lot* of time together – just the three of us –laughing, talking, joking, and just *enjoying* each other again," Faith said with a big warm smile on her face as we drove home from one of my lab appointments. "It's important to me, E. I mean, we're essentially making up for the time lost during this painful year and a half and we're somehow even closer as a result. Dr. Wilmott-Davis' advice to keep the lines of communication open among us was the best strategy I could have used for us. It helped us build trust, a sense of stability and a bond that is absolutely unbreakable. With the girls as my number one priority, I do everything necessary to ensure their overall mental and emotional well-being. I'm *so* glad I'm doing it, it's definitely worth it," she said smiling.

After Faith put him out of the house, DiMarco tried everything possible to get her attention and to talk to him but Faith vehemently refused.

He sent flowers, cards, and chocolates along with long letters expressing his "deepest apologies" for what he'd put her through. Sadly, he even enlisted Kennedi and Harper to deliver messages telling her he started counseling which proved to be false.

None of it worked because Faith was D-O-N-E, *DONE!* and she wanted nothing else to do with him. Her trust in him was gone and she'd lost all respect for him. She told me her love had turned to hate and "I want him out of my life *forever*."

When all of his superficial efforts failed and the divorce proceedings began, the counseling sessions he claimed to have been attending stopped and the *real* DiMarco Rathers emerged. When honey didn't work, he tried poison and did whatever he could to make Faith's life a living hell and break her financially.

During their divorce proceedings, D tried to play hardball in court. He lied about his income and desperately tried to hide large sums of his money so his child support responsibilities would be significantly reduced. He claimed he was entitled to the classic car Faith had purchased for him, until he learned his name was never added to the title. And, he and his lawyer attempted to obstruct justice by telling Chelsea Patterson, the "little girl" who called Faith to apologize, not to show up to court to testify against him.

Faith's attorney, however, was a pit bull and shooed away these "Hail Mary" legal antics DiMarco and his lawyer presented to the court. The defense strategies of endless motions and legal arguments didn't impress the judge either. He dismissed most of them and even threatened to find DiMarco in contempt at one point after one of his outbursts. Given that Faith filed for divorce on the grounds of adultery and could prove it with her taped confession, the judge had significant leeway in deciding how the distribution of the property, custody and visitation would go in the case.

In the end, Faith got everything she asked for plus attorney fees. No surprise, she *was,* however, responsible for paying him a lump sum of $50,000 for the clothes and other "donations" she made on his behalf, because the "donated" booty were only *his* items and didn't include any of the girl's things or hers. The judge felt the "donations" were made without DiMarco's consent so he deserved to be compensated for them.

But Faith wasn't bothered by any of this one bit because she received half of everything else including his 401(k) plans and a savings account she didn't know he had! She also got to keep the house, receive alimony, child support and all the gifts, fine jewelry and the Mercedes SUV he had given her the previous Christmas. As a bonus of sorts, she was also given the option of suing his paramour for damages based on a new law whereby spouses of adulterers are entitled to sue the paramour for damages to her and the family caused by the affair. Needless to say, it's an option Faith is *seriously* contemplating.

As the judge read his ruling in the closed courtroom, Faith exhaled a long, *long* sigh of relief once the proceedings came to an end. Visibly upset, DiMarco, her now ex-husband and his attorney loudly stormed out of the courtroom. Faith just sat in her seat and quietly wept while her attorney hugged her and reassured her she would be just fine. "While I believed her, the tears I shed were for my children -- not for me," Faith said later when we gathered at her house. "I never wanted them to become a statistic and now they – *we* – are." This, I know, rocked Faith to her core because for a long time she *really* wanted DiMarco to simply own his shit and come clean. But he was just too immature and too narcissistic to do it. The possibility of growing old with her husband, the father of her children, was no longer an option and this devastated her.

Adrienne, Krishna, and I immediately went over to her and embraced and comforted our sister-girlfriend in the way only best friends can.

"I'm divorced," Faith somberly whispered.

"Yes, yes you are, girl, and it hasn't been easy getting here, I know, but you and your beautiful girls are going to be fine. We got your back, Faye," Adrienne said.

"Faye, we're not here to celebrate anything. We're here to support you and lift you up. We stood with you on your wedding day and we're here to *lift you up* on the day of your divorce," I explained sincerely.

"You know we wouldn't let you go through this alone, Faye. We love you," Krishna added.

Every word we spoke resonated with Faith that afternoon. I could tell our presence in that courtroom – just as on her wedding day – meant *everything* to her. Faith can be stubborn and the final day of her divorce was no exception. She was determined to do it alone and insisted we all wait at her house until she returned from court. We kept our promise for about ten minutes and then the girls and I, along with Luke and Mr. and Mrs. St. John, piled into our cars and drove straight to the courthouse so we could all be there for her.

Then Faith's mother, Bridgette, said, "I've been there for every milestone and turning point in your life, baby. The majority of it has been wonderful and you've made your father and me so very proud. But it's the turning points in our lives that can either make us or break us. You're *not* broken. This is a turning point in your life and yet at the same time, it's an opportunity to begin anew."

"As long as I have breath in my body, I will *always* be here for you and my grandbabies. I know you may not feel it right now, but I want you to know you're *strong*. D tried every sneaky trick in the book to break you and *nothing* worked. You clung tightly to your faith, believed and trusted in God and *He* delivered you today. So, let's praise Him and give Him all of the Glory and then, go home because *I need a drink*! And I *don't drink!*" Mrs. St. John's words had us all in tears and then laughter. She has a way of doing that and we all love her for it.

"I'm so happy that on *this day* I have four of the most amazing women in my life at my side – crying with me, laughing with me, praying for me and loving me. I am so blessed," Faith said.

The first couple of months after Faith's divorce were difficult and uncomfortable for her at first. Along with dealing with hundreds of legal details, she had to get used to referring to DiMarco as "my ex-husband" or as "my kids' father" instead of her husband and I know this saddened her.

"Evey, it feels so weird when I look down at my bare ring finger, because for years I'd identified myself as part of a unit based in part on that big piece of jewelry – it symbolized a union – and now, I'm not part of a unit any more."

She was right. Her divorce was an adjustment for all of us, but as time went on, Faith got used to it, as did we. She had her up days and her down days, (including days when she didn't want to get out of bed), but thanks to her children's school schedules and activities, she had no choice.

Adrienne, Krishna, and I (as well as her family) did our best to keep her strong. We helped her maintain her routines so she wouldn't wallow in self-pity or get swallowed up by feelings of emotional abandonment. There were many days when it felt like depression was trying to become her new companion and we helped her get through those.

Those days were really tough – she did a lot of crying, but with time, Faith's outlook improved and she began to feel better. Without a doubt, she did *a lot* of praying during those periods and frequently met with Dr. Buckingham in order to get things off of her chest and the anxiety she was feeling out of her head and spirit. This combination helped Faith not to become jaded or irrevocably bitter and she really worked hard *not* to become *that* woman! I'm so proud of her!

"I don't care, Faye. You haven't been out in months! In fact, as far as I know, you haven't been out since your divorce! That's been at least six or seven months, right?"

Adrienne and I were on the phone with Faith, pressing her about meeting us for drinks and dinner at the opening of a swank Cuban-themed lounge and bar in the DC metro area.

"I really don't feel like going, Dre. I'm good. You guys go and let me know how it is," she insisted.

"No way! You're not getting off the hook that easily. We've let you slide for *months*, but not this time. I'm giving you three days to get yourself together so be ready to roll out by 6:30p on Friday. I'm working from home so I'll swing by then to pick you up and you better be ready to go!" Adrienne threatened.

"OK. Geez! You're so damn annoying!" Faith whined but agreed.

"Yeah, I know. I love you too, girl. Remember, Friday 6:30p sharp and don't have me waiting for you either. You know I'm prompt. By the way, this event is invitation only. I know the partners and a couple of the investors so we'll sit with them," Adrienne name-dropped as only she can.

"It's definitely going to be well attended," Adrienne continued. "This is their second location so word is already out. The first one opened two years ago in Chi-town and it's booming. If this one is anything like that, it's going to be *hot*! The food and drinks are awesome – Cuban and South American, the décor puts you in a South Beach frame of mind *and* they have a walk in, sit down humidor with a cigar bar that's off the freakin' chain. Nothing but top shelf *everything* and all types of Cuban rolled cigars on deck! You know when I indulge, I like either the torpedo tip ones or the big fat George Burns cigars dipped in a smooth glass of aged Cognac!

"Wow! That *does* sound nice," I added. "Maybe, *I'll* even have a cigar!"

"What do you need a cigar for? You're already on the good shit! That medicinal weed ain't no joke, E!" Faith joked.

"Whew! I can see it now," Adrienne said. "Any way, it'll definitely be an experience! We're gonna have a great time. My friend, Don Burgess and his partners are tons of fun and we will want for absolutely nothing! Y*ou're* going Faith, so be ready! Alright, gotta go, bye!" And with that, Dre hung up from our conference call before Faith had the chance to come up with another excuse not to go.

"Come on Faye, it'll be fun. You deserve to have a little fun," I said, encouraging her to shake the bad mood she was in. Thankfully, by the time Friday afternoon rolled around, Faith had worked her way out of her funk and decided to just go and have a good time. She hadn't hung out with us girls in a while and we were all excited to see what this new lounge, *Socio*, was all about. And Faith knew if the owners were friends of Adrienne's, they were either Ivy Leaguers with deep pockets or self-made men comfortable in any environment so that alone made the place worth checking out. We just *knew* it was going to be a fun evening. But, like anything else, deciding what to wear wasn't going to be easy.

"What the hell am I going to wear to this thing tonight?" Faith called me frantically.

"I would have been quite content taking in a quick erotica read and a nice bottle of wine. Erotic short stories set the mood and get me thinking about the type of man I want to be with next time," she confessed.

"Well, who knows? Maybe you'll get lucky tonight and meet someone like that!" I quipped. "Now put on the right attitude and a killer pair of heels."

"Nope! Get it out of your head because it's gonna be the same ol' type of folks just dressed up in a different suit. Argh! Any way…!" Faith snapped as she filed through her outfit options and tried to focus.

"All right, Faye, just start with the shoes," I told her.

"OK, Will it be you Mr. Manolo or you Mr. Choo? Stuart, are you calling out for some attention tonight? I haven't worn these black Stuart Weitzman's in a while.

"Oh, well, decisions, decisions… Funny, if this is the hardest decision I have to make today or the only thing that's going to get me a little frustrated, then it has been a *great* day!" she mused.

"Faith! Congratulations, girl, you are really turning the corner! Now, get dressed to go out there and meet some new people, Dr. Faith St. John," I jokingly ordered.

We remained on the phone as she contemplated what to wear and I remained undecided on what shoes to put on. I could hear her thinking through her choices out loud. Some things about us *never* change.

"If I can't figure out which shoes to wear, the entire outfit is up in the air," she continued. "I'm torn between my fringed Stuart Weitzman high heel sandals and my deep blue Aquazzura platforms with the ultra high chunky heel."

"I vote for the Aquazzura platforms – with something funky. Color outside of the lines," I told her.

"Damn, now I wish I would have gotten D to buy me those banging Danielle Michetti fringe pumps when he was trying to buy my love back! What the hell was I thinking?"

Before I could chime in she said, "It wouldn't have mattered," she thought out loud "Cause I wouldn't have taken his cheating, lying ass back anyway *and* I can buy my own damn shoes!" she snickered and I laughed with her.

Scanning her now expansive "all me" walk-in closet, Faith decided to ditch the fringes and the chunky heels and opted for a sleeker, more French Fashion Week type of style. She said she wanted to feel fashionably sexy, confident, alluring and maybe, *just maybe*, available so she switched gears entirely and decided to keep it, what I call, *sexy simple*. Eventually wearing her white Emilio Pucci lace up silk blend jumpsuit and Giuseppe Zanotti three strap high heel gold metallic stilettos and carrying a matching oversized gold metallic envelope clutch accomplished everything she needed to feel tonight – confident and very sexy. She pulled her hair back into a chic chignon and by 6:20p made her way into the kitchen where she poured herself another glass of champagne, waited patiently for "her date", Adrienne, to arrive and Face Timed me to check my status.

At 6:30p Adrienne was ringing the doorbell. "That's one chick who is *always* on time!" Faith said to me.

I could hear Adrienne's reaction at the door to Faye's appearance, she couldn't contain herself. "Damn chick, I don't know *who* he is, but he's gonna sure be happy to see *you* tonight! Wow! Faith you look amazing! Divorce suits you," Adrienne teased.

"Oh, shut up, crazy!" Faith snapped back. "And, remember, I'm not *looking* for anybody. I just figured if I'm going to go out to this 'exclusive grand opening' event," she gestured with air quotes, 'as a guest of the owners', I might as well look like I belong," she said coyly as she swung herself around for Adrienne to see her entire ensemble.

"Oh please. You can *never* look out of place but I am glad you got out of those daggon sweatpants!" Dre teased and I laughed. "Now, pour me a glass of something. I don't care what it is. Looking like that, I *know* you've got a bottle of wine or something open," Adrienne said.

"Perseco!" Faye announced as she grabbed another champagne glass from the cabinet.

"Perfect! Evey, are you and Krish still driving together? When I spoke to her about an hour ago, she didn't sound too good," Dre informed us.

"Yeah, I know. I spoke with her too. It's her medication. She did it again and took it on an empty stomach, so now she's paying the price. Something tells me I'm riding solo tonight because I haven't heard from her yet and she's supposed to be here in about half hour," I told them.

"OK, well, we'll probably arrive within fifteen minutes of each other," Adrienne added. "You guys have your passes already, so you'll be fine," and then continued, "These passes are sleek; they're made out of titanium! Here's yours, Faye," Adrienne said as she handed Faith her exclusive guest pass. "The guys spared no expense with this opening. Apparently, the passes *we* have are like American Express Black Cards. They'll not only give us access to the event tonight, but they also come with a membership to their cigar club with that walk-in humidor area I was telling you about. *And,* apparently it includes free passes to private pop up concerts they've got lined up in the next few months. I'm so excited," She explained.

"I'm just so happy for them. Most places don't last longer than a year or two and they're going into their third year with the original lounge and now the second one here! OK, let's go," Adrienne said right before she logged off.

Our sister/girlfriend night was not as we planned. Shortly before our scheduled departure time, Krishna called me and said she wasn't going to make the event. Krishna has been dealing with a lot of issues since her assault on Frank - one of which is finding the right drug cocktail to balance her moods. While this particular mix seems to work well, if she doesn't eat a proper meal it can make her feel nauseous and light headed and that is what was happening this evening.

When I arrived at *Socio*, I could see giant Hollywood searchlights, valet parking attendants and hordes of people. The scene felt very much like a movie premier and was very exciting. I lucked out and arrived at the same time Dre and Faye pulled up, and as a result, after we valet parked the cars, the three of us walked into the lounge together. We were amazed and impressed by the décor.

Two statuesque beauties in black dresses and armed with iPads greeted us. They scanned our passes and rolled an invisible inked stamp across the top of one of our hands.

" You're part of the VIP list. This stamp gives you unlimited cigars and access to our '*Cohibas Bar*' – our completely ventilated *members' only* cigar bar. Enjoy your evening," one of them said as we were handed very tall glasses of champagne.

The lounge upstairs was spacious, dimly, yet well lit and *very* sexy. Large white swaths of chiffon curtains separated spaces throughout the venue, while white leather bar seats lined the twelve-foot long crystal clear bar whose base doubled as a saltwater aquarium. There were no less than six televisions on the wall above the liquor shelves. Opposite the bar were lovely, intimate geometrically shaped pewter tables with double couches, oversized and single chairs, and leather benches with squat stools. Seating was *not* an issue.

A twelve-foot long partial wall of fire encased in glass divided the bar and the dining areas. In the main dining area, the tables and the booths were a mixture of whites, deep velvet blues and shades of grey. Music could be heard faintly in the background but between chattering voices and clanging glasses and silverware, it was difficult to make out what was being played. I assumed it was Latin music. Everyone was obviously having a great time.

We made our way through the lounge and wound our way downstairs to the *Cohibas Bar* just to check it out. I must say, I've never seen anything like it. It was a walk-in humidor with a bar, plush lounge seating, two televisions and incredibly ventilated as described. The top of the lighted white opaque bar had retractable ashtrays inlayed at various intervals. Earth tones and metallic finishes braced the furniture and furnishings and the Latin music made the experience feel even more authentic: it truly was a lounge inside of a lounge!

As we exited the cigar lounge, Adrienne ran into her friend, Don Burgess, who's one of the club's six owners. After introducing himself, he immediately escorted us to the member's only elevator, which brought us directly into the VIP section of the restaurant. About twenty people were already there when we entered and dedicated servers passed hors d'oeuvres and champagne or took drink orders.

Don quickly introduced us to his partners. I learned through the introductions these six guys have known each other since middle school, played sports together and eventually three of them attended the same college. Over the years, they've remained a close-knit group and had gone into the club business together as well as investing in each other's ventures all the while remaining close friends just like me and my girls are.

Of the six partners we were introduced to, the one who obviously caught Faith's eye and kept her attention the entire night was Marcus "Q" Jamieson. When she described their introduction to Krishna later on that evening via a conference call I was also in on, Faye sounded like she'd written her own romance novel.

"While the introduction was being made, I immediately thought to myself, 'Wow! He's *really* handsome!' Q gave me the warmest smile I've ever seen Krish, and it instantly made me feel warm all over. By then, I'd been in the lounge about twenty minutes and had scanned the entire place. No one stood out to me more than Q," she remarked.

She was right. Q *is* very handsome. "He is fine, Krish! That's no lie," I added.

He *did* make quite an impression. He's over six feet tall, with a caramel complexion, bearded and bald.

That night he wore a nicely tailored navy blue suit, micro checkered lavender dress shirt with jeweled cufflinks and a silk pocket square, no tie and Ferragamo driving loafers and I remember his appearance spoke of confidence, not arrogance. He was strong yet quiet and had a notable presence that wasn't screaming "Hey! Look at me!" He just didn't have to be the center of attention like his friend, Don (who was a nice enough guy, just extremely extroverted). Q appeared to be comfortable with who he was and had a gentleness in his eyes that drew Faith in.

Faith continued to fill Krishna in on our evening. "He said to me, 'I'm sorry, but with all of the noise I really didn't catch *your* name. Please, tell me again,' he asked me as he continued shaking my hand and then leaned in closer in order to hear me speak.

" I told him again and he introduced himself as Marcus Jamieson but everyone calls him Q. He welcomed me to *Socio* and asked if I was enjoying myself so far.

"I thanked him and said yes, I was. I congratulated him on his beautiful club. I'm sure those guys will do well here. DC needed a place like this.

"He and his partners are excited about opening this one because DC is home for all of them. Then he asked if I had had a chance to walk around and check things out yet and suggested the *Cohibas Bar* since it's a lot more intimate and a *lot* quieter.

"I immediately wanted to lie and tell him I hadn't seen it yet so he'd have to assume the role of tour guide and take me there, but then I remembered we had been exiting the cigar bar when we ran into Don. 'Damn!' I thought in that millisecond before I responded, 'Only briefly. Based on what I *did* see, though, I was intrigued by the "lounge inside of a lounge" concept. I must admit, I've never seen *that* before" I confessed to him.

"Q said, 'If you're interested, I'd like to show you around, Miss St. John. It is *Miss* St. John, right?" Immediately I knew that was his way of cleverly inquiring about my marital status and I also saw him trying to peek at my left hand in search of an engagement or wedding ring.

" 'Well, technically, it's 'Ms.' now. I'm divorced,' I told him and it felt great to have that out upfront.

" 'Good', he said in his sexy baritone voice while he flashed that gorgeous smile again. 'I wouldn't want to create any problems for you while I give you a tour of my restaurant.'

"I leaned over to Adrienne and told her, 'I'm getting my own *personal* tour, girl!'

"She smiled and replied, 'I *knew* you guys would hit it off!'"

I remember thinking Dre's comment sounded as if she *had* pre-arranged their meeting – like a blind date or something -- but just as Faith was about to inquire, Q stepped in and in a gentlemanly way signaled for her to walk ahead of him. Faith shot Adrienne a quizzical look like "What are you up to?" and Dre shot back a sheepish smile with a fake wave that screamed, "I set you up on blind date you didn't know about and it's working!"

"He's divorced, too, Krish. Six years. He joked he should have told me that before kidnapping me," Faith continued.

"I told him that's good to know because I'm a 'no drama' kind of chick but I admit I felt excited and relieved after he said that, but all I could say was, 'Things could get really ugly and I wouldn't want to create a problem for you on your big night.'

"Q told me, 'As beautiful as you are tonight in that killer jumpsuit, I could see how that could happen. But, I'm not that kind of guy. If I'm with you, I'm with *you*, period. Otherwise, I'm single. And currently, I am. I don't have time to play silly games, *especially* when it comes to affairs of the heart. That's dangerous territory and, excuse my language, but karma's a bitch!' he told he me.

" 'That's for sure!' I agreed. "We're definitely on the same page with that one.'

"Wow! So that's how your 'little "tour' went. He's seems quite intense –

but in a good way." Krish observed while we were on the call. I didn't pay much attention to the rest of Faith's debrief with Krish as I witnessed it.

Q and Faith wove their way through the crowd until they found their way downstairs to *Cohibas*. By the time they returned, Adrienne, Don and I were having drinks. Q and Faith sat with us but seemed very much to be into themselves. From his conversation, I could tell he had a warm personality, a good sense of humor and was interested in learning about her. I could tell he didn't seem guarded and he volunteered some things on his own without making the entire conversation about him.

"You're stunning," he told her. "You look absolutely beautiful tonight. I'm happy you came." The music in that part of the lounge was a lot quieter and I could hear quite a bit of their conversation. I wasn't trying to be nosey and they didn't seem to notice anyone else in the lounge any way!

"Thank you. You clean up pretty well yourself," she joked. "I must admit. I wasn't going to come because I just wasn't in the mood initially. But Adrienne practically threatened me, so I didn't have much of a choice," Faith told him honestly. They laughed and she concluded, "But, I'm glad I did."

After enjoying our drinks and a few hors d'oeuvres, we all made our way back upstairs, joined the group and ate dinner. It was obvious Faith was really enjoying Q's company.

By the end of the evening, Faith learned quite a bit about Marcus "Q" Jamieson. Adrienne told me a little about him as well and I could also hear parts of their conversation over the course of the evening.

In addition to being an owner of *Socio*, he's a bio-medical engineer who owns a small but very successful company that manufactures prosthetic devices for orthopedic patients. He's a widower and divorced. Seventeen years ago, his first wife, Amanda, a journalist, died while giving birth to their twin boys, only one of which, Quest, survived. Amanda and Q agreed the first born would be named Quest – representing a life long pursuit of knowledge and growth, and the second, Quill – representing her love of writing. She was blessed to meet both of her sons before going into septic shock but sadly died thirty-six hours later, shortly after Quill passed away as well. Within seventy-two hours, Marcus became a father, a widower and the parent of a deceased child.

Q keeps the memory of his deceased wife and son alive with a tattoo over his heart of a quill completing a drawing of God's hands holding a woman who's holding a baby. He was given the nickname "Q" in high school because his friends used to say he was always on a *quest* to achieve more in life. After his son passed away, he adopted the nickname again as a tribute to the child he never got to raise but whom he believes is *always* with him.

Three years later he married Charise. He explained that marriage "... probably shouldn't have happened because I was still grieving and looking for someone to help make the pain go away. I never really dealt with the loss of burying Amanda and Quill because I suddenly found myself a single parent, raising Quest. Charise is a really nice lady but not someone I should have married," he explained. "We were only married three years and I admit I wasn't ready to remarry so soon. After we divorced, I began seeing a therapist and that really helped my son and me a lot. Charise and I never had any children but we're still good friends."

Then he switched gears and started speaking about his surviving son, Quest. When he did, he beamed with pride. I could tell Quest was the most important person in his world and he's invested a lot of himself in that young man.

While the conversation seemed heavy given how festive the evening was, it was obvious they were genuinely interested in learning about each other. They'd moved beyond physical attraction and dove feet first into sharing their personal experiences – each wanting to know more. As a result, the evening began to feel more like a date than the grand opening of a swank new club, *his* club. He didn't seem to mind and neither did Faith!

By the end of the evening, Faith knew that Marcus "Q" Jamieson was a God-fearing, humble gentleman who valued life, family and relationships. He was honest, intriguing and definitely someone she wanted to get to know better. Dre's match making worked and we both saw the immediate attraction between the two.

Faith was on a *quest* to learn more about Q! The pain of her recent ugly past, relative to her marriage and the pain of her divorce, was quickly dissipating and the possibility of a new chapter with a new man was beginning. Her "seasons" were changing and she could feel the seasons of her old life beginning to fade away and a new season – filled with hope – rolling in. Faith deserves it and I pray that the changes she is beginning to see in her life will occur in *all* of our lives.

CHAPTER 12

EVEY – LOVE <u>ALWAYS</u> WINS!

After initially receiving the divorce papers from Len, I extended my stay in Nags Head a few extra days. I just couldn't see myself going back home and seeing him. I was shocked, hurt and angry. He called several times every day to talk to me but I refused to take his calls. He also called my girlfriends too, but none of them would speak to him except to be civil and polite, Faith being the only exception. She told Len I had decided to stay on for a few more days but I wouldn't be alone and needed time to process everything. Faith also promised him she, Dre and Krish would ensure I ate and took my medications. Once more, my sister/girlfriends were there for me.

We kept to our morning routine of walking the beach and doing at least thirty minutes of yoga each day. Krishna made sure I ate properly and Adrienne insured I took my meds. Faith manned the music and refused to allow anything slow or romantic to be played so I wouldn't wallow in self-pity. Because it's just what we do, the drinks flowed but considerably less than the previous week. My girlfriends made sure I wasn't getting drunk and losing my mind during that time.

While Adrienne and Krishna altered their schedules so they could support me as much as they could through this ordeal, understandably, their work demands and impending travel schedules dictated they had to leave by mid afternoon on their second extended day. Faith was able to rearrange her calendar and make arrangements for her girls so she could be with me as long as I wanted to.

They were all wonderful, but the most memorable part of those last few days was the time spent with Faith after the other girls left.

It took those days with just Faith for me to process the shock of Len filing for divorce and for all of the emotions I'd buried inside of me to finally surface.

At first, I had fits of raw anger and bouts of uncontrollable crying. I prayed incessantly, trying to find peace and Faith prayed *with* and *for*, me too. There were several times when *she* lead the prayers and reminded me God didn't bring me this far to leave me. I never lost my faith in God or what he has in store for me, but my faith was definitely being tested.

Overall, I was disappointed because I felt Len gave up on his faith and as a result, had given up on *us*. I had believed he was stronger spiritually than I'd given him credit for because I really thought we'd be together until the end. But I eventually concluded I was wrong about that and the temptation of just wanting to live a "normal life" without living under the looming shadow of cancer was too much for him.

Unfortunately, cancer was the "normal" part of my life and the card I was dealt with. I had no choice, but I see how *he* did. I had only hoped, prayed and came to expect Len was strong enough to deal with it as well. Isn't that what marriage is all about?

Faith showed me how a true friend can put aside their own feelings and be 100% supportive to ensure your happiness.

"Evey, if you want to call him and try to understand what he's thinking, *do it.* He's *your* husband. This is *your* family, he's the father of *your* children and this is worth fighting for," she told me.

"But, why?" I said. "I've been patient with him, expecting he'll come around. And, although I have no proof, I've even tolerated his cheating. I've talked to him and even *begged* him not to destroy our marriage and our family and *this* is how he repays me, Faith? He can't even tell me he wants a divorce to my face? He has some *stranger* deliver his dirty work to me at our vacation home, the one peaceful place he knows I have in this country? -- The one place away from my home in the islands where I *always* feel cancer free.

"I've been a fool thinking this man was truly my husband. 'Through sickness and health'! Yeah, right! Those were just *words* to him. They meant absolutely *nothing!* You were right, why didn't he abide by *that* part of the vow? I would have been there for him if it were the other way around. I had *cancer*! I didn't cheat on him or steal from him. I got *sick*. That isn't my fault," I screamed. "So why is he *punishing me?!"*

"Evey, I shouldn't have been so vocal with my feelings about your marriage. Me and my big mouth! I was out of line and I'm sorry. Whatever you decide to do, I'll be there for you no matter what. My marriage didn't work out but that doesn't mean yours can't," Faith said.

"Len *really, really loves* you, Evey and I *know* you still love him. He's just having a difficult time right now and he's confused and afraid," she reasoned.

"You know the universe only has two real emotions – love and fear," she continued. "Through all of this, you've experienced both. Len loves you but now *fear* is clouding his thinking. That's all. He's *afraid* he's going to lose you to that disease and instead of loving you through his fear this time – because he was there for you the last two times – he caved. Please, give him a chance to explain himself. Just hear him out and return his calls, *please,*" she begged.

I allowed her advice to soak in because she spoke as if she knew something I didn't.

But I was conflicted. Isn't filing for divorce the legal way of saying, "I don't love you any more and I don't want to be part of your life any more?" So, if that is what he "said" through his actions, why was she telling me "Len *loves* you"? And why was he continuously calling? If you're going to walk away, walk away!" These were my thoughts and nothing else made any sense.

"I was always taught you don't give up when you claim to love someone. You stick around and fight – together!" I told her.

"Just hear him out, Evey, please, just hear him out," she pleaded.

"No, I think he's 'said' enough, don't you? And there's really nothing for me to say to him either. There's too much *noise* around this issue. I can't think. I need peace." I said as I walked away, shaking my head with tears streaming down my face.

The hurt and pain I felt was too much to bear and I just wanted to be left alone to rest.

I went into my bedroom, laid down and fell asleep. When I awoke a couple hours later, the direction I should take was clear. I knew what I needed to do in this situation, at least in the short term. I packed my bags and told Faith I would be ready to leave in the morning.

"I'm going home tomorrow morning, Faye. I've already packed my bags." I told her over an early dinner.

"OK, Did you speak with Len?" she asked sounding slightly optimistic as if having a conversation with him was the reason why I suddenly wanted to go home.

"No, and I don't intend to. I'm just going home. I *need* to go home and begin working on releasing myself from the emotional cripple I've become. This is a weakness I have to work on," I told her.

" 'Emotional cripple'? What does *that* mean?" she asked but before I could respond she immediately followed up with another more pressing question.

"So, you're not planning on having a conversation with him at some point about the divorce papers and his plans? You can't ignore it," Faith said with surety in her voice.

"I'm not ignoring anything, Faith. I'm just being *obedient* and that means I have to go home, keep my mouth shut and work on *me* for a while. I'll retain an attorney just so that he knows I have representation but that's it. I have absolutely nothing to say."

When I arrived home Len wasn't there and I was relieved. I was prepared for him to attempt to start some type of dialogue with me but I wanted none of it. My only plan was to stay in the house, retain an attorney and not initiate any communication with him.

I began to rebuild my emotional pillar, which I believe is linked to my spiritual pillar, part of the three primary pillars: mind, body, and spirit. *The Bitch* robbed me of all of these and tried to kill me, but, I worked really hard to overcome those obstacles and I am stronger because of it.

I've become more centered and have a deeper connection with my Maker through this experience, which has strengthened my spirit. But my emotional self was still crippled and when Len abandoned me in the hospital that day, I nearly didn't survive my cancer diagnosis that time because I had relied on him emotionally for so long. I had looked to him almost exclusively for my joy and happiness instead of seeking it from the universe.

Now that Len has filed for divorce, not being fully dependent on my relationship with God has slapped me in the face. I know for sure now that man will always disappoint you but God *never* will. As a result, I vowed to become less dependent on Len emotionally and completely surrender myself to the spirit and allow Him to order my steps. Once this became clear to me and I began *listening and being obedient* to the spirit that has guided me my entire life, things started turning around.

The less I did to convince Len that I need him, the more *he* began to initiate conversations with me (and our sons) and extended invitations to meet at places so we could talk. Len and the boys are very close so it didn't surprise me that they accepted his invitations to talk. I, on the other hand, wasn't interested and therefore showed no interest in his offers initially, but he persisted. "Just please listen to me, you don't have to say a word," he would say, so he would speak and I listened. I offered absolutely no assistance or commentary during his monologues.

As the weeks passed by, I used my training for my impending Triathlon to get me stronger physically while I used prayer and mediation to build and repair my spiritual and emotional health. Through my difficulties, I drew strength by helping my girlfriends who were doing their best to sort out their own lives. But the turning point came and I realized I couldn't continue in this state of flux and I needed to make a decision. I felt a sense of restlessness and unease so I decided to go back to the beach in order to think through things and decide what to do next. I invited the girls to join me for a long weekend on the back end but only Faith was available.

I spent most of my private time in Nags Head alone walking the beach, thinking, praying and allowing myself to feel every emotion. When Faith arrived she, too, used this time to be alone and reconnect spiritually. It was a very different atmosphere from the festive girls week we'd had a couple of months earlier.

When Faith and I talked about the issues surrounding my marriage and plans going forward, it only came up when I wanted it to. I think she realized she had said all she could say about the matter during our last stay and now the rest was left to God and me to figure out.

I prayed for guidance, strength and patience. I begged God to order my steps and show me what I should do. My marriage and our family mean *everything* to me but I knew I couldn't stay in a relationship that was not healthy for me or one God wanted me to let go. I realized this situation was bigger than me so being at the beach was very cathartic. By the end of the week, I felt an overwhelming sense of peace and calm which gave me the emotional and mental strength I needed to deal with going forward and, if necessary, make some very hard decisions.

On the very last day of our stay, I woke up earlier than usual and chose to walk the beach alone. Faith's company on those walks each morning was always welcomed and on several occasions she was even literally my crutch, physically holding me up when I couldn't stand or take another step because of the emotions that commandeered my body left me physically weak in the knees. But that morning, I felt the strength to do it alone. As I walked the length of the beach, I didn't feel sad, worried or confused. All of those feelings seemed to have left my spirit. Instead, I felt an overwhelming sense of peace and calm the way I felt on the last day of treatment; it was so serene, it made me smile. Given everything I'd *been* through and was *now* going through, it felt like *joy*. I felt lighter and no longer weighed down by the issues I was facing. Finally, I had peace.

As I looked up from the sand washing away from my feet, I saw the most amazing morning rainbow – a nearly complete arc – and just beneath the arc was a burst of color -- like a shooting star of rainbows. I stopped and gazed in amazement. I'd never seen anything like it before, and it made me feel hopeful.

I dropped my head and prayed for wisdom, discernment, patience and strength. I *still* love my husband but I told God that whatever *He* decides, I would accept, but for the sake of our children, "Please allow Len and I to always keep them first and foremost." When I finished and looked up again at the sky I noticed the color burst was gone but had been replaced by a *double rainbow!*

"Oh my goodness! Wow! Two miracles in the space of minutes," I said aloud and in awe. I looked around to see if anyone else had witnessed this and when I did, I saw Len walking toward me, ripping and shredding what appeared to be the divorce papers.

"Oh my God, Len!" I said as I automatically ran toward him. I couldn't help it. It just felt so right, so natural. At that very moment, I no longer felt abandoned, angry, frustrated or hurt. The feelings of pain and despair had vanished. All I felt was joy, relief and love for *my husband and best friend.*

He grabbed me and squeezed me into his body.

"I'm sorry, baby. I'm so sorry," he told me repeatedly as he held me.

I couldn't speak. I was in shock and at the same time, I was incredibly relieved he was actually there, *holding me* and telling me he *still* loved me!

"I love you, baby," he said. "I don't want to live my life without you. I know I wasn't there for you this time and I am so sorry. Please forgive me, please. I'm *so* sorry. I've talked to the boys and apologized and asked for their forgiveness and I've apologized to our parents and asked for their forgiveness as well. Baby, I love you and I am truly sorry.

"I don't want a divorce, E. I just want *you*! As soon as the papers were filed and the Process Server told me you got the papers, I immediately knew I'd made a mistake," he franticly told me as we clung to each other.

"With each day you refused to speak to me, I thought I'd lost you for sure. And when you came back down here, I just felt that you were coming here to agree to the divorce. But something inside of me kept saying, 'Get down there before she leaves.' I didn't know what to do or say because I'd been trying to talk to you but you wouldn't say anything. I didn't know how to get through to you but a voice kept saying, 'Get down there *before* she leaves or you'll lose her forever.' So, I grabbed the first flight out of DC, called Faith and told her not to let you leave," he revealed.

He put me down but continued to hold me close, looked me in the eyes and said with all seriousness and tenderness,

"Evey, I want you to know that I *never* cheated on you. The nights I wasn't at home or would leave early I was either working or at the condo sleeping. I haven't been with or even *confided* in another woman other than a therapist since marrying you. It's *really* important to me you believe that. I've been working on the weaknesses in me that made me do what I did. I was trying to figure things out and leading you to believe I was having an affair by being absent was a stupid method to get *you* to divorce *me* because I didn't have the guts to do it. After I filed the papers and you were served, I realized I made a terrible mistake but I didn't know how to make it right with you. I just thank God you didn't agree to it.

"I'm sorry I put you, the kids, our parents and everybody through all of that unnecessary nonsense. I failed you and abandoned you when you needed me most and I'm sorry, babe. Please forgive me. I know we can't get that time back and that's my fault.

"I *promise* you I will spend the rest of my life making it up to you, but I can only do that if you agree to *remain my wife*, *my partner in life*, and *my best friend*. I *need* you in my life and I *love* you with all my heart Evelyn Montague," Len confessed as he got down on one knee and presented me with the biggest diamond ring I'd ever seen.

Frankly, while it was incredibly beautiful, I could care less about the ring. I wanted *my husband and soul mate* so I grabbed him and told him "Yes, babe, yes! I *will* remain your wife. I love you too, Len Montague, and I forgive you." He picked me up and held me as tightly as possible. I could hear him exhale a *very* long sigh of relief and whispered in my ear "*I love you, Evey.*"

Just then we heard,

"Whoooo hooooo!! Yeeeeeessssss.... Whooooooo hoooooo!!! Go Len... Whoooo hooooo!! Yeeeeeessssss.... Go Evey!"

He put me down and as we turned around, still clinging to one another, we could see Faith jumping up and down, clapping her hands and then pumping her fists in the air like Rocky Balboa, yelling and shouting from the wraparound deck at the house.

"Whoooo hooooo!! Yeeeeeessssss.... Yeeeeeessssss.... Whooooooo hoooooo!!! Love WINS, Love WINS! Look at the double rainbow!! God is GOOOOOOOD!"

We smiled, waved back looked at each other and instinctively yet calmly replied in unison, "All the time." And then *my husband and the love of my life* kissed me with all the passion he had in his body.

Faith *was* right, love did win and without question, today was definitely one of the best days of my life.

EPILOGUE

The End of a Season

"For everything there is a season, and a time for every matter under heaven."

Ecclesiastes 3:1 (ESV)

"I can't believe it's been almost two years since I've been on a plane and traveled out of the country," Krishna lamented. Time really flies. I don't know how in the world I let that happen."

"I do!" Adrienne replied. "It's called LIFE!"

"Ha! Two years for you and almost four for me!" I confessed.

"Everything has been so crazy. Our lives have been a *real* mess the last few years. But fortunately, especially in this past year and a half, things have really turned around for the better for all of us," I added with relief in my voice.

"Thank God! And *that's* why *this* trip is going to be one of the best I've taken in a long while; especially since we're all traveling together! No more craziness and no kids! Just sun, beach, rest, good food, great drinks, and good looking men to look at all day long (I hope)!" Faith said excitedly.

We were all excited about this girls' trip. We needed the escape and change of scenery and it was the first *real* trip out of the country we've taken together in years. The biggest difference this time is three of the four of us are divorced now.

We were traveling to attend Symphony and Emile's wedding in Cannes. Given Emile's status and influence in the European film industry, their wedding was initially going to be a huge production but as the planning activities began, both Symphony and Emile decided to scale the 550 count guest list down to a modest 75! This considerably shorter list consisted of family and close friends only.

Their wedding planner took care of all of the details. Extravagant invitations were hand delivered to our homes accompanied by a signature bottle of wine from Emile's vineyard in Provence, France and included a complete twenty-page program, featuring the couple and a narrative on how they met, photos of each of them individually and with family and friends, and all of the activities for the week artfully outlined. With the exception of Symphony's sister and her family and one of Emile's business associates, we were the only group flying in for the occasion from the United States.

Symphony and Emile took care of every detail – from our first class airfare to our individual suites at our hotel in the heart of Cannes (this hotel is where all of the celebrities and movers and shakers stay during the Cannes Film Festival each May) to spa appointments, shopping excursions, tours to nearby Monaco and Provence, and a day on the Mediterranean on a yacht – Symphony and Emile spared absolutely no expense ensuring all of their invited guests were comfortable, pampered and had a memorable time. The plans were spectacular and we couldn't wait to arrive.

When we landed in Nice, Symphony met us with a car and driver. It was so nice to see her, glowing with excitement and beautifully sun kissed. Summer months in Europe can be hot and after all of the mayhem associated with the film festival in May and finalizing the wedding details in time for a July wedding, she still looked amazing!

After checking in and seeing our magnificent accommodations, Symphony escorted us to *her* quarters; a palatial 1,200 square foot suite with a near panoramic view of the Mediterranean Sea from ceiling to floor French windows that opened onto an amazing balcony overlooking the sapphire sea. The suite was exquisitely decorated in contemporary French provincial furniture and bedding and had its own maid and butler service. The color palette was a coordinated mixture of ivory, soft gray, and ecru hues that complimented the wood finish, ceiling to floor silk and organza draperies and beautiful crystal chandeliers. It was truly spectacular.

"Oh my goodness, Symphony, this suite is absolutely gorgeous," Krishna commented as we all agreed and walked around.

"Thanks. I love it. Emile chose well, huh?" she responded softly as we were each handed a glass of champagne by the butler.

"Emile gets major kudos from all of us any way because he is such a nice guy and he *loves you to pieces, girl.* His face lights up when you walk into a room. It's a beautiful thing to see," Adrienne said to Symphony.

"Aww… thanks. I'm so happy right now at this stage in my life. I'm finally *really* happy again. There was a time when I didn't think it would be possible, but Emile has been such a blessing and I love him so much. OK, don't get me started with the water works because once I start I won't be able to stop," she said as her eyes welled up.

"Oh! No tears girl! You'll ruin your makeup which is beat for the freakin' Gods right now! Damn, it looks so good!" Krishna added.

Just then the butler reappeared with lunch. "I figured you ladies would probably be hungry and tired after your flight so I had lunch brought up," Symphony announced.

"Great, because I'm famished," I replied.

"After we eat, you guys can rest, unpack, or hang out for a while and we can meet either back here or downstairs in the lobby around five o'clock for cocktails and then dinner with Emile and some of his friends. You'll like them. They're lots of fun, not stuffy 'cause they're artsy, movie types and a real bunch of cuties, Adrienne, Krish, and Faith!" she said as she pointed to the now single ladies.

"Evey, I *know* you're spoken for. Len is a very lucky man. I'm so happy for you guys" she said as she gave me a big hug.

"Wow! That ring is GORGEOUS girl!" she observed.

"Thank you," I replied with a huge smile as she peered down at my left hand and I recalled Len's romantic proposal and rededication to me on the beach in Nags Head.

"Hey, why are you calling us out – Krish, Faith, and me – and telling *us* about Emile's single friends? Do we look like we need some fine European men breathing down our necks, showering us with attention?" Adrienne joked.

There was a brief silence in the room after Adrienne made that comment and then we all shouted, *"Hell yeah!"* and burst out laughing.

"Well, I know I don't have to tell you ladies this, but you don't have to worry about a thing here because what happens in Cannes…" Symphony began, "…stays in Cannes" the five of us said in unison, laughing hysterically and giving each other a bunch of high fives and fist bumps before sitting down to our wonderful lunch.

As we took our seats, Symphony said, "Hey, I just want you guys to know I'm *so* happy you were able to come. I know with all of our crazy schedules, kids and other things happening, it's not always easy to get away for ten days but I'm *so* glad you did. You're the closest girlfriends I have, so it means a lot to me. And the best part, as far as Emile and I are concerned, my family and his don't arrive for another three days so we can just relax and hang out before all of the wedding festivities begin. We haven't done anything like this in a very long time. Thank you for making all of this even more memorable by just being here. I really appreciate it."

"Well, you paid for every damn thing! What the hell did you expect us to say, 'No?!' I know *I* wasn't going to say no! I don't know about these chicks but I was coming regardless!" Krishna broke the seriousness of Symphony's words with this off the cuff comment that made us all laugh.

"OK, but seriously, Symphony, we love you," Krishna continued. "And, as far as we're concerned, *you're one of us*. You've been through some serious stuff of your own and you've bounced back beautifully. I mean *look* at you! You're beautiful, healthy and in love. Your career is soaring and the man you've chosen to marry *adores* you and without a doubt, he will spend the rest of his life loving *you*. You can't ask for more. We'll always be here for you just as we are here for each other – always remember that. So let's stand up, raise our glasses and toast to living the rest of your life *in* love and *being* loved by your man and your friends and to living a purpose *filled* and *driven* life. May God continue to bless and keep you, Symphony Walton," and with that, we clanged glasses in honor of our friend, Symphony Walton – bride and sister-girlfriend.

By the third day we'd met quite a few of Emile's friends and had a great time hanging out with everyone. We ate at some of the poshest restaurants in Cannes, toured and drank wine at Emile's vineyard in Provence and gambled in Monte Carlo. It was awesome. Several of the guys were smitten with us for sure but while none of the single ladies made any love connections, they did develop several professional contacts and solid friendships.

When the rest of the wedding party and guests arrived, the festivities outlined in the program began. Cocktail receptions, formal dinners and brunches, tours, beach outings and shopping excursions for those who wanted to go all led up to the big day.

On the day of the wedding, the weather was perfect. It was 85 degrees and the sea breeze made it incredibly comfortable for July, The ceremony was held in the hotel's grand courtyard and began promptly at 1:00p. Having been married once before, Symphony opted not to wear a traditional wedding gown and instead chose a beautiful, silk nearly form fitting blush pink Valentino cape gown with an altered horizontal neckline and a detachable floor length cape. Her ensemble was breathtaking.

After the ceremony, she removed the cape to dramatically reveal a completely exposed back that dramatically dropped to the very small of her back. The dramatic sexiness of the back of that gown was something to behold. The gown fell gracefully to the floor; elegantly concealing her five-inch, off white rhinestone studded small platform "Red Bottoms" with an artful jewel encrusted heel. So as not to take away from the beauty and drama of the gown, Symphony chose to accessorize it with 10mm pearl stud earrings, a four row pearl and diamond bracelet on each wrist, and a 10mm solitaire pearl ring surrounded by a sphere of diamonds on her right ring finger; all part of Emile's wedding gift to her! Her hair was styled in a tight chignon and her milk chocolate skin was completely aglow thanks to the Mediterranean sun and her absolutely flawless make up. She was stunning and an absolute beauty on her wedding day.

Emile, also marrying for the second time, was visibly taken back when she entered and I saw him wipe a tear from his eye. He, too, was well put together in his custom made Kiton midnight blue tuxedo with peak lapels, crisp white custom made monogrammed shirt, sapphire and diamond cufflinks (Symphony's wedding gift to him), an untied bow tie reminiscent of Sean Connery playing James Bond and black leather lace up tuxedo shoes. His salt and pepper wavy hair was perfectly combed back and his goatee, trimmed with precision, graced his deep olive complexion.

The reception that followed in the grand ballroom was extravagant. A variety of passed hors d'oeuvres, champagne and wine started things off while a string quintet and a harpist provided the entertainment. The sit down, seven-course meal included everything from caviar, butternut squash soup and arugula salad with a citrus dressing to lobster, truffle mac and cheese, filet mignon and an assortment of tarts and sorbets for desserts. Between the courses, the chef interspersed a few amuse bouches to keep us eagerly awaiting the next course.

It was an amazing afternoon which seemed to quickly turn into the evening. Those of us who chose to, agreed to change clothes and meet in the lobby an hour later in order to see the newlyweds and meet some of Emile's friends. Once there, Emile told us we'd all be going out via limo bus to a jazz club and then to one of the hottest clubs in Cannes to finish off the night. Fifteen of us took him up on this offer and we all had a spectacular time. By midnight Symphony and Emile left the group and went back to the hotel while the rest of us hung out until the wee hours of the morning.

Fortunately, the brunch on a yacht the following day didn't begin until 1:00p because I doubt anyone would have made it any earlier without being completely hung over. I was a little concerned with the size of the boat because I'm prone to seasickness, especially on smaller vessels (even without a hangover) but when we arrived at the dock we saw it was a *101-foot yacht!* Needless to say, I was *very* relieved and oh so excited!

This lavish brunch was held on the En Su Punto (Just Right), and hosted by one of Emile's good friends and business associates, Marcio Aderemo. The brunch was a perfect way to end the wedding festivities and allow the newlyweds to formally say goodbye to every one prior to leaving on a three week honeymoon in the Seychelles.

The day before our departure, Faith, Adrienne, Krishna, and I decided we'd simply "veg out" by the pool. We wanted to end our ten-day vacation relaxing and enjoying what was left of our time in Cannes. Faith and I arrived at the pool before everyone else, selected our lounge chairs, ordered our drinks, got comfortable and then Faith began reflecting on her budding relationship with Q. It's interesting how distance can tug on the heartstrings of two people who are no longer in regular contact because she was quite the chatter box! I guess I prompted her with my initial question,

"So, Faye, how's Q? Have you been staying in touch him while you're here?"

She smiled and said, "Since we've arrived, he's surprised me by keeping in touch and we've spoken nearly every night. I had assumed I wouldn't hear from him more than a few times over the course of our trip but without fail each morning, I wake up to 'Good Morning' texts and a few 'Missing you' ones throughout the day as well," she beamed.

"And, when we were preparing to go out at night he'll remind me to 'Be safe' and 'I'm thinking of you' before saying 'Goodnight, babe' each evening! I have to admit, E, I like the attention I'm getting because he is definitely courting me – even while I'm overseas. I'm excited. He's a real gentleman – strong, thoughtful, courteous and serious about the people he allows in his life. I like that," she said with a huge smile on her face as she reached for her phone.

"Who are *you* texting, Faith, *Q*?" Adrienne teased with a smile while dragging his name like a schoolgirl, as she asked this question while she and Krishna arrived and got comfortable on their lounge chairs, drinks in hand. This question got our attention as we all smiled and sat around the infinity pool at the hotel, drinking cocktails and taking in the beautiful Mediterranean.

"I just knew you guys would hit it off," she added. "The moment I heard he was single I told Don we had to connect you two. The funny thing is neither of you knew we were setting you guys up. It was masterful," she taunted, sounding a bit like a mad scientist.

"Really? And just what would you have done if I didn't go, 'Miss Masterful'?" Faith retorted.

"Oh, *you were going!* Trust me, if I had to throw you in the shower and dress you *myself* you were going to go to that opening and meet *that man that night* because it was time for you to get out and meet people. Plus, he is fine, smart, single and an all around *nice guy!* The time was right," she insisted as she adjusted her oversized sun hat and began applying sunscreen.

"Evey, Krish, do you hear this craziness? Miss Matchmaker over here thinks she knew it was time for me to meet someone!" Faith said in search of someone to take her side.

"Well, it *was* about time you got out of those sweat pant things you started wearing like a uniform every day, Faye," I said laughing.

"Yeah, I hope you threw those things out, girl. They were… well, I'm not even going to go there but let's just say they weren't *you!*" added Krishna, also laughing.

"Oh, whatever! All of you guys can go to hell. I was going through something and I didn't feel like going any where so I just wore those," Faith explained as she adjusted her sunglasses and took a sip of her second caipirinha for the day.

"*All* the time! No, seriously, I mean you wore those things *all the damn time, Faye!* You wore them in the house, to the store, in the yard. It was getting to be a bit much, frankly. Seriously. Thank *God* for that opening at *Socio* because I thought we were gonna have to go into your house and tie you down in order to get you out of those things," Krishna added as she, Adrienne and I broke into hysterics.

"Yeah, well it all worked out the way it was supposed to, I guess." This response was funny because for a person who is never short on words, Faith could only muster that in her defense.

"Well, since we're all in catch up mode, Ms. Adrienne, and you started it by getting in *my* business, what's going on with *Mr. Chef Boyardee,* I mean Marcel?" Faith shot back while laughing.

We're really good at teasing each other and not getting upset about it. We have tough skin and know whatever is being said is not meant as a personal attack but to simply bring humor to a situation, lighten a mood, or make you laugh at yourself. "Life's too short… and when it gets hard LAUGH!" we always say.

"Ohhhh!! Ooooo!!!" Krish and I squealed in unison and broke into rib breaking laughter.

"Wait a damn minute," Adrienne replied trying not to laugh. " 'Chef Boyardee?' " Oh my goodness I'm gonna tell him you said that and the next time you go into one of his restaurants, you better have your credit card ready, bitch, 'cause *you're* paying!" she immediately shot back after spitting up half of the rum punch she tried to drink while laughing.

"Now look what you made me do!" she said with the liquid dripping down her chin.

"I'll be damned," Faith replied. "Marcel is Len's boy from undergrad, remember? (After hours and hours of conversations, Adrienne found out Marcel and Len know each other from college. They had met for dinner and drinks a few times before Marcel landed that coveted seat next to Adrienne on that now infamous flight to London.)

"And as of right now I can do no wrong in Len's book because I was the *only* one who talked to him and helped him get his wifey back. I doubt my ass will be paying for anything *ever* in that damn place! Am I right, Evey?" Faith snapped back confidently.

"Yeah, Dre, I think she may have a point there!" I said agreed.

"Yeah, whatever. I'm sure I can change his mind about that with one good romp in the sack. When I'm done with him he'll be asking me, 'Um, babe, who's Faith?'"

She laughed and swung her arms up so abruptly she almost toppled over her drink and then she and Krishna high fived each other in agreement.

"Any way, he's doing just fine, Missy. We talk all the time and he's educating me on how to go about choosing a location for my art gallery. Speaking of that, you guys, I think I've narrowed it to two locations now. I'm so excited. I want you girls to help me decide. Everything else is falling into place nicely and if all goes well I plan to say goodbye to big Pharma within six months, ya'll!! Ahhh!!!" she squealed, kicked her feet and waved her hands over her head in sheer delight.

"Oh my goodness, Dre, that's awesome! We gotta celebrate and get Ken to plan the opening." I said. "Wow! You're finally gonna do it, girl," we all expressed our joy for her simultaneously.

"Thank you. I can't wait," she blushed.

"Oh and Marcel will be back in DC in a few weeks. We'll definitely see each other when he's there," she continued, getting us back on track with the guy updates.

"We'll see how it goes. I'm gonna take my time with this one. I really like him," she said.

"OK. Now, what about *you*, Miss Krishna?" Faith's inquiries continued.

"What about me? You can take your sights off of me. I'm good," Krishna speedily replied while repositioning herself on her lounge chair, adjusting the straps on her bikini and reaching for her wine.

"Oh no, not so fast. How is Officer Winsome doing?" Faith followed up.

"Has he used his handcuffs on you yet?" Adrienne added with mock innocence.

Krishna looked at Adrienne and rolled her eyes. She then smiled and finally responded to the barrage of questions we were shooting at her.

"Charles is fine, I guess," she said.

"Ooo! *'Charles'*," Bratty Faith repeated, dragging his name out. "Please continue," she teased.

"A few weeks ago, he called to tell me he's no longer on the police force," Krish admitted.

"Why? What happened?" Adrienne said concerned.

"You know he's a jazz musician and plays like five instruments. Music is really his passion. Doing the police thing just paid the bills, he says. Any way, he's releasing his second CD soon. He told me he's going on tour and opening for Diana Krall in a few weeks." Krishna seemed really excited to share this news with us but still appeared a bit cautious with her emotions.

"Wow! We *love* jazz, especially Diana Krall!" Faith said, already self-inviting us to his next concert!

"He can save your life and then lull your ass to sleep with a song," Adrienne added and we all laughed.

"Diana Krall! That's major. I love her," I added.

"Yeah, I'd like that too, Faith. I've been really impressed with him and everything he's told me about himself. But with everything that had been going on with Lauren on the West Coast, it's taken me some time to really connect with him. We've been playing a lot of phone tag. We talked for a while the other day though, and I met him for lunch the day before I left," she finally admitted.

"I confess," Adrienne said. "I don't remember much about him other than he was the cutie who was talking to you the day you busted Frank's teeth out with that hammer? And the *same* officer that pulled you over that night Frank acted like a fool after the gala, right? He was really nice and I could tell he *really* liked you."

"I *do* like him. He's really nice, kind of soft-spoken but very strong at the same time," Krish answered. "He has a gentle quality about him I like and probably *need* in my life. He's absolutely *nothing* like Frank. He's comfortable not being the center of attention and I *really* like that. He's never been married but he's the single parent of an 18 year old son, Charles, Jr. but he calls him CJ. His son lives with him and I can tell he absolutely adores him.

"Apparently, he was engaged to the boy's mother and they'd planned to marry right after CJ was born but then he learned his fiancé had a really bad cocaine habit. As a result, he called off the wedding. Six months or so after CJ was born, and probably in an effort to get him back for calling everything off, he learned she was going to put the child up for adoption. Charles intervened and was able to get full custody of his son. And with the help of his mom, sister and her husband, he's been raising him alone ever since. It's sad, but the mother has never been in CJ's life since she lost the court case," Krishna told us.

"Wow, that's terrible," I said.

"I can't imagine not being in my children's lives," Adrienne added.

"So it seems that Officer Winsome may have the potential to '*serve* and protect' more than just our community after all, huh?" I teased in order to break up the seriousness of the conversation and we all laughed and clanged glasses to toast Krishna's good fortune with this new man.

"And, now, Ms. Evey. Well, we know all about your *Lifetime* story and how wonderfully amazing your life is now that you and Len are back together. I'm surprised you came up for air and agreed to come on this trip with all of us!" Faith joked.

"Yeah, if you're not careful you and Len may end up having another baby!" Adrienne teased.

"Oh, absolutely *not!*" I snapped. "That ship sailed long ago. There ain't *nothing* coming out of this port ever again!" We all laughed and agreed that proverbial "ship" I was referring to had sailed for all of us and we have neither interest nor intention of ever venturing down that canal ever again.

"Len and I are doing just great," I said calmly and a wide, warm smile stretched across my face as I talked about our relationship.

"I believe there is a season for everything in life. And things happen for a reason, too. My cancer brought me closer to God, there's no question about that and, as strange as it may sound, brought Len closer to God and to me, as well. It tested his faith and his commitment to his family and me. It was painful and it wasn't an easy road, especially this last time around, you guys know that, but I'm still here and in full remission – Praise God – and Len and I are *still* together and *still* in love. That's nothing but God's mercy and His grace at work. We're good and doing really well. I'm very blessed."

"No, doubt. You are most certainly blessed, Evey. Heck, as I look back on all of our lives and this past year and a half in particular, I *know* we are all blessed and we're all *still* here because of God's mercy and grace. We have a lot to be thankful for. I know I do," Faith acknowledged.

"That's for sure, me too," Adrienne and Krishna replied together while I nodded my head in agreement.

"Our lives have been crazy… *absolutely* crazy but lots of fun too… and we have *tons* of stories to tell our grandchildren, that's for damn sure. Heck, with all that's happened to each of us over the years it's definitely a story worth telling."

Faith paused and then blurted out, "Why wait? I should write a book!" she said as she took a long sip of her drink. The idea came to her just like that!

"A BOOK?!" we all screamed.

"Oh, hell no!" emphasized Adrienne. "I got waaaayyy too much shit for you to be writing about in a damn book. I should kill you now to be sure nothing gets written," she laughed.

"A book about what? Who?" Krishna asked with paranoia in her voice.

"It would be 'inspired by actual events,' " Faith quipped, motioning air quotes, and then continued.

"It would be about four fabulous women, who live wonderfully 'perfect lives'. They're jetsetters and movers and shakers, married to the 'perfect guys', they have 'perfect kids' and live in beautiful houses. They're living what appears to be the American Dream, plus some. To all those on the outside, their lives appear to be perfect in every way. But in actuality, all hell is breaking loose in *each* of their lives but *only* they know how bad things really are among them. They're thick as thieves, been friends forever and they've helped each other through every possible situation life has thrown their way. As life gets complicated and things unravel, the friends realize almost *everything* about their lives, with the exception of their kids and their sisterhood bond and friendship, is all a sham and inauthentic because they all got caught up in the material side of life – labels and titles. The ladies come to learn first hand that all the trappings really don't mean anything if you don't have your family and closest friends with you when things go haywire," Faith explained.

"That's true. I like the premise of the book. Just remember to include the importance of having and maintaining your faith and a spiritual connection with God – whatever you call him: God, Allah, Jehovah, Yahweh, etc. It's *everything*. *He's* everything." I added.

"Amen," we said collectively.

"What would you call it?" asked Adrienne.

Faith paused for a minute, sat up on her lounge chair and peering over at each of us but beginning with herself, pointed and said, "F"."A"."K"."E". – F A K E!"

"Whoa! That's *deep*, Faye. But, are you saying we're 'fake'? And there's nothing authentic about *us?*" Krish asked, concerned.

"Not at all. First of all it stands for the first letter of each of our names (but, of course, I wouldn't use our *real* names) and it *does* represent aspects of our lives that simply weren't real or authentic - like our marriages. Faking orgasms and faking happiness in our marriages just so we can say we're married, living in the big house with the big diamond ring isn't being *real – if you're not happy and there's no love.* Dreams deferred and not living up to our fullest potential with the gifts God has blessed us with isn't living the lives God intended us to live. It's all just *fake!* And if you're not being true to yourself, and what makes *you* happy and pursuing those things, like *your* dreams that brings real joy to your life and your mandate to *share* your gifts with the rest of the world, then you're not fulfilling your purpose and you're a FAKE, plain and simple!" Faith insisted.

"I mean, lets be honest you guys. We weren't living real and authentic lives. It may have started off that way, but somewhere along the road we got sucked into foolishness and allowed 'the Joneses' to define what our lives should be. Designer bags and shoes shouldn't define us or give the illusion of happiness. They can't take the place of the love and support of a real friend or a loving man in your life when things get difficult. I think we *all* learned that first hand. And after everything I've been through, I'm on a mission to change all of that and just keep shit REAL from now on. So, the title – FAKE! – has a double meaning.

" 'For everything in life there is a season', right, isn't that what the Bible says? And I'm telling you my season of living a fake life is *over!* We only get *one* life to live. Damn it, *mine* isn't going to be *fake* any more. It's too exhausting and I'm tired of it. From my perspective, DiMarco's cheating on me and ruining our marriage was a fucking blessing – sorry Evey, I mean no disrespect. But all of that shit opened my eyes to the lie I was living. Whether it's through divorce, the death of a child or loved one, illness or whatever, the universe has a way of getting our attention and opening our eyes to things. Needless to say, mine are WIDE OPEN now!"

As Faith made her impassioned plea for living an authentic life, we all nodded in agreement and it was obvious she'd captured our attention. The stunned looks on each of our faces were priceless because the *truth* seemed to hit each of us like a ton of bricks.

Krishna broke the awkwardness of the silence with a suggestion, "While I like the concept, Faye, I'm only on board with it if Evey writes the story. At least we won't sound so dysfunctional," she reasoned and I looked at her with a quizzical eye and attempted to shift the focus a bit.

"But there *are* happy endings to our stories for the most part, Faye. We're all in a new season now and I'm sure we will *all* live our lives much differently going forward. So, I hope there will be a sequel to that book that'll wind things up on a positive note, *right*?" I added and, in my own way, demanded happen.

"What would you call *that* one… the sequel," Adrienne poked fun with curiosity in her voice and then immediately offered a title. "How about 'Happy Ending'?" she suggested as she thrust her pelvis backwards and forwards mocking a sex act and everyone burst into a roaring laughter.

"You're hilarious! But, that one is easy," I replied quickly and with a huge smile. *'A Season for Love.'* "

"Oh, that's nice. I like that," Faith and Krishna replied in agreement. Faith sounding optimistic and Krishna a bit relieved.

"Hmm…?" Adrienne pondered as she drank what was left of the rum punch in her glass and swished the ice cubes around. "Yeah, I guess, but I like 'Happy Ending' 'cause at least I know I'm gonna get me some!" she blurted out and we all laughed until we cried.

"And there's definitely *nothing* FAKE about that!" I said.

LIVE AUTHENTICALLY!

THE END

ABOUT THE AUTHOR

Mom, daughter, and a REAL FRIEND!

Made in the USA
Middletown, DE
23 December 2018